SORCERER'S HOUSE

Sinister events in the village of Fern-cross have given the inhabitants good reason to respect the legend surrounding derelict Threshold House: whenever a light appears in the window of the Long Room, they know from experience that a corpse will be found the next day. For two years the mystery has remained unsolved — until there comes a time when the killer strikes once too often. Because helping the police in their investigation of the latest murder is the unorthodox but astute Simon Gale . . .

GERALD VERNER

---◆---

SORCERER'S HOUSE

Complete and Unabridged

LINFORD
Leicester

First published in Great Britain in 1956

First Linford Edition
published 2015

A catalogue record for this book is available
from the British Library.

ISBN 978–1–4448–2341–7

Published by
F. A. Thorpe (Publishing)
Anstey, Leicestershire

Set by Words & Graphics Ltd.
Anstey, Leicestershire
Printed and bound in Great Britain by
T. J. International Ltd., Padstow, Cornwall

This book is printed on acid-free paper

1

The poplars at the end of the garden formed a line of dark spearheads against the deepening blue of the sky. Below them the shrubbery was brushed in with an almost solid black; a background for a bed of tobacco plants that stood out with startling clarity, as though their white, starry petals had caught and held all that remained of the fading light.

The hot, airless night was thick and oppressive and heavy with scent. The faces of the group of people, sitting in deck-chairs on the small, oblong lawn, were pale, almost indistinguishable ovals; featureless as a gathering of ghosts. Even Flake's scarlet dress, which earlier had made a splash of colour on the green of the grass, had changed to a blackish-purple and become almost lost in the gloom.

The American, Alan Boyce, had a sudden feeling that the garden had acquired a queerly spectral quality, with something that was vaguely sinister about it. The thickening dusk had, all at once, become tangible — something with weight and substance that was pressing in and down — and there was a deep stillness that was somehow disquieting.

A few seconds before — until, in fact, Avril Ferrall had made that extraordinary and disturbing remark — everything had seemed normal. She had said, in that rich and resonant contralto voice of hers, and without reference to anything that had gone before: 'There was a light in the window last night. I wonder who is going to die *this* time?'

And it was during the rather breathless hush which followed that Boyce experienced the odd sensation that something menacing had crept into the peace of the darkening garden . . .

A chair creaked loudly. Henry Onslow-White was mopping at his face with a large silk handkerchief and breathing heavily. His daughter, Flake — her name was Joan, but everyone had called her 'Flake' since she was a child for an obvious reason — stopped her whispered conversation with Paul Meriton and turned her head sharply. Dr. Ferrall, sitting beside his sister, fingered the thin black line of his moustache nervously. Boyce, who had only arrived in Ferncross that morning, looked from one to the other, although he could not see them very distinctly, and wondered what in hell the woman was talking about. Only Mrs. Onslow-White, placid as usual, made neither sound nor movement. Her small, thin figure was almost lost in the deck-chair.

'What do you mean by that, Avril?' Paul Meriton's voice, usually pleasantly deep, but now suddenly sharp and metallic, came out of the gloom.

'My dear Avril ... ' Henry Onslow-White's chair creaked again as he twisted his huge body round towards her. 'You saw a light ... ? You actually *saw* a light ... ?'

'Imagination!' snapped Meriton angrily. He had dropped in unexpectedly a few minutes before, and Boyce thought they had all been rather surprised to see him.

'It must have been a trick of the moonlight, Avril,' said Dr. Ferrall.

The pale glimmer of her face moved in the darkness as she looked up at him. She sounded acutely embarrassed as she said, hesitantly: 'I — I don't know . . . It wasn't that *kind* of light . . . '

Henry Onslow-White shifted uneasily and began mopping his face again vigorously. A breeze, like a puff from a blast furnace, stirred the trees and died away. The heat was stifling. Alan Boyce's thin shirt clung, damply and stickily, to his body, and the palms of his hands were clammy. Flake snapped a lighter into flame, and her face leapt out of the dark into momentary startling clearness as she lit a cigarette.

'What,' said Alan inquiringly, 'is there so extraordinary about a light in this place?'

'Threshold House is empty. It hasn't been occupied for *years*.' Flake's voice, cool and clear, answered him. It was, he thought, a very attractive voice.

'But, surely — ' he began.

'Oh, of course that isn't all,' she

interrupted. 'There's a lot more to it than *that* . . . '

'All nonsense,' said Henry Onslow-White. His thin tenor was jerky, as though he had been running. He suffered from shortness of breath due to his stoutness, but Alan wasn't sure that it was entirely the cause of his laboured diction. 'Just a stupid superstition, that's all . . . Lord, it's like an oven! What about some more drinks, Flake?'

She got up silently from beside Meriton, collected empty glasses, and went over to the veranda. A shaded light spread a soft amber glow over a table laden with bottles as she pressed a switch. There was a pleasant sound of ice tinkling and the cool splash of liquid . . .

Alan rose lazily to his feet and strolled over to join her. 'Let me help you,' he said.

She thrust cold tumblers into his hands. 'The left one's Mother's, the right one's Avril's.' She looked at him and there was speculation in her dark eyes. 'You're curious, aren't you?' she said.

'I guess I am,' he answered. 'What did

she mean by — people dying . . . ?'

Flake shook back her thick, glossy black hair. 'It's queer, you know,' she said seriously. 'I don't believe in it, but it's queer . . . Hadn't you better take those drinks before the ice melts?'

He nodded. The light had almost completely gone now, and the tall poplars looked like funeral plumes. From where Meriton sat, a cigarette glowed redly in the dark, waxing and waning as he drew on it intermittently. A winged night thing bumped blindly into Boyce's face and he jerked his head aside with an exclamation of disgust.

Mrs. Onslow-White took the glass Alan held out to her and thanked him. Avril Ferrall was leaning sideways, talking in an undertone to her brother, and barely acknowledged the drink he gave her. Two words of what she was saying came to him clearly: ' . . . it's dangerous . . . '

He wondered, as he went back to Flake, what the rest of the sentence was from which those two words had detached themselves. *What* was danger-ous, and had it any connection with that other remark Avril Ferrall had made? *'There was a light in the window last night. I wonder who is going to die this time?'*

Flake had mixed the other drinks when he joined her. 'You take Paul's and your own,' she said. 'I'll bring Daddy's and Dr. Ferrall's.'

'What about yours?' he asked.

'I'm not having another,' she said, switching out the veranda light.

A flicker of lightning whitened the sky briefly as they walked back across the grass side by side, and a hot breath of wind rustled the dry leaves of the trees. The white blossoms of the tobacco plants danced wildly for an instant and were still.

'I think,' said the placid voice of Mrs. Onslow-White, 'there's going to be a storm.'

'Good thing,' grunted her husband. 'Break up this infernal heat.'

'We ought to be making a move,' said Ferrall, getting up abruptly. 'It's nearly eleven.'

'I've just brought you a drink, Dr.

7

Ferrall,' said Flake.

'I won't refuse *that*,' he said, taking the glass from her, 'but I think we ought to go just the same, don't you, Avril?'

'Yes, I suppose so,' she answered undecidedly. 'Yes, perhaps we had — '

'Care to drop me at my place?' asked Meriton. He stood up and drained the glass which Alan had just given him.

'Yes . . . of course.' There was the faintest trace of irritation in Ferrall's reply.

'Then I'll say good night, too,' said Meriton. 'Don't bother to get up, Henry.' A battery of protesting creaks heralded Henry Onslow-White's laboured efforts to heave himself out of his chair.

'Come and . . . see you . . . to the gate,' he panted. 'If you . . . must go . . . '

They said good night all round, Avril with a curious reluctance, the American thought, and Onslow-White escorted them to the gate.

'I think I'll go inside, dear,' said Mrs. Onslow-White as soon as they had gone. 'There are one or two things I want to do before I go to bed.'

'Do you want any help, Mother?' asked Flake.

'No, dear, thank you,' replied her mother. 'You stay and look after Mr. Boyce.' She got up, tripped daintily away and was lost in the shadows of the house. Flake collected the empty glasses, took them over to the veranda, and came back and sat down in the chair her mother had vacated. After a moment, Alan dragged up another chair and sat down beside her. A little gust of wind went whispering through the tree tops, and low down on the distant horizon a stealthy rumble of thunder grumbled in silence. Alan gave Flake a cigarette, took one himself, and lit them both.

'Now,' he said. 'What *is* the story about this place what-do-you-call-it . . . Threshold House?'

There was quite an appreciable lapse of time before she answered his question, and then she said: 'Have you ever heard of Cagliostro?'

'Cagliostro?'

'He was quite a famous late-eighteenth-century character,' she said. 'Among other

9

things, he claimed to be two thousand years old, from drinking his own elixir of life. He was a wizard — or said he was . . . '

'Oh, that guy!' His brow cleared. 'I remember something about him . . . '

'Well, he's the beginning of the story,' she said. 'He was a fat little Italian charlatan and pretended that he was possessed of magical powers. He postured his way successfully from Paris to St. Petersburg, prophesying the future, making gold, and founding his cult of Egyptian Masonry . . . He must have been clever because he was never exposed as a fake. It was the affair of Marie Antoinette's diamond necklace, with which he had nothing really to do, that ruined him.'

'You seem to have made a pretty close study of him,' remarked Alan as she paused.

'I've read nearly everything that's ever been written about him,' she answered surprisingly. 'The most intriguing thing he's alleged to have done was the famous Banquet of the Dead in that mysterious house in the Rue St. Claude.'

10

Another mutter of thunder went rumbling round the sky, and the trees whispered again uneasily to each other. There was a tension in the air, and the heat was getting thicker and more oppressive. Alan felt the perspiration trickling down his face. He sensed rather than saw a movement beside him and looked up to find Henry Onslow-White mopping his face as usual.

'You're telling him the story, eh?' he grunted. 'There's nothing in at all. Just a fable like vampires and werewolves and witches — children's fairy tales.'

'What,' said the American, 'was the Banquet of the Dead?'

'He is supposed to have summoned the ghosts of six great men to dine with six living people,' answered Flake. 'Rather an embarrassing situation for all concerned — '

'And what happened?'

'One biographer — I forget which — writes, 'At first, conversation did not flow freely'.' She laughed, but he thought it was rather forced. 'I don't think *my* conversation would have flowed at all.'

11

'Stuff and nonsense,' commented Henry Onslow-White. He lowered his huge bulk cautiously into a creaking chair. 'Sheer unadulterated rubbish.' He was breathing heavily and unevenly.

'He's supposed to have attempted something of the same sort at . . . Threshold House,' said Flake. She drew quickly on her cigarette and her face showed up dimly red in the dark. 'He came to England twice, you know. On the second occasion he rented Threshold House.'

'It's a queer name,' said Alan.

'It was originally called Meriton Manor. Cagliostro renamed it Threshold House . . . They call it 'Sorcerer's House' in the village.'

'Meriton Manor?' said Alan. 'That's the name of the guy — '

'Paul Meriton?' she interrupted. 'Yes, that's right. Threshold House belonged to his family. It still does for that matter.'

'But he doesn't live there!'

'Nobody lives there,' she answered. 'The place is a ruin. I'll show it to you tomorrow. You can see part of it from here — from the room we've given you.'

'The famous window,' said Henry Onslow-White thickly. 'You can see *that*.'

There was a pause. The sky lit up brightly for a second, and the thunder, when it came, was louder and nearer. Flake threw away her cigarette and it hit the grass with a little shower of reddish sparks.

'Is that the window,' said Alan, 'where you see the light?'

'According to the local superstition, legend, or whatever you like to call it,' answered Onslow-White. 'It's the window of the Long Room. Cagliostro used it as a kind of wizard's den. The villagers say he *still* uses it . . . '

'Do you mean that his ghost is supposed to haunt the place?' asked the American sceptically.

'No,' replied Flake slowly. 'Only the ghost of . . . a light.'

Another gust of wind hissed through the trees. The garden was swept by a thick, hot breeze. Alan took out his handkerchief and wiped his wet face and the palms of his hands.

'Ridiculous, isn't it?' growled Henry

Onslow-White with a sudden expulsion of breath. 'But they nearly all believe in it round here.'

'What sort of a light?' asked Alan. He remembered Avril's reply to her brother's suggestion that it had been a trick of the moonlight. ' . . . *it wasn't that* kind *of light* . . . '

'A dim, bluish glow,' said Flake. 'It's supposed to come from the lamps of the Magic Circle used by Cagliostro to invoke the spirits of the dead.'

'And when this light is seen, it's taken to be a sign that somebody is going to die?' said Alan.

'Only that somebody is going to die . . . *violently*,' she answered. 'Not otherwise.'

'I don't quite get that,' he said.

'It wouldn't signify an ordinary death,' she explained. 'Like old age or . . . or pneumonia or anything like that. It would have to be an accident or . . . murder . . . '

'Like that chap on the motorcycle who smashed himself to pieces against the parapet of the bridge over the Dark Water,' said Onslow-White. 'Several

14

people swore they'd seen a light the window the night *that* happened.'

'They said the same thing when that tramp was found dead in the grounds of Threshold House two years ago,' said Flake.

'*I've* never seen a light,' grunted Onslow-White.

'How did *he* die?' asked Alan curiously. 'The tramp?'

'His head was crushed in,' she answered. 'Dr. Ferrall thought he must have fallen from . . . ' She paused.

'They found him under the window of the Long Room,' remarked Onslow-White.

'Maybe he thought the place was a good spot to sleep in,' said Alan. 'If anybody saw a light that night, I guess it was easy to explain . . . '

'They did,' said Flake. 'Two people.'

'Well, if they'd investigated they'd have found it was only this poor devil of a tramp trying to make himself comfortable with an end of candle, or a fire.'

'Investigate!' echoed Onslow-White. He uttered a short laugh. 'You wouldn't get anybody from the village to go near Threshold House after dark — not for all the money in the Bank of England.'

'There was no trace of a candle-end, or of a fire,' broke in Flake quietly. 'I thought the same as you, and I asked Inspector Hatchard.'

The sky flared whitely, and there was a deafening crash of thunder. Big, oily drops of rain began to fall spasmodically.

'Here it comes,' said Henry Onslow-White. 'We'd better be getting in.'

2

Alan Boyce sat on the side of the bed in the room which had been given him at Bryony Cottage, smoking a cigarette. Outside the rain was sheeting down into the dark garden and drumming steadily on the roof. Through the wide-open casement window came waves of coolness, mercifully driving away the thick, heavy, oppressive heat. Thunder was still rumbling and muttering in the distance but the violence of the storm had passed.

He was thinking about Flake's story. It was curious, he thought, how it had gripped his imagination. In the noisy bustle of America with its broad highways, rashed with filling stations, its neon signs, and its general air of practical efficiency, he would hardly have given it a second thought — except, maybe, to deride. Here, in the deep hushed greenness of the English countryside, it was different. Such a tale seemed to *fit*, somehow, in this land of legend and tradition where the real and the unreal walked hand in hand and the earth was still old and enchanted. He had got the same impression in London during the two days he had spent there — that the famous figures of history and literature might step at any moment from the dark courts and alleys.

When this trip to England had first been mooted, his father had said: 'I'll write to Onslow-White. You've never seen an English village and it would do you good to spend a week or two in Ferncross. It's got everything.'

And back had come the reply inviting him to stay at Bryony Cottage. Henry Onslow-White and Halliwell Boyce were friends of long standing, though they seldom saw each other. Business had first brought them together, for Onslow-White, now retired, had been a literary agent, and Boyce was still an active member of the firm of Boyce and Wade, the New York publishing house. It was partly business that had brought Alan to England, but before attending to the business side of his trip he had arranged to spend a month's holiday with the Onslow-Whites. And here he was.

He looked round the raftered room with approval. There was a soothing atmosphere of rest and peace. It had enveloped him when he stepped out of the train at the little railway station and it had remained with him during the drive through the winding leafy lanes and twisting white roads. His father had been right, he thought. It had everything . . .

Even a haunted house . . .

He got up and went over to the window. Beyond the veil of rain that glistened in the light from the lamp was dense blackness. He could see nothing of Threshold House now, but he *had* seen it: a great gabled house in a half-screen of trees on the brow of a hill, momentarily visible in the blue-white glare of the lightning. It had been so clear that he had seen the window of the Long Room, which almost directly faced him, half hidden by a smother of ivy.

The gutters were gurgling and water was splashing somewhere from a blocked drainpipe, but the air was blessedly cool and fresh after the abnormal, prickly heat of the day. He pressed out the stub of his cigarette in a little beaten brass ashtray. He didn't feel like sleeping, but there was nothing else to do but go to bed. The Onslow-Whites had gone an hour ago — Flake had gone to bed early. By now she was probably fast asleep.

Flake . . . ?

When she had told him her name, she had seen his eyebrows rise and laughed.

'I was called Flake because my name's White,' she explained. 'It's a kind of English humour that I expect you'll find hard to appreciate.'

He had not found it hard to appreciate Flake. He liked her soft, black, glossy hair and the way she had of crinkling her nose when she laughed, and the neatness of her feet and ankles. He had been told that the majority of Englishwomen had clumsy feet and thick ankles, and generally lacked the smartness of the American woman, but, even before he had met Flake, he had decided that this was an exaggeration. He had seen plenty of smart women during his two days in London.

Only, Flake had an appeal for him that these had not. She was so cool and fresh — like the English countryside with the dew on it . . .

He wandered about the room, smoking and thinking of Flake and trying to make up his mind to undress and get into bed. A moth flew in through the open window and bumped against the lampshade. Its shadow, huge and distorted, was reflected on the white-washed wall. He paused to watch it as it crawled up the shade, with wings fluttering busily, and then it flew round and under, banging itself again and again against the naked bulb. A gust of wind bellowed the flimsy curtains and he looked round, startled, to stand suddenly rigid.

There was a light in the window of the Long Room . . .

He stared out through the curtain of rain at that dim oblong of light shining in the darkness, while the moth battered itself uselessly against the lampshade. There must be some mistake, he thought.

There *couldn't* be light there. His eyes were playing tricks, or had he mistaken the direction of Threshold House . . . ? But he very quickly realized that there was *no* mistake. There *was* a light, dim and misty, but unmistakably real. And it came from the window of the Long Room . . .

He glanced at his wristwatch. It was nearly one o'clock. The story told to him by Flake and her father came surging up in his mind, and once again he heard Avril Ferrall's odd remark: '*There was a light in the window last night. I wonder who is going to die this time . . . ?*' And suddenly an overwhelming desire to *know* took possession of him.

Hurriedly, he put on a pair of thick shoes and struggled into a raincoat. He would find out what caused that light; see for himself *what* there was in the Long Room of the ruined house.

Quietly, he opened his bedroom door and slid out into the darkness of the passage. The whole house was still and he paused for an instant to get his bearings. The staircase was to his right. He guided himself towards it with his fingertips lightly touching the wall, felt with an exploring foot for the first stair, and descended cautiously.

It took him some time to draw back the front door bolts and unfasten the chain without making a noise, but he managed it, and opening the door, stepped out into the rain. It wasn't quite so violent as it had been, but heavy enough. He groped his way to the gate and stood for a moment, irresolute. There was no sign of a light now to guide him. The window of the Long Room was not visible from ground level. However, he knew roughly the direction in which Threshold House lay, and he set off as quickly as he could through the drenched darkness.

The rain got in his eyes and blinded him, and he splashed through puddles and semi-liquid mud. He bore to the left, which he knew was the direction he should go, and blundered into a fence. The impact made him gasp, but he recovered himself and with difficulty clambered over. On the other side was a steep and muddy bank down which he slithered, and found himself ankle-deep in water. Floundering through it, he came to long grass and, although he could see nothing, guessed that he was in a meadow. His hair was hanging in wet streaks over his forehead, and he brushed it out of his eyes. His shoes and trousers were sodden and the water was trickling down his neck in cold rivulets.

The meadow ended abruptly, and he was suddenly in the middle of a thicket that tore at his coat and scratched his hands and face. Brambles twined about his ankles and nearly tripped him up, and then the ground began to slope upwards, and he knew that he must be getting near his destination. He peered through the rain, striving to catch a glimpse of the light which had brought him out on this lunatic errand, but there was nothing but darkness — a darkness that was so intensely black that it looked solid. He felt that another step forward would bring him sharply up against it like a wall. With his arms stretched out before him to give warning of any obstacles in the way, he stumbled and groped his way onward.

The ground rose under his feet more and more steeply, and presently he actually came to a wall. The weeds grew thickly at its base and it was covered with ivy, but his fingers felt the brick beneath.

He paused, a little breathless from his exertions. He had no idea how high the wall was. With his arm stretched up to its full extent he could feel no sign of the top. His best course would be to follow it in the hope that he would come across an opening of some kind.

He moved along by the wall, touching the ivy every foot or so to make sure that he had not strayed away from it in the dark.

The ground was rough and uneven, and once he fell over a piece of rubble and smothered himself from head to foot with mud.

The rain had increased. It was coming down again in a cataract of water that drummed and hissed around him and splashed up from the sodden earth. It seemed that he had been following the wall for miles before his finger suddenly touched wet and rusty iron and he knew, from the feel of it, that it was a gate.

He pushed, and it opened stiffly and unwillingly. Beyond, in that cavern of blackness, he concluded, there must be some sort of path up to the house — probably the main drive, judging from the size of the gate. The falling rain was less heavy here and he thought that this was probably due to the thick foliage of overhanging trees. He pulled out his lighter and snapped it on, sheltering the feeble flame in the cup of his hand. He caught a glimpse of wet bark and a dense shrubbery with a curving weed-grown drive vanishing into it, and then the flame of the lighter went out as a raindrop fell on the little wick. But he had seen enough to show him the way, and pressed forward.

He hoped that he would know when he came in sight of the house by the light, but nothing dissipated the intense darkness. It occurred to him that he might have lost his sense of direction and come to the wrong house, but he remembered the momentary sight of the neglected drive before the lighter went out, and decided that it was unlikely there would be two empty houses of such a size in close proximity.

And then there was a sudden flicker of lightning and he knew that he had come to the right place. The house rose up before him less than ten yards away, ivy-covered, with broad, broken steps leading up to an overhanging porch. The darkness swallowed it up again but he had seen enough to be assured that he had made no mistake.

The window of the Long Room must be round at the side. As near as he could tell, that would bring it in a direct line with Bryony Cottage.

The drive divided in front of the steps, going right and left. Alan took the left, and found that his calculations had been correct. The thick shrubbery and trees ended abruptly, and out of the waste of blackness, bleary from the falling rain, shone a lighted window — the window of his bedroom at Bryony Cottage, in which he had left the lamp burning.

But there was no light from the dark mass of Threshold House. It blended with and was lost in the night. Whatever had originally caused that dim, uncertain glow in the window of the Long Room was no longer there.

He stood looking up with the rain beating down on his face, trying to distinguish the outline of the gable from the surrounding darkness. He must, he thought, be standing almost under that oblong window from which the light had glimmered, but he could see nothing.

He took a step forward, wiping the water from his eyes with a wet hand, and stumbled over something that was soft — like a sodden sack filled with grain. His heart jumped in his chest and he felt suddenly breathless.

Like a sodden sack of grain but *different* . . .

He stooped, groping frantically in the darkness. His hands felt a cold face and wet hair and the slimy chill of a wet mackintosh . . . his fingers touched something about the head that was a *different* wetness . . .

He crouched, motionless, and a coldness that was not of the rain crept stealthily up his spine.

The tramp who had died . . . from a smashed-in skull.

He fought the panic of fear that suddenly came over him. This thing that lay soaking in the rain and mud was *real*. It had substance.

A sound reached him — a sound that was superimposed on the beating and hissing of the rain — and he jerked up his head and listened.

Somebody was coming up the drive.

A flicker of a light shone among the dripping bushes, and he called sharply and curtly, 'Who's there . . . who's that?'

'Is that you, Mr, Boyce?' came the answer, and he realized, with a flood of relief, that it was Flake.

'Yes,' he said. 'Don't come any further. Stay where you are — '

'What's the matter?' Her voice was high-pitched, betraying the state of her nerves.

'There's been some sort of an accident,' he answered. 'There's somebody here — on the path. It's a man, I think.'

He heard her sudden gasp. 'Do you . . .

mean he's dead?' she asked.

'I . . . don't know. I can't see. If you give me your torch I'll have a look.' He straightened up and moved towards her.

'Where is he?' she said as he came into the light. 'Under . . . under the . . . window?'

'Yes,' he said. 'Give me your torch and stay where you are.'

She thrust it into his hand and he retraced his steps. The torch was not very bright, but it was bright enough. A man lay sprawling on his back, his eyes wide open to the wet sky, the sodden ground red under his head . . .

It was Paul Meriton.

3

Alan Boyce felt suddenly sick. The light of the torch wavered over the wet ground and the thing that lay there, as his twitching nerves reacted to the shock.

Paul Meriton . . .

He steadied the light with an effort and forced himself to look at the upturned face.

'What's the matter? Why don't you say something?' Flake's voice, with a queer little catch in it, dispelled the wild images that were forming in his mind.

'I'm coming,' said Alan. He walked unsteadily over to where he had left her. 'Where does Dr. Ferrall live?' he asked abruptly.

Her dark eyes, curiously enlarged and luminous in the white oval of her face, looked up at him inquiringly. 'Dr. Ferrall? Why? Has there . . . ?'

'Yes,' he nodded. 'Your friend Meriton's over there.'

'Paul?' She sounded suddenly shrill with surprise and alarm.

'Yes. He's . . . dead, I'm afraid . . . No, don't go.' He stopped her as she made a movement forward. 'It's not a very nice sight.'

'How — ' she said in a voice that now had a peculiar *flat* quality, 'how did . . . he die?'

'I don't know,' he answered evasively. 'That's for the doctor to say.'

'How do you *think* he died?' she insisted.

He remembered the sticky feeling of the head under his touch, and the red pool in which it lay. 'From a smashed skull,' he said. 'Look here,' he added quickly, taking her arm, 'hadn't we better find Ferrall? We ought to do *some-thing* . . . at once.'

'Yes, I suppose so.' She was staring into the darkness beyond him with a look so intent that, involuntarily, he half turned. 'I wonder what he was doing here — ?'

'Maybe he saw the light, too,' he suggested, and she nodded.

'You saw it, didn't you?' she said.

'That's why you came.'

'Yes, I was curious.'

'I heard you go out,' she went on, almost as though he hadn't spoken. 'I guessed you were coming here and followed you. I was curious, too.'

'You saw the light from your window?' he asked, and without waiting for her answer he added: 'There was no light when I got here.'

He felt her give a sudden shiver. 'Let's go,' she said, turning sharply.

They hurried down the dark drive, the falling rain glistening in the light from the torch.

'Which way did you come?' asked Flake as they reached the gate, and he explained as far as he was able.

'I know,' she interrupted him. 'I came the longer way round. It's longer but it's easier . . . No, not that way. I'll show you.' She bore to the right outside the gates, along a rutted road that dipped steeply. 'This takes us straight down to the village,' she said. 'Dr. Ferrall's house is on the green.'

The road was little more than a series

of rivulets in semi-liquid mud. They had to walk on the rough grass verge, and even then it was so slippery they found it difficult to keep their feet. Flake was wearing tennis shoes with crepe soles, sodden and mud-stained.

'How do you think it happened . . . Paul, I mean?' she said, breaking a short silence. 'How *could* he have hurt his head like that?'

'It looked to me,' answered Alan slowly, 'as though he had fallen from the window.'

'Like the tramp,' whispered Flake. 'Just like the tramp . . . '

'There must be a natural explanation,' he said. 'Anything else just isn't possible.'

'That's what *I* thought. I didn't *believe* there was anything in the story of the light.'

'Go on believing there isn't,' said Alan. 'Meriton may have gone to have a look over the house for some reason or other — after all it *was* his property, wasn't it? That would account for the light.' He felt that it was rather a lame suggestion, and Flake evidently thought so, too, for she said:

'On a night like this — at one o'clock? Don't be silly!'

'It's not as silly as believing in ghosts,' he retorted. 'Supposing he *did* go there. He could quite easily have fallen out the window in the dark.'

'But why *should* he go there at all?' she said.

He tried to think of a reasonable explanation and failed. 'What's the good of speculating? He *did* go there . . . and he met with an accident in the dark.'

'Avril won't believe it was an accident,' she said. 'Not when she hears how . . . how it happened.'

'Stop thinking about it,' said Alan, almost roughly. 'There's nothing to it, I tell you. Only a coincidence — '

'You're not really trying to convince me,' she said with unexpected shrewdness. 'You're trying to convince yourself.'

The denial that came swiftly to his lips remained unuttered. Was she right? *Was* he trying to convince himself that Meriton's death had nothing to do with the local superstition?

'I understand how you feel about it,' Flake went on. 'It's not a *practical* explanation, is it? And you're very practical.'

'I suppose I am — in some things,' he admitted. 'I don't like my credulity strained too far.'

She was silent. They came out through a short lane to the fringe of the green. 'Dr. Ferrall's house is over there — on the other side,' she said.

They crossed the green diagonally. The rain was falling heavily and running in little streams from the rats'-tails of Alan's hair. Flake's transparent mackintosh looked as if it had been dipped in oil. Somewhere, a long way away, thunder was still rumbling at intervals.

'Here it is,' said Flake. They stopped before a closed wooden gate set in a neat hedge. Beyond, they could see a short flagged path between beds of flowers. Alan pushed the gate, and it swung open. He held it for Flake to pass through.

'They'll be asleep,' she whispered.

'He's got a night bell, hasn't he?' said Alan, and she nodded.

He let go of the gate and it shut on a spring with a thud. The porch of the house faced them: an oblong black smudge that changed into a green painted door, with brass knocker and letter box, under the light from the torch. Two brass bell-pushes labelled 'day' and 'night' were set in the right-hand frame.

Alan pressed his finger on the 'night' push, and waited. After a little while, as nothing happened, he pressed it again. Almost before he could remove his finger, the door opened and orange light flooded them.

'Who is it?' demanded the voice of Dr. Ferrall curtly, and then: 'Flake! What the devil are you doing here? Is — ?'

'Something's happened to Paul,' interrupted Flake breathlessly. 'Can we come in for a minute?'

'Of course.' Dr. Ferrall, in a dark red dressing gown, stood aside. 'Oh, it's you, Boyce. Good lord! You're both soaked. What the deuce is the trouble?'

'Meriton's dead,' said Alan bluntly.

'Dead . . . *Meriton?*' Ferrall's face was almost stupidly astonished. 'Good God!

How did it happen?'

'His . . . head was smashed in,' said Flake, and her voice we not quite steady. *'His head was smashed . . . '*

'His head?' echoed Ferrall. He shot a searching glance at each of them in turn. 'Where . . . how?'

Alan shook his head. 'We don't know how,' he answered. 'We found him like that — under the window of the Long Room — at Threshold House.'

★ ★ ★

They were back in the wet darkness of the drive, only now that darkness was seared by bright wedges of light from the headlights of Ferrall's car. The leaves of the bushes glistened against the black background with a startling greenness where the light caught them, and the sprawling figure of Meriton threw a long, deep shadow, elongated and distorted, over the muddy gravel.

Flake, clutching Alan by the arm, stared at that shadow, morbidly fascinated by its queer shape. Dr. Ferrall moved to

38

the sharp, white ray, and his own shadow obliterated that other. He stood looking down for a moment and then he stooped, feeling and pressing with sensitive fingers.

The soaked leaves around them dripped water, making strange little sounds as though something was moving and creeping stealthily through the shrubbery.

'The back of his skull is crushed to a pulp.' Ferrall spoke without looking up. 'Though how — '

'He fell,' said Flake. 'He fell . . . He *must* have fallen — '

'From there?' demanded Ferrall. His head jerked up and he stared above into the darkness.

'Yes — from the window,' she answered. 'He must have fallen from the window . . . '

'Supposing he'd tripped and fallen heavily,' suggested Alan. 'Couldn't he have hurt his head *that* way?'

'It must have been a very heavy fall,' answered Ferrall, 'and he'd have to have fallen *backwards*.'

Alan felt Flake's fingers tighten on his arm. He glanced quickly, down and sideways, at the dim white oval of her face. She looked on the verge of tears. 'You mean something *hit* him?' she whispered huskily.

Ferrall shook his head. 'Perhaps — perhaps not,' he replied. 'That's what it looks like. I can't tell without a closer examination.'

'If he fell from the window, he might have fallen on his head,' said Flake. 'He *could* have done that.'

'Yes, it's possible, I suppose.' Ferrall sounded doubtful. 'It looks a . . . well, a different kind of injury to me.' He hesitated, cleared his throat, and added: 'We ought to get in touch with the police, you know.'

'The police?' Flake's tone sharpened. 'The police — ?'

'Of course.' Ferrall's voice was reassuring and matter-of-fact. 'It's the proper thing to do in a case like this. It's up to them to make up their minds how Meriton came by his injuries.' He looked at Alan. 'Will you wait here?'

'Sure,' said the American, though he didn't relish the proposal.

'Good. I'll go and tell 'em. I can drop

you at home on the way, Flake.'

'I'll stay,' she said quickly.

'You won't,' declared Alan firmly. 'You're soaked through and you've had enough for one night. You go along with Ferrall.'

She looked rebellious for a moment and then, reluctantly, she walked over and got into the car.

'Won't be long,' said Ferrall. He backed the car into the semicircle of the drive, swung the long radiator round, and was gone.

The darkness was intense now that the headlights no longer served as an illumination. Alan fumbled in his pocket for a cigarette, remembered that the rain had put his lighter out of action, and slid the packet back again. His hand came in cold contact with the torch which he had taken from Flake, and he pulled it out and switched on the light. It wasn't very bright but it was better than being in the pitch blackness. He might as well, he thought, try and get some shelter from the rain. Not that he could get much wetter.

He made his way round to the front of the house and walked up the broken steps to the porch. The weather-beaten oak door was shut and he leaned against it to rest. It gave under his weight and he nearly fell backwards into the hall, only saving himself by an instinctive clutch at the frame.

When he recovered his balance, he saw that the big door was wide open. He thought that the lock was rotten and had given way under his weight, but when he examined it he found that it had been unlocked. Curiously, he looked round the great, yawning cavern of the dilapidated hall. The old panelling was rotten and broken away in a dozen places and there were heaps of dirty white plaster where parts of the ceiling had fallen in. Everything was covered in dust, and huge cobwebs swayed in the draught from the open door. The place smelt of damp and decay. An enormous staircase, black with age and grime, led upward into darkness, and there was a big open fireplace with a pile of soot in the hearth.

Alan stared up the staircase. On the

floor above was the Long Room from the window of which he had seen that dim light; from the window of which Paul Meriton might have fallen . . .

He suddenly caught his breath. The light of the torch had shown him something on the broad, dusty treads of the stairs.

Footprints — *damp* footprints in the thick dust!

There were quite a lot of them. They led back from the staircase to the door. And there was more than one kind. Two people had been in the house that night. If one set had belonged to Paul Meriton, whose were the others?

Alan moved forward slowly, taking care not to obliterate any of those marks in the dust. He reached the foot of the staircase and, after a momentary pause, began to ascend, keeping to the side of the treads. He heard a scurry of rats, and something flew over his head. There were bats here, then, as well as rats. Well, one expected such things in an old derelict mansion like this.

He came to a landing on either side of

which was a broad corridor. The damp footmarks led to the left, and to a partly open door — the only door in that wall of the corridor. He pushed it fully open and stepped across the threshold. He was in the Long Room.

It was very long and, in consequence, looked narrow. The whole of one end — the end farthest away from the door — was taken up by a great window that reached from the floor to the high ceiling. Dust and dirt and cobwebs were here also, but the air smelt fresher and cleaner. He saw the reason for this when he went nearer to the window. Most of the glass was out.

It occurred to him, as he stood there staring at the window, that if anyone should chance to be looking in that direction now, there would be a light visible — the light from the torch he carried. Was that what *he* had seen from his room in Bryony Cottage? The light from a torch that *somebody* had carried?

He looked down at the floor. The footprints here were in wild confusion. Close to the great window was something

44

that glistened in his light, and when he stooped to look closer he saw, with a sudden constriction of his throat, that it was blood — *wet* blood. There were several spots of it.

Something ugly and horrible had happened in this room that night. Paul Meriton, lying down there on the sodden ground, had *not* met with any accident. His death had been deliberate . . .

Alan's face was white as he straightened up. He felt a sudden panic take possession of him — a violent desire to rush away from this horrible room with its hideous evidence. The shadows and the dust and the cobwebs all concealed something that was malignant and evil. The whole room was evil . . .

Although he was not normally an imaginative man, he seemed to feel a gathering of forces — potent forces — that had been locked up for centuries in these ancient walls. The shadows hanging blackly round the great carved cornice seemed to have thickened oddly, and he fancied that a queer smell which was neither damp nor mildew had seeped into the dank atmosphere . . . a pungent spicy smell that reminded him of a church . . .

The story he had listened to on the lawn, in the dark garden at Bryony Cottage, filled his mind with disquieting images and he understood the superstitious dread of the villagers for this house . . .

Sorcerer's House . . .

And then the silence of the night outside was broken by the hum of a car engine. Dr. Ferrall was returning with the police.

4

Sunlight streamed into the living room at Bryony Cottage; strong, hot sunlight, although it was barely nine o'clock in the morning.

There were, gathered in that pleasant room, six people: Alan Boyce, Flake, Dr. Ferrall, Henry Onslow-White, Major Chipingham, the chief constable for the county, and Inspector Hatchard of the local C.I.D. With the exception of Major Chipingham, fresh and rosy from his morning bath, and Henry Onslow-White, sat and smooth-shaven, they looked pale and tired.

The chief constable cleared his throat. He said, speaking in a clipped, staccato manner: 'Got the gist of it, I think. Queer business altogether. Like to hear more details.'

Inspector Hatchard raised eyes that looked out from under bushy, overhanging brows. His greying head had a little round bald spot on the top of the skull. When he was thoughtful or worried, he had a habit of gently rubbing it with the middle finger of his right hand. 'There doesn't seem to be much doubt that it was murder, sir,' he said. 'He was struck on the back of the head with some heavy, blunt instrument, and pitched out of the window. I've got the report of the police surgeon. That's right, isn't it, sir? You agree?' He appealed for confirmation to Dr. Ferrall.

'That's right,' agreed Ferrall. 'Quite a considerable amount of force must have been put behind the blow. His skull was badly fractured. In my opinion the fall could not have been responsible for the injuries.'

'Weapon?' queried the chief constable.

Hatchard shook his head. 'We haven't found it yet, sir,' he said. 'We're still looking.'

Major Chipingham smoothed a hand over a hairless head. He frowned, pursed his lips, and turned his pale blue eyes towards Alan. He said: 'You were the first to find the body, eh?'

The American nodded. Had he got to go over it again? he thought wearily. Waves of tiredness kept breaking over him and his eyes felt hot and prickly.

'How did you come to find it?' asked the chief constable. Alan told him. He had already told Inspector Hatchard and Ferrall and the police doctor. When he mentioned Flake, Major Chipingham gave her a sharp look which, although he may not have intended it, was entirely disapproving.

'Huh!' he grunted when Alan had finished. 'Wondered what you were doing at this place, so late, in that storm. Heard something about this legend, or whatever you call it. Lot of poppycock, of course. People talked a lot of nonsense when that poor devil of a tramp was found.'

'His skull was badly fractured too,' put in Ferrall quietly. Major Chipingham glared at him.

'Coincidence — nothing more,' he said irritably. '*That* was an accident. Snooping round the place and fell out of the window. Probably drunk . . . What was this light you saw like?'

49

'Just a dimmish kind of light,' answered Alan.

'What impression did it give you? Candle, torch . . . ?'

'It didn't seem like either.' Alan tried to fight back a yawn and failed. 'That may have been the distance . . . and the rain . . . I couldn't really tell.'

'I think I ought to mention,' said Ferrall, 'that my sister saw a light in that window the night before last.'

Major Chipingham's mouth, which had partly opened to put a further question to Alan, remained open as he turned his eyes towards Ferrall. 'Your sister saw a light — the night before last?' he repeated. 'What time?'

'Between twelve and half past,' replied Ferrall. 'She had been out to dinner with some friends and was on her way home.'

'Knowing the house was empty, didn't she attempt to investigate the cause of the light?'

'She was on the Mersham Road. That's a fairish way from Theshold House,' said Ferrall. 'Besides,' he shrugged his shoulders, 'some things are best left alone.'

The chief constable stared at him frostily. He said: 'Mean to say you believe in this . . . this rubbish?'

'I neither believe nor disbelieve,' said Ferrall. 'I prefer to leave it alone, that's all.'

Major Chipingham gave a snort. 'Let's get back to something practical,' he said curtly. 'I understand that Meriton spent part of the evening here?'

'That's right.' Henry Onslow-White spoke for the first time. 'We'd invited some people to meet Mr. Boyce, who is staying with us for a few weeks. Meriton called in for a drink. He was only here for a short while.' He looked over at Alan.

'Who were the others?'

'Ourselves: my wife and my daughter, and Dr. Ferrall and his sister.'

'What time did Meriton leave?'

It was Ferrall who answered: 'About eleven. He asked if I would give him a lift home and left with us.'

'Did he say anything about going to this place — Threshold House?'

'Nothing.'

'No mention was made about the house at all?'

'Not then.' Ferrall moved in his chair, uncrossed his legs and recrossed them. 'The fact that my sister had seen a light in the window on the previous night was mentioned earlier in the evening.'

There rose in Alan Boyce's mind a vivid memory: the dark garden and Avril Ferrall's deep contralto coming suddenly, in the pause that had followed a murmur of light conversation, *'There was a light in the window last night. I wonder who is going to die this time?'* and that later whisper which he had caught when he had brought over the drinks ' . . . *it's dangerous . . .* '

'What did Meriton say about it?' The chief constable's voice brought his mind back to the present with a jerk.

'He appeared to think that she had imagined it,' replied Ferrall.

'What I'm trying to get at,' said Major Chipingham, 'is whether he was sufficiently interested in this talk about lights to go and investigate for himself.'

'I couldn't say. Possibly,' Ferrall's tone was noncommittal.

'Surely,' said Henry Onslow-White, 'he wouldn't have chosen such an hour on such a night?'

'Don't know about that,' said the chief constable. 'It didn't deter Mr. Boyce when *he* saw the light — or Miss Onslow-White,' he added.

'But Meriton couldn't have *seen* the light,' said Henry Onslow-White. 'Not from *his* house . . . '

'Perhaps he became anxious about his property,' suggested Major Chipingham. 'After all, the house belonged to him.'

'I'm afraid that won't wash,' interrupted Onslow-White, shaking his big head. 'Meriton didn't care a tinker's curse for Threshold House. It's a white elephant and always has been.'

'Well, something must have taken him there,' said the chief constable, making the obvious statement with an impatient gesture. 'That's what we want to get at. What took him to this empty house, in the pouring rain, at one o'clock in the morning?'

'It's my opinion, sir,' remarked Inspector Hatchard, who had been listening quietly and occasionally making a note in the open book before him, 'that he went there to keep an appointment.'

'You think so, eh?' The chief constable seized on the suggestion with the eagerness of a drowning man clutching at a lifebelt. 'Inclined to agree with you. Had the same idea myself. Queer place to choose, though!'

'That depends, sir,' said the inspector quietly, 'on the way you look at it. If Mr. Meriton had wanted absolute privacy and secrecy, he couldn't have chosen a better place. Nobody was likely to disturb him *there.*'

Shrewd guy, the inspector, thought Alan. More brains in *his* head than in the bald dome of his pink-faced superior.

'What was the object of all this secrecy?' demanded the chief constable. 'Eh?'

'You have me there,' sir,' said Hatchard. 'I don't know. But the footprints show that there were *two* persons there last night and one of them was Meriton.'

'It's the other we're interested in,' said the chief constable. 'Who could Meriton have gone there to meet — ?'

He was interrupted by a commotion outside in the hall. Through the closed door, Mrs. Onslow-White's voice reached them raised in protest.

'Don't be silly, Maggie,' cried a deep booming voice. 'Of course I'm going in.'

Alan Boyce saw the chief constable stiffen and the pink of his face grow deeper. He made a clicking noise with the tip of his tongue against his teeth; a noise of irritable disapproval.

The door was flung open violently — so violently that it crashed against a chair — and into the room marched an extraordinary figure. It was a huge man, dressed in very stained and very baggy corduroy trousers and an open-necked shirt of a vivid and startling shade of green. His shock of unruly hair was the colour of a freshly ripened horse-chestnut, and he had an aggressive beard of the same vivid hue which projected belligerently from an out-thrust chin.

'Mornin',' boomed this apparition, in a

voice that set all the ornaments in the room rattling. 'Now, Chippy, what's this blasted nonsense about murder?'

Henry Onslow-White's fat face creased into innumerable wrinkles and he uttered a soft, throaty chuckle. Major Chipingham was a study in outraged dignity.

'Really, Gale,' he said severely. 'You can't come bursting in here like that.'

'Nonsense!' retorted the newcomer, throwing himself down in an armchair so heavily that it shook the house. 'I'm in, aren't I? Don't you try an' get all official with me, Chippy, my lad! I want to know what all this is about, d'you see? Shoot!'

The chief constable looked as though he would like to comply with this demand literally. The blood suffused his face until Alan thought he was going to have a stroke. He said, in a strangled voice: 'This is *outrageous!*'

'Keep calm, Chippy,' advised the bearded man soothingly. 'Bad for your blood pressure to get excited.' He whipped a battered tin box from his trouser pocket, extracted from it a pinch of black tobacco and a cigarette paper, rolled a cigarette with amazing dexterity, and lit it with a match which he struck on the sole of his shoe. 'Now then, let's have it — *all* of it.'

'Look here, Gale,' said the chief constable, when he was again capable of coherent speech. 'This is a serious investigation — '

'I know,' interrupted Gale, blowing out a cloud of acrid, evil-smelling smoke with great enjoyment. 'That's why I'm here. Now tell me all about it.'

Major Chipingham gulped. He looked as if he were swallowing something sour. He made a sudden, helpless gesture. He said with an obvious effort at self-control: 'All right, all right. We'll *tell* you all about it.'

'Go ahead,' said the bearded man coolly. 'An' don't dither!'

The chief constable looked at Inspector Hatchard. 'You tell him,' he said.

Rather to Alan's surprise, the inspector seemed only too willing. He laughed, turned back the pages of his notebook, and began, gently massaging the bald spot on his head while he talked. His recital, the American thought, was a model of what such a recital should be. It was clear and concise and omitted nothing that was important.

Gale listened intently, puffing furiously at his foul cigarette When Hatchard's voice finally ceased, he flung the end of the cigarette into the fireplace and rubbed his hands. 'Chippy,' he said, 'this'll give you something to chew on! Who bashed Meriton over the bean in the haunted room at Sorcerer's House? A nice hefty little problem, eh? Don't worry, you port-swilling old rascal, I'm going to help you with it.'

'I should prefer, Gale, that you kept out of it,' broke in the chief constable, clutching at the remnants of his dignity. 'And I object most strongly to your unfounded reference to port-swilling.'

'A form of endearment,' said Gale, waving an impatient hand. 'I always liked you, though I did have to do the difficult work for you at school. Just you relax an' leave it to Simon Gale. This isn't robbing hen-houses or impounding straying cattle. This is something big — B.I.G.' He clutched at his beard and frowned ferociously. 'Have you been up to the house yet?'

The chief constable, rendered speechless, shook his head helplessly.

'Then what are we waiting for?' exclaimed Simon Gale, leaping to his feet with a single bound. 'Come along — let's go! I want to see the haunted room.' He strode out the door, taking it for granted that they would follow him.

Major Chipingham sighed and got to his feet. 'We might as well go with him,' he said resignedly.

Alan found himself beside Flake as they straggled out into the hall. 'Who is he?' he asked in a whisper.

'Simon?' she said. 'A little startling, isn't he?'

'You're telling me,' he said. 'I thought the chief constable was going to have a fit.'

'Oh, they're great friends, really,' she laughed. 'They went to the same public school and were at Oxford together.'

'What is he — an artist?' he asked.

'He's a little bit of everything,'

answered Flake. 'He paints and he writes, but mostly he just does anything that appeals to him at the moment.' She stopped abruptly as they joined the others, who had congregated in a group by the front door.

'You don't want me, do you?' said Henry Onslow-White.

'No, Henry, no,' answered Simon Gale, flinging the words over his shoulder. 'You can stay at home and put your feet up! I don't want anybody but Chippy and Hatchard . . . oh yes, and you, young feller,' he added, swinging round on Alan. 'You found Meriton, didn't you? I want you.'

'I was there, too, Simon,' said Flake.

'You can come along if you want to.' His gesture dismissed her as unimportant. 'Let's get a move on. We don't want to waste all day.'

'I'm going back home,' said Ferrall. 'There's no need for me to come, and I've got plenty to do.'

'You'll be hearing from the coroner's officer, sir,' said Inspector Hatchard, and Ferrall nodded.

The huge, ungainly figure of Simon Gale was already several yards away up the road. He had seized the chief constable by the arm and was dragging that perspiring individual along so fast that he had to keep on breaking into a trot to keep up with him. They heard little breathless gurgles of protest, which Gale completely ignored.

Inspector Hatchard hurried after them, and once more Alan found himself alone with Flake.

'Tell me some more about our friend,' he said. 'I'm interested. What do you mean by 'he just does anything that appeals to him'?'

'Exactly that,' she answered. 'His idea is that, in order to enjoy life, you should have no fixed occupation, but be able to do exactly as you please, when you please.'

'That's all right if you've got enough money.'

'Simon realized that. He decided to work really hard for years so that he could spend the rest of his life as he liked. He invented and patented a new breakfast food — 'Gale's Golden Flakes'.'

'Gee, is that *his?*' exclaimed Alan in surprise. 'They sell all over the States.'

'All over the world,' said Flake. 'Simon formed the original company and at the end of his five years he sold out. Since then, he *has* done as he likes.'

The object of this conversation was still striding along at a great pace, gesticulating violently, and they could hear the booming bass of his voice.

'What's made him so interested in this business?' asked Alan, after a pause.

'Just a passing craze, I expect,' she answered. 'He's like that. He takes up something new, gets wildly enthusiastic about it, and then drops it like a red-hot brick. A month or two back it was fireworks — '

'Fireworks?'

'Yes. He made them, and gave a display on the green. They were lovely. That's one of the things about Simon. Whatever he takes up, he's successful.'

'Lucky man,' Alan said.

She looked at him quickly. 'You don't like him?' she challenged.

'Not very much,' he admitted.

'You will when you know him better,' she said. 'Don't take any notice of all that bounce and bluster. That's just a pose, like the beard and the emerald shirt. Mind you, *he* doesn't realize he's posing, but that's all it is.'

Alan felt a rush of irritability flood over him. '*You* seem to like him, anyway,' he remarked curtly.

'I do,' said Flake. 'Most people do when they really know him.'

They continued in silence. Alan knew that there was no excuse at all for his bad temper, because this girl beside him happened to like a man she had known for years — known before she was even aware that *he* existed. It was ridiculous and childish . . .

They came to the entrance to Threshold House, looking different now in the bright sunlight from how it had on that night of storm and rain. Simon Gale, the chief constable, and Inspector Hatchard had stopped just inside the drive. Gale's strident voice reached them as they came up. He was saying with a wealth of gesticulation: ' . . . You've got to get an idea of the pattern, that's what you've got to get. Or the rhythm, if you prefer it.'

'That's all very well,' Major Chipingham snorted. 'It sounds very impressive. But all we've got here is a man who's been bludgeoned to death and thrown out of a window. Where's your pattern and your rhythm in that?'

'There's *bound* to be pattern an' rhythm, d'you see?' said Gale. 'It had a beginning an' it's got an end. Meriton's murder is *part* of something else — '

'Not necessarily,' broke in the chief constable, argumentatively. 'Supposing he was killed by a tramp?'

'It applies just the same,' retorted Simon Gale. 'If it was a tramp, something led up to murder, didn't it? An' the tramp's going on living his life, isn't he? He existed *before* the murder and he'll go on existing until the hangman drops him. The murder was only a dot on the line of that existence. D'you see? Like a station on a railway line. An' the principle's the same *whoever* killed Meriton. Come on, let's get up to the house. I want to see that blasted room.' He turned on his heel and the chief constable, his face flushed, shrugged his shoulders and followed.

The drive, with its carpet of weeds and moss, was still soggy from the rain, and the leaves of the bushes and trees shot sparks of fire in the sunlight as though they had been set here and there with diamonds. The porch yawned blackly behind a bored-looking constable standing on guard, and who hastily stamped out a cigarette as he saw Inspector Hatchard — an action which the inspector diplomatically pretended he hadn't noticed.

Inside the great hall, where the light filtered frugally, it was cold and dank. Alan experienced some of the sensations he had felt on the previous night when he had stood there looking up the gloomy staircase.

'Now, don't move, anybody.' Simon Gale's voice was tossed back from walls and ceiling so that it sounded hollow and unreal. He stood a little in advance of the others, sniffing the mildewed air like a great shaggy dog. 'Those are the foot-prints, are they? Meriton's and the other man's? Two lots of the other man's. One set going up and one set coming down. By the Seven Plagues of Egypt, who messed 'em all up like that?'

'I'm afraid we did,' said Inspector Hatchard apologetically. 'We've got tracings of them, though, and photographs.'

'You have, eh?' cried Gale. 'Well, *that's* something anyhow.' He stooped, almost bent double, and his eyes darted back and forth. He muttered to himself, a completely unintelligible rumbling. After two or three minutes he suddenly straightened up. 'Come on upstairs,' he said abruptly.

They followed him over to the staircase. He shook the balustrade as he went up, pulled out a couple of banisters that were loose, looked at them, and flung them down into the hall, where they hit the floor with two hollow thwacks.

They entered the Long Room. Sunlight was streaming in through the great window, making the trailing ivy outside almost translucent and tingeing the light with green. Its only effect was to make more evident the signs of decay and dilapidation which were visible everywhere, and to show up with greater clearness the dark spots on the dirty boards.

'So this is where it happened, eh?' muttered Gale, staring about and tugging at his beard. 'This is where somebody smashed in Meriton's head and pitched him out of the window. What did the murderer hit him with?'

'We haven't found the weapon yet,' said Major Chipingham.

Gale ignored the remark. He went over and peered down at the confused scrabble of footprints and the spattered blood spots. Then he stood up and looked out of the window, still tugging ferociously at his beard.

'Shall I tell you where the weapon is?' he said suddenly, twisting round and facing them. 'Somewhere down there in that tangle of shrubbery.' He jerked his thumb over his shoulder. 'That's *where* it is. Now I'll tell you *what* it is. One of those heavy banisters from the staircase. There's one missing near the top. Did you notice *that*?'

★ ★ ★

Inspector Hatchard and the constable, after a comparatively short search among the bushes, found the banister, and Simon Gale was as delighted as a child who has done something clever. He chuckled, rubbed his hands, and looked triumphantly at Major Chipingham. 'There you are, Chippy,' he said. 'What d'you say *now*, hey?'

'I don't see how you knew,' grunted the chief constable.

'Brains, my little man, brains,' cried Gale, thumping his forehead violently. 'If you'd just socked a man a wallop over the head, pitched him out of a window, and wanted to get rid of the weapon, what would *you* do with it, hey? You'd chuck it out too, as far as you could fling it. Here, let me have a look at that thing.'

'Be careful, sir,' warned the inspector anxiously. 'There may be prints — '

'I shouldn't think there was a chance in hell,' grunted Gale, 'but I'll humour you.' He laughed, snatched the immaculate wash-leather gloves that Major Chipingham was carrying, and before that annoyed and long-suffering gentleman could protest had thrust his large fingers into them.

'Really, Gale . . . really . . . ' stuttered the chief constable.

'Don't fuss! Give 'em you back,' said Simon Gale, and he took the heavy banister from the reluctant hand of the inspector. His eyes darted along its length and back again. 'No blood,' he remarked. 'Rain would have washed it off, of course. Done the same for any prints, too, I'll bet.' He thrust the banister back at Hatchard, pulled off the gloves and tossed them over to the chief constable. 'The Sorcerer's den,' he said, striding about the room with great energy. 'The house of hocus-pocus, charlatanism, abracadabra, sigils, chants, incantations and what not.' He pounced suddenly on Alan. 'That light, young feller. What was it *like?*'

'It was just a light,' answered Alan, feeling so tired that his mind almost refused to function at all.

'Just a light, eh? What d'you mean by that?'

'Well, it's difficult to describe.'

'Did it look like a torch?'

'No.' Alan shook his head. 'It may have been, but I don't think so.'

'It was very dim and looked bluish,' said Flake.

'You saw it too?' Simon Gale swung round on her.

'Yes, from my window. That's why I followed Mr. Boyce here. I guessed that he had seen it and that that was where he had gone.'

'You heard him go out.' He tugged at his beard. 'I wonder if anybody else saw that light?'

'Avril Ferrall saw it the night before last,' began Flake.

'What's that?' cried Gale. 'Avril Ferrall saw a light here — from *this* window?'

'Of course. Do you think anyone in Ferncross would be interested in a light from any *other* window?'

'Did you know about this, Chippy?' demanded Simon Gale.

'Yes, of course — ' began the chief constable irritably.

'Then why,' broke in Gale, 'didn't you tell me before? Why leave out the thing that's important?' He waved his arms impatiently and strode over to the door. 'Come on,' he said. Don't stand there like petrified dummies — come on.'

'Where are you going now?' demanded the chief constable.

'To the Ferralls', of course,' bellowed Gale, already clattering down the staircase. 'I want to hear more about this light, and I want to hear it straight from the horse's mouth.'

His long legs covered the ground at such a rate that they struggled to keep up with him. The result was a queer kind of straggling procession headed by Simon Gale, a good twelve yards in front, with Major Chipingham gamely bringing up the rear, very red in the face and gasping for breath.

'Heck,' said Alan huskily, falling into step beside Flake, 'I am tired.'

She gave him a quick sidelong glance. 'So am I. I'm going to bed after lunch and I'm going to sleep and sleep and sleep.'

'Do you think we shall be allowed to sleep — any of us?' he said.

'I'm not going to ask anybody's permission,' she answered. 'I'm just going to lock my door and go to bed. If you're wise you'll do the same.'

Dr. Ferrall had gone out on his morning round of visits when they reached the house on the green, but Avril was at home and received them in a house-frock of *eau de nil* velvet with long princess sleeves that made her look, Alan thought, like Lady Macbeth. Her face was pale and there was a faint puffy redness about her eyelids as though she had been crying.

'Isn't it dreadful,' she said, and her deep, rich voice was marred by a slight huskiness, 'about poor Paul? Peter told me.'

'Murder is always dreadful when it actually happens and you don't read about it in books,' broke in Gale. 'I'm told you and Ferrall drove Meriton home last night?'

Avril, who had flinched at the word 'murder', nodded slowly.

'What happened?' he demanded.

'Why . . . nothing happened,' she

answered quickly, but she looked uneasy. 'We . . . just dropped him at his gate, that's all.'

'You didn't go in?'

'No. It was getting late and the rain was beginning. Peter and I were very tired.'

Simon Gale picked up a vase from the mantelpiece, looked at it with an expression of loathing, and put it down again. 'The night before last, you saw a light in Threshold House,' he said suddenly. 'What time was it and what was it like?'

Why *was* he so interested in what the light was like? thought Alan irritably. What the hell did it matter what it was like, anyway? A description of the light wasn't going to tell them who had killed Paul Meriton.

'It was about half past twelve,' said Avril. 'I'd been out to dinner and I was late coming home. It was a very dim light — '

'Bluish?' asked Gale quickly.

'Yes.' She nodded. 'I told Flake about it last night, when we were all sitting in the garden. Didn't I, Flake?'

'You did,' agreed Flake. 'You also said you wondered who was going to die *this* time.'

Avril caught her breath and pressed a hand against her breast.

'You said *that*, did you?' cried Gale. 'Why did you say that? Did you *expect* that Meriton was going to be murdered?'

'No, no,' she said. Her hands, smoothing down the sides of her housecoat, were trembling. 'Of course I didn't. But every time there *has* been a light in that window *somebody* has died!'

'My dear Miss Ferrall,' said Major Chipingham. 'You surely don't believe that there can be any connection?'

'Why not, Chippy?' cried Gale. 'Why not?' He leered ferociously at the chief constable.

'Because it's ridiculous,' snapped Major Chipingham. 'How can a sort of child's fairy tale — '

'There was a light when the man was killed on the motorcycle,' interrupted Avril Ferrall. 'There was a light when the tramp died — '

'And there was a light *last* night when

Meriton was killed,' said Gale, rubbing his hands together almost gleefully. 'You can't get away from that, Chippy, old boy. Ridiculous, rubbish, fairy tales — all the words that mean the same thing, don't explain *that* away.'

'You're not going to tell me that *you* think — ' began the major.

'I do — frequently,' interrupted Gale, with a burst of laughter. 'And you'd be surprised at some of the things I think about, you old mule.'

'Nothing concerning you would ever surprise me,' retorted the major stiffly. 'And I object strongly to being referred to as a — '

The remainder of the sentence was lost in a prodigious gasp as Simon Gale gave him a hearty slap on the back and knocked all the breath out of him. It was intended for an affectionate pat but was rather like the kick of a horse.

'Don't get huffy, Chippy,' he said. 'I'll see this thing through for you. I feel like beer — a lot of beer! Let's all go down to the pub and have a drink. You come along, too, Avril.'

75

'I'll have to change.' She hesitated, but the suggestion obviously appealed to her.

'Well, go on then. What are you waiting for?' He strode over to the door and held it open impatiently. 'We'll give you three minutes.'

'Look here, Gale,' said Major Chipingham as she went out. 'Hatchard and I can't waste time drinking. This is a murder investigation. We've got to see the coroner about the inquest.'

'All right, all right,' said Gale, sweeping aside the objection with a wave of his huge arm. 'What time did it start raining last night, hey?'

'About ten to twelve,' answered Flake before the major could reply. 'It was just before we went indoors. Do you remember, Mr. Boyce?'

Alan nodded. He remembered everything about that evening very vividly.

'What time did Meriton leave with the Ferralls?' inquired Simon Gale, cocking a disapproving eye at a picture over the mantelpiece and suddenly making a hideous grimace at it.

'Just before eleven,' said Flake.

'Ah-ha!' Gale swung round with such a violent movement that he nearly knocked over a small table beside him. 'The plot thickens. They left just before eleven, did they? And *she* said' — he jerked his head towards the door — 'that it was just *starting* to rain when they left Meriton at his gate. Get that? It's only five minutes' run by car from Bryony Cottage to Meriton's house. *Five minutes.* And they took nearly an *hour.* By the nine lives of Grimalkin, what did they do in the interval?'

5

The village of Ferncross, considering its size, was very well provided with public houses. There were three in all: the Red Lion, facing the small railway station; the Horse and Groom, at the upper end of the short and narrow High Street, and the Three Witches on the fringe of the green.

The Three Witches, if not the largest and most imposing of the trio, was a pleasant-looking white-washed building of great age, with a thatched roof and oak beams, and full of shining copper and old pewter. It stood on the site of an ancient cottage — part of the original building still remained — that had once belonged to three sisters who were accused of practising witchcraft by the infamous Mathew Hopkins, and subsequently burned at the stake.

The bars were low-ceilinged and raftered; the fireplaces, of ancient, mellowed brick, wide and deep, with oak settles; and in the principal bar, dignified with the title 'Saloon Lounge', there was a cosy ingle-nook. The entire atmosphere was a pleasant mixture of age and solid comfort, and the majority of the residents of Ferncross forgathered in the oblong bar for such refreshment and company as they desired outside their own homes, under the genial auspices of the landlord, Mr. Jellyberry.

Simon Gale was a regular and popular frequenter of the Three Witches. The quality of the beer was better than at either of the two rival establishments, and on most evenings he was to be found leaning against the bar, consuming vast quantities of this delectable brew, and holding forth in his booming bass upon a variety of subjects to the edification and, it must be admitted, the amusement of those present. His views on most things were anything but conventional and he had a passionate hatred of all forms of cant and humbug. He delighted in taking a tradition, or an established institution, and twisting it inside-out so that its ridiculous aspect was the only thing that remained. Whatever his opinion, he would always take the opposite side of an argument for the sheer love of controversy, and when he had demolished his opponents' arguments completely, would blandly turn round and declare that he entirely agreed with everything they had said and order up fresh drinks.

When he strode into the bar, followed by Alan Boyce, Flake and Avril Ferrall, he was greeted by the stout, rubicund landlord with a beaming smile.

'Mornin', Mr. Gale, sir,' he said without stopping the vigorous polishing of the glass he was holding in his chubby hands. 'Goin' ter be another powerful 'ot day, I'm thinkin'. Mornin', Miss White. Mornin', Miss Ferrall.'

'Good morning, Jellyberry,' greeted Gale, in a voice that set the bottles and glasses ringing. 'I want beer — lots of beer! What are you going to have?'

'I'd like a large gin and French,' said Avril. 'Booth's gin.'

'I'd like one, too, please,' said Flake.

'Beer for me,' said Alan. 'I've heard a lot about English beer — '

'Oh yes, you're American, aren't you?' said Simon Gale. 'No such thing as decent beer in America. Wishy-washy stuff without any body in it. And they *can* it. Bah! If this is your first taste of *real* beer you've come to the right place, eh, Jellyberry?'

'Well, Mr. Gale,' said the landlord, wiping his hands on the cloth with which he had been drying his glasses, 'though I say it as shouldn't, I don't s'pose you'll find a better drop o' draught bitter anywhere.'

'Dish it out, man,' said Gale. 'Fill the flowing bowl. I've a thirst — a real, full-grown, hundred-percent thirst! Produce two of the largest tankards you've got.'

The landlord complied. He set before them, on the age-blackened oak of the bar, two gins-and-French and two gargantuan tankards topped with frothing foam.

'Ah!' cried Gale. He seized his tankard, lifted it to the level of his bearded lips, threw back his head and poured a prodigious quantity down his throat, apparently without bothering to swallow. 'That's better,' he said, banging the tankard down on the bar and wiping the froth from his beard with the back of his hand. 'I needed that.' He looked at Alan. 'Well, young feller, what d'you think of *real* beer, eh?'

Alan nodded over the top of his tankard. 'I guess I like it,' he replied.

'You'd like it better if you *drank* it instead of sipping it,' grunted Gale. 'Go on, swallow it, man! Beer was made to be quaffed, not sipped like a parson taking tea with an old maiden aunt.' He drained the contents of his own tankard in one gulp. 'That's the way to drink beer, my lad. Fill it up again, Jellyberry.'

'We haven't *all* got your capacity, Simon,' said Flake.

'Or practice,' murmured Avril maliciously.

'It's neither capacity nor practice,' retorted Simon Gale. 'It's an art! We'll teach Boyce to acquire it, if he stays here long enough. Swallow it down, young feller, an' have another.'

The tankard must have contained

nearly a quart, but Alan dealt with it valiantly, if a trifle breathlessly.

'We'll all have another — on me,' he said, gasping a little as he set down the empty tankard.

'That's the stuff,' cried Gale, slapping him on the back with a huge hand and knocking all the remainder of his breath out of him. 'We'll make you a beer-drinker, yet — eh, Jellyberry?'

The beaming landlord nodded as he refilled the glasses and tankards. 'There's them that's beer drinkers an' them that ain't,' he said. 'Now, poor Mr. Meriton — 'e liked whiskey.'

'Why do you say 'poor' Mr. Meriton?' demanded Gale quickly.

'Well, I did 'ear that 'e'd met with an accident,' said Mr. Jellyberry placidly. 'Up at that there 'ouse of 'is on the 'ill, it 'appened, so I'm told.'

'And who told you all this?' asked Gale.

Mr. Jellyberry pushed forward two full tankards and picked up a bottle of *Noilly Prat*. 'Well, it was the wife,' he said, 'but she did 'ear it from Tanner's boy.'

'And Tanner's boy heard it from the

postman, who got it from the baker,'
interrupted Gale, with a huge grin. 'In
other words, it's all round the village,
hey?'

'I suppose that'd be about it, sir.' Mr.
Jellyberry's large fat face creased into a
smile. 'Is there any truth in it?'

'I'm afraid there is,' said Simon Gale.
He took a huge gulp of beer, and Alan
watched in fascinated amazement. The
capacity of this huge bearded man was
extraordinary. 'And it wasn't an accident.'

The beaming expanse of Mr. Jellyberry's face changed. His smile vanished and
was replaced by a look of concern. 'You
don't mean as it was . . . ?'

'It was murder,' answered Simon Gale.
'Somebody bashed Meriton's head in an'
threw him out the window.' He picked up
his tankard, glared at it ferociously, flung
back his head, and swallowed the
remainder of its contents. 'More beer,' he
said, banging the tankard down on the
bar.

Frowning thoughtfully, the landlord
mechanically refilled it. Alan thought that
he looked more puzzled than surprised.

'That's a queer thing to've 'appened, now, ain't it, sir?' he remarked.

'Queer?' echoed Gale. 'By the cloven hooves of Pan, it's remarkable. There was a light in the window the night before it happened.'

'Yes, sir — I did 'ear about that,' said Mr. Jellyberry. 'That's what made me say it was queer.'

'Do you believe in the local superstition?' put in Alan.

'Well, sir . . . ' The landlord was hesitant. 'Most o' the folk these parts do.'

'Answer the question,' said Gale, like a Q.C. with an unwilling witness. 'Mr. Boyce said, 'Do *you* believe in it?'

'I don't really know 'ow ter answer,' said Mr. Jellyberry. His small eyes were perplexed and wary. 'Yer see, there be some things that folk can't explain, now, ain't there?'

'That's how I feel about it,' breathed Avril Ferrall. 'I don't actually *believe* . . . but there *might* be something in it.'

'Ah-ha.' Gale grinned down at her, his beard almost bristling. He really was, thought Alan, a most objectionable man.

'Of *course* there's something in it.'

'Does that mean that *you* believe it?' asked Flake.

'Lights *have* been seen in that window,' replied Simon Gale, '*and* people have died — violently. That's an irrefutable fact.'

'But is there a connection?' said Alan sceptically.

Gale looked at him. He said, in a voice that was no longer deep and booming, but low and thoughtful: 'Ah, that's the question . . . *Is* there a connection? Fill up those tankards, Jellyberry, and let's have two more gins-and-French.' The latter part of this was a reversion to his former boisterous manner. The change was so sudden that Alan looked round for the cause. Somebody had come quietly into the bar. He was a middle-aged man with a straggling greyish-ginger moustache, rather shabbily dressed, and possessing a large nose, the reddish colour of which spread over his thin cheeks which were otherwise very pale, producing a rather startling effect. The mouth below the unkempt moustache

86

was loose, with wet lips, and under this was a very small pimple of a chin. He was rather like a photograph of George Moore that Alan had once seen in his father's office.

He came over to the bar with a curious hesitant step, as though he wasn't quite sure where he was going.

'Good morning, Mr. Veezey,' greeted the landlord. 'The usual, I s'pose?'

The newcomer nodded jerkily, his watery eyes moving restlessly over the four other occupants, but with such a dull, dead-fish expression that Alan was convinced he had no idea what he was looking at.

'Yes . . . yes, please,' he murmured tremulously, fumbling in his pocket.

Mr. Jellyberry turned to his stocked shelves, selected a bottle of Scotch whiskey, poured out a generous double, and pushed the glass gently across the bar.

Mr. Veezey continued to fumble in his pocket, apparently failed to find what he was seeking, and transferred his search to another. Eventually, first from one pocket and then from another, he produced a number of coins which he laid in a row before the landlord. Then he picked up his glass and with one swift movement swallowed the contents.

'Again, please,' he murmured, pushing the empty glass across the counter.

Mr. Jellyberry, preparing to execute the order, caught Alan's eye and winked, slowly and ponderously. He poured out another double whiskey and placed it before Mr. Veezey. Once more the previous performance was repeated to the astonishment and secret amusement of the American. Mr. Veezey found, with apparent great difficulty, sufficient money from his various pockets to pay for his drink. As before he carefully placed the amount in front of Mr. Jellyberry, swallowed his whiskey and, politely raising his battered straw hat, drifted out with his peculiar, uncertain step.

'Say, that's quite a character,' remarked Alan when the back of Mr. Veezey had disappeared from view.

Mr. Jellyberry rested his large forearms

on the counter and uttered a rumbling chuckle. 'That he be,' he agreed. 'That's 'is breakfast . . . Two double whiskies,' said the landlord, nodding. 'Day in an' day out.'

'Does he always go through that queer act of searching for the money?' asked the American.

'Yer'd think 'e was 'ard up, wouldn't yer?' grinned Mr. Jellyberry. 'Bless yer, 'e's got more money than what I 'ave. That just be 'is way, that be.'

'Poor Mr. Veezey,' said Flake. 'He always looks dazed — as if he hadn't quite woken up.'

'Drink,' said Alan laconically.

'You're wrong, m'lad,' said Simon Gale, shaking his head. 'Those two drinks are the only ones Veezey'll have today. That rosy flush that suffuses his nose and cheeks is not the result of alcoholic intemperance but of acne — common or garden acne.'

'Tha's right, sir,' said Mr. Jellyberry, nodding in agreement. 'Not another drop'll pass 'is lips until the same time termorrow.'

'Peter says he's crazy,' Avril Ferrall's voice joined in the conversation. 'Living all alone in that little hut . . . '

'Hut?' said Alan.

'Well, that's all it is,' said Avril. 'It was an old army hut when Veezey bought it.'

'He's made it look very nice,' remarked Flake.

'Aye, that 'e 'as,' said Mr. Jellyberry. 'Proper nice bit o' garden 'e's got.'

'But if he's well off, why does he want to live in a hut?' said Alan.

'Because he likes it — and that's the best reason in the world.' Simon Gale waved the eccentric Mr. Veezey out of existence. 'Drink up, all of you. We'll have another an' then I must be off. I want to see Meriton's housekeeper.'

* * *

On either side of the narrow rutted lane were thick woods and the great trees met overhead, their leaves vivid and translucent in the sunlight. On the dusty path splashes of bright yellow, like the spilled pieces of a jigsaw puzzle, flickered and danced as the breeze stirred the branches overhead.

Alan Boyce, walking along this leafy green tunnel with Flake beside him, thought that all he had heard about the restful beauty of the English countryside had not been an exaggeration.

His eyes were hot and heavy, but the tiredness which had overwhelmed him earlier had given place to a restless, nervous energy. He knew this was but an extension of his previous weariness — that what his whole mind and body craved was rest — but he also knew that his present state of nervous overstrain would not allow it.

Flake felt the same. She had told him so when he had suggested that she ought to go home and lie down. 'It wouldn't be any use,' she said, shrugging. 'I've gone past it. What I need is fresh air, lots and lots of it.'

They had left Simon Gale to seek his interview with Mrs. Horly, Paul Meriton's housekeeper, and Avril to return home, and set out on a desultory, circuitous ramble back to Bryony Cottage.

The countryside surrounding the village was lovely in the haze of that hot morning. The oppressive heat of the previous night had gone. It was still very hot, but it was a different heat. There was more energy in it, and everything looked fresh after the heavy rain. The scent from hot sun on the rain-soaked earth came refreshingly to their nostrils and partially, if not quite, drove away the memory of the horrors of the previous night. The moment when he had found Meriton lying wet and dead under the window of the Long Room at Sorcerer's House would never fade entirely from Alan Boyce's mind, but it was no longer a vivid terror. Curiosity had taken the place of fear.

'How long have you known the Ferralls?' he asked suddenly, breaking a long silence.

Flake wrinkled up her nose in the delightful way which he found so attractive. 'About three years, I think,' she answered. 'Since Dr. Ferrall bought old Dr. Wycherly's practice.'

'What do you think of them?' he said.

92

She gave him a quick sidelong glance, looking up under her long dark lashes. 'What *do you* think of them?' she answered.

'I don't quite know,' he said, after an interval. 'Avril made a queer remark last night in your garden.'

'About the light?' she said. 'She's always doing that sort of thing. I wouldn't — '

'No, *not* about the light,' he broke in quickly. 'It was after that, when I was helping you with the drinks.'

'What did she say?' asked Flake. 'I didn't hear her say anything.'

'I don't think anyone heard her except me and her brother,' he answered. 'I wasn't *intended* to hear what she said. But I did — while I was handing her the drinks. She said, 'It's dangerous.''

'She said *what* was dangerous?' asked Flake.

'I don't know. That was all I heard. Just, 'It's dangerous.''

Flake pursed her lips. She said, frowning: 'I wonder what she meant by that?'

'I wondered at the time,' said Alan, 'and I've wondered quite a lot since. Particularly after last night.'

'It might not have anything to do with *that*,' said Flake. 'If you'd heard all she said it might not really be anything at all . . . I mean, she might have been referring to something in the house — a loose board or — or the leg of a chair . . . something like that.'

Alan's imagination conjured up that shadowy garden with the queer, sinister atmosphere that had suddenly come into it. He thought it was very unlikely that those two words which had floated up to him so clearly were merely the end of a trivial sentence. He said doubtfully: 'Well, you may be right.'

'You're not suggesting that the *Ferralls* could have . . . had anything to do with Paul's murder, are you?' said Flake. 'What reason could they have?'

'What reason could anybody have?' said Alan. 'There must have *been* a reason, you know.'

'Yes, I suppose so.' She made the admission, he thought, a little reluctantly.

'But the Ferralls . . . it's ridiculous.'

They walked on for a while in silence. The lane emerged from the screening woods into open country, and the hot sun beat down full on them. The sky was a clear bright blue, without a cloud anywhere to break its smoothness. Somewhere the faint drone of a tractor seemed, curiously, to enhance the stillness. Alan slipped off his jacket and slung it over his arm.

'Out here it all seems like a bad dream, doesn't it?' said Flake. Her face, he thought, was looking a little strained.

'Yes . . . only it wasn't,' he answered. 'Somebody really *did* kill Meriton at that old house last night.'

Flake shook back her thick hair. 'Your introduction to our peaceful English countryside hasn't been very successful, has it?' she remarked.

'I guess I'm satisfied,' he said, and she flushed slightly. 'Look here,' he went on, 'tell me more about the people around here, starting with Meriton.'

'They're a queer lot, some of them,' said Flake. 'You'll find the same types in most English villages. The Meritons, of course, are almost part of the village.'

'The Meritons,' he repeated. 'Are there any more?'

'Not now,' said Flake. 'Paul was the last of the line. But years and years ago the Meritons owned the whole village and a good part of the surrounding land as well. Old Percival Meriton lost all that at dice one night, and for a long time after they were very poor. Then one of the sons, Martyn Meriton, won a lot of money at cards, bought back the manor, and settled down to live there with his wife. He died from an apoplectic stroke.'

'Too much port?' interjected Alan.

'Yes — I expect that was it.' She smiled. 'They were all heavy drinkers in those days.'

'Was Paul Meriton a heavy drinker?'

She shook her head. 'No, not really,' she said. 'After old Martyn's death there wasn't much money, and, when Cagliostro offered to rent the house, Martyn's widow was only too glad to accept the offer. She moved out with her family — two sons and a daughter — into

Ferncross Lodge, a much smaller house on the outskirts of village, where Paul lived.'

'None of them went back to Threshold House?' asked Alan.

'No. Mostly, I think, because they never had enough money. They tried to sell it after Cagliostro had gone, but nobody would buy it. There were a lot of rumours about it.'

'Nobody has lived there since?'

'No. It's just been left to decay.'

'Pity,' said Alan. 'It must have been a fine house in its day. Couldn't Meriton sell it?'

'I don't know that he ever tried,' said Flake. 'Paul hated the place but he disliked selling anything that belonged to his family. He owned a lot of the land round here but he wouldn't sell any of it.'

'And he lived alone at Ferncross Lodge?'

'Only recently.' Flake paused and hesitated. 'Until about two years ago, he lived there with his wife.'

'His wife!' exclaimed the American.

'He married Colonel Ayling's daughter.

You'll meet Colonel Ayling — nobody can stay here long without meeting Colonel Ayling. Paul was terribly in love with her.'

'What happened? Did she die?' asked Alan as she stopped.

'She ran away,' said Flake slowly. 'She left a note saying that she had gone, and it was no use trying to find her. There was another man, of course, but nobody ever discovered who he was.'

'Did Meriton take it badly?'

'He went all to pieces,' replied Flake. 'Shut himself up and wouldn't see anybody. He recovered a little after a time, but was never really the same since.' She frowned.

'And didn't anybody ever find out why she went, or who she went with?' asked Alan. 'Surely she said *something* in the note she left?'

'Not anything very helpful,' answered Flake. 'Paul showed us the note. It said: *I'm going away and it's no use your trying to find me. You will never see me again.*' She paused and added: 'Nobody ever has.'

Alan pursed his lips. 'Didn't anybody try?'

'Oh yes. Colonel Ayling was furious — he liked Paul — and he went to the police. But they never found her.'

'Did anyone suspect who the man was?' asked Alan.

She shook her head. 'No. It couldn't have been anyone in Ferncross — '

'Why not?' he said quickly.

'If it had been he would have gone, too, wouldn't he?'

'Perhaps there wasn't a man,' suggested Alan.

'There usually is, isn't there?' said Flake. 'If there wasn't, why did she go?'

'There *could* have been some other reason,' he replied.

'I suppose there could,' she said without conviction. 'Everybody here was certain there was some man at the bottom of it. Fay was very beautiful — '

'Fay — that's quite a pretty name,' said Alan.

She gave him another of those infernally disturbing sidelong glances and said with a peculiar intonation: 'It suited her.

Somehow you'd *expect* her to be called Fay.'

'You didn't like her?

'Well, no, I didn't,' she answered candidly. 'I don't think many women did — not round here, I mean.'

Alan pulled out a packet of cigarettes, gave one to Flake and took one himself. He snapped a lighter into flame and lit both.

'Why?' he asked. 'What was wrong with her?'

'When you first met her you thought she was sweet,' said Flake. 'It was only when you got to know her better that you began to realize that it was all on the surface. Underneath she was mean and selfish.'

The lane turned sharply and they came out onto a road. Coming towards them along the road, and walking on the rough grass verge, was an elderly man in grey flannels and a worn sports jacket patched with leather at the cuffs and elbows. He was hatless and the sun shone on the baldness of his head, which was relieved from complete nakedness by a trace of white over his ears.

Flake pressed her arm against Alan's. 'That's Colonel Ayling,' she said. 'Fay's father.'

As they drew nearer, Alan saw that the man's face was bronzed and very lined. An aggressive nose dominated it, jutting out almost like a beak, under which the thin mouth lay straight and lipless beneath a closely trimmed moustache.

Colonel Ayling, he thought, looked formidable. He could not imagine anything turning him from his purpose once he made up his mind on a course of action. The determination of face was repeated in his walk. There was nothing hesitant about it. He strode forward as if he knew exactly where he was going and meant to get there in the shortest possible time.

When they were almost up with him, he smiled and stopped. 'Hello, Flake,' he said, and his voice was rather harsh. 'What a lovely day.'

His sunken eyes under the ragged white brows looked at Alan interrogatively, and Flake introduced them.

'American, eh?' remarked Colonel Ayling. 'This your first visit to England?'

'Yes,' answered Alan.

'Well, what do you think of it, eh?'

Alan answered, truthfully, that he liked it very much indeed.

'You couldn't have chosen a better time, except maybe the spring,' said Ayling, looking round as though he were personally responsible for the beauty of the country. 'And, of course, this is unusual weather — we're not always so lucky, eh, Flake?' The expression in his eyes changed suddenly. 'I say, you must be the feller who found poor Meriton last night?'

'We both found him,' said Flake.

'Terrible thing to have happened,' said Colonel Ayling. 'I couldn't believe it when I heard about it. Still think there must be some mistake. Who could want to murder Meriton?'

'Somebody not only wanted to, but did,' said Alan.

'Surely it might have been an accident?'

'I'm afraid there's no chance of that,' said Alan.

'He was hit on the head with one of those loose banisters,' augmented Flake. 'And Simon found — '

'Simon? You mean Gale?' broke in Colonel Ayling. 'How did *he* become mixed up in it?'

Flake told him.

'Good heavens, does he fancy himself as a detective now?' exclaimed Ayling. 'What the devil will he take up next?'

'He's very enthusiastic,' said Flake, smiling.

'Enthusiastic!' echoed the colonel. 'He's always enthusiastic over every fresh notion he gets in his head. We shall be treated to an immense display of energy and he'll probably have half the village arrested before he's through. Do you remember the fireworks?'

'They were very good fireworks,' murmured Flake.

'They burned down two haystacks and set fire to the thatched roof of Mrs. Gumsol's cottage!' said Colonel Ayling grimly. Quite obviously, thought Alan, he did not approve of the blustering Mr. Gale. He discovered that he was rather pleased at this. He felt like shaking Colonel Ayling warmly by the hand.

'How did you two come to find Meriton?' went on Ayling, looking keenly from one to the other, and finally fixing his eyes on Alan.

'I saw a light in the window of the Long Room from my room in Bryony Cottage,' Alan explained. 'We'd been talking about the legend, or whatever you call it, earlier in the evening.'

'He was curious and went to see what it was,' chimed in Flake. 'I heard him go out and followed him.'

'And you found poor Meriton lying under the window?' asked Ayling. His lined face puckered up in a frown. 'With a fractured skull?'

'Yes,' said Flake.

'Extraordinary,' muttered the colonel, his face clouding. 'What the devil was he doing at Threshold House on a night like that?'

'If that were known, we'd probably know who killed him,' said Alan.

'H'm, very probably. Damned queer business altogether. Which way are you going?' Ayling finished abruptly.

'Back home,' answered Flake. She looked at the watch on her wrist. 'We'll just get there in time for lunch.'

'Mind if I walk along with you?' asked Ayling. 'I was going home myself, but I can easily cut across Penny's Meadow.'

Alan would have preferred to dispense with his company, and he had a satisfying idea that Flake would, too, but there seemed to be no way out of it without being rude. With Flake between them they walked along the hot road. Alan had been rather curious to learn how Colonel Ayling had become so well informed about the events of the previous night, and he discovered that he had got his information from Peter Ferrall. Mrs. Ayling had been suffering from a bilious attack — Flake told him, afterwards, that she was always over-eating — Ferrall had called in to see her, and during his visit had told them the news.

'My wife is very distressed, as you can imagine,' said Ayling. 'Paul was a great favourite of hers — as, of course, he was of mine. A nice fellow, a very nice fellow.'

He shook his head sorrowfully and for a little while there was silence. It was Flake who spoke first.

'Oh, look,' she exclaimed suddenly. 'Now we are in for it.'

A bicycle had suddenly shot out of a side lane. It was a very decrepit lady's bicycle and everything on it that could be loose was, judging from the noise it made, very loose indeed. Mounted on this appalling contraption, sitting bolt upright and gripping the handlebars firmly with her mitten-clad hands, was an elderly lady whom Alan stared at in fascinated astonishment.

She looked exactly like a photograph of somebody's Victorian aunt. Her hair was screwed up on the top of her head in a grey bun; her blouse was fastened at her throat with a small bow of black velvet, and the sleeves were genuine leg-of-mutton. Her skirt was very wide and long and billowed out on either side of the ancient bicycle, allowing fleeting glimpses of elastic-sided boots as they moved up and down on the pedals. The skirt was secured at the waist by a broad belt of shiny patent leather which encased her narrow midriff very tightly, producing a curious waspish effect.

'Who is it?' asked Alan, without removing his eyes from this astounding apparition rattling rapidly towards them.

'Miss Flappit,' answered Flake. 'She's awful! But we can't do anything about it now.'

The bicycle added a loud squeal to its other collection of noises as Miss Flappit applied the brakes and stopped with a jerk beside them.

'What a truly delightful morning,' she said in a voice that was like the echo of the squeaking brakes, as she slid off the saddle. 'How are you, Colonel Ayling, and my dear Miss Onslow-White?'

'I'm very well, thank you, Miss Flappit,' said Flake. 'This is Mr. Boyce; he's staying with us.'

'And you're showing him the beauties of our delightful neighbourhood?' beamed Miss Flappit, with a smile that reminded Alan of a vicious horse. 'Don't you think the countryside here is charming, Mr. Boyce?'

Alan said he thought it was very charming indeed. He wondered how often during his stay he would have to say this.

'I've been hearing the most dreadful rumours,' went on Miss Flappit eagerly. 'Of course I don't suppose for one moment it's *true* — they exaggerate things so in Ferncross — but they say that Mr. Meriton has been murdered!'

'I'm afraid it *is* true,' broke in Colonel Ayling.

'Dear me, how very shocking,' said Miss Flappit. She didn't look the least bit shocked, Alan thought. Her eyes opened very wide behind her steel-rimmed spectacles with an expression of avid interest. '*Do* tell me how it happened and who did it.'

As briefly as possible they told her all that was known.

'And so it isn't known who did it?' said Miss Flappit. 'Dear me, it's *exactly* like a detective story, is it not? I'm so *fond* of a good detective story, Mr. Boyce. You know, I've always *said* that house was unlucky. Don't you think it's strange that poor Mr. Meriton should have died almost *exactly* in the same way as that unfortunate tramp? Do you think there *could* be any connection?'

'I should doubt it,' grunted Colonel Ayling. 'This doesn't happen to be a detective story, you see,' he added drily.

'I'm sure I'm probably being very silly,' said Miss Flappit, who quite obviously didn't think anything of the kind, 'but it seems to me that the *first* thing to look for is the *motive* — don't you think so?'

This was so obviously true that they had to agree. 'Why should anyone *wish* to kill Mr. Meriton?' she continued, screwing up her angular face into a tortured expression of concentration. '*That* is the question.'

'To which, I very much doubt, if *we* can provide an answer,' said Colonel Ayling pointedly. It was evident that he had no wish to continue the discussion. But Miss Flappit was not to be put off so easily.

'Well, it might be Mr. Veezey, you know,' she said thoughtfully. 'He's a very peculiar man and nobody knows very much about him, do they?'

'I don't think that's a good enough reason for suspecting him of murder,' said Alan.

Miss Flappit turned her long face towards him. Her expression was one of strong disapproval. She said severely:

'*I* should hardly consider it a good and sufficient reason myself, young man, but it doesn't happen to *be* the reason for my suggesting Mr. Veezey.'

'What *is* your reason, then, Miss Flappit?' inquired Flake politely.

Miss Flappit's eyes gleamed. She moistened her lips in anticipatory relish of the tit-bit she was about to impart. She said: 'Well, you see, I overheard Mr. Veezey threaten to kill Mr. Meriton four days ago.'

countryside . . . '

Colonel Ayling, who looked as though he wished something especially shocking might happen to Miss Flappit right there and then, could contain himself no longer. He said with impatience: 'Veezey and Meriton, I suppose?'

'Yes,' said Miss Flappit, making two quick little forward movements of her head, like a bird pecking at a worm. 'It is so very *dark* there, because of the overhanging trees, that I didn't recognize them immediately. They were quite unaware of *my* presence in the vicinity, and I had no wish to attract attention to myself. I drew back into Hanger's Lane, and then I heard Mr. Veezey say, in a *very* excited manner: 'If you do that, I'll kill you!' Mr. Meriton laughed, and Mr. Veezey shouted: 'I will! I warn you, I'll kill you!''

'Are you sure it *was* Veezey and Meriton?' interrupted Ayling.

'Oh, yes indeed,' said Miss Flappit with conviction. 'There is no *doubt* about that at all. I recognized Mr. Veezey's voice at *once*!'

6

Miss Flappit surveyed them triumphantly, her small eyes bright behind her spectacles. She had fired her broadside and awaited the result with evident enjoyment.

'Rubbish!' snorted Colonel Ayling. 'Nonsense! Veezey? It's ridiculous.'

Miss Flappit drew herself up with dignity. A faint flush coloured her sallow cheeks. 'I am only telling you what I heard,' she said in a voice that was like chipped ice falling into a tin pail. 'If you do not *believe* what I say — '

'Oh, indeed we do,' interrupted Flake soothingly. 'It isn't that at all, Miss Flappit. Only it's so difficult to imagine poor little Mr. Veezey threatening to kill *anyone*.'

'Well, he did,' said Miss Flappit decisively. '*And* he sounded as if he meant it. I am the *last* person to propagate *gossip*' — she made this utterly fallacious assertion without even the tremor of an eyelid — 'but if there *is* a murderer at large in Ferncross, then I consider it the duty of everyone to frankly disclose anything that might lead to his apprehension.' Her attitude defied them to contradict her.

Alan Boyce, catching Flake's eye, very nearly choked. He said in a slightly strangled voice: 'I guess that's the duty of every good citizen.'

'How did you come to hear Veezey utter this threat?' asked Colonel Ayling abruptly.

Miss Flappit drew a deep breath as though preparing for verbal battle. Her mittened hands closed firmly on the grips of the decrepit bicycle.

'I wouldn't like you to think that I was *eavesdropping*,' she said with great earnestness. 'It was only *quite* by accident that I heard what Mr. Veezey said. I was coming home rather late from the church hall — there had been a meeting of the bazaar committee, and the agenda was rather a lengthy one, and the old Mrs. Wardle *would* keep on interrupting the proceedings with the most *ridiculous* questions — the poor vicar had the greatest *difficulty* in keeping his temper — such a trying woman . . . ' Miss Flappit took a quick gulp and continued: 'I had not got my bicycle with me — the rear tyre had developed a puncture when I was shopping earlier, and I had to walk home. There is a short cut through Hanger's Lane which brings one out at the foot of the bridge over the Dark Water — I should *never* have gone that way, only it was *really* getting so very *late*, and it *does* save fifteen minutes . . . ' Miss Flappit took in more air, and Alan wondered whether she would ever get to the point.

'One cannot *see* the bridge,' Miss Flappit's high-pitched voice began again, 'until one is right *out* of Hanger's Lane, so I had no *idea* there was anyone on it until I was scarcely more than a few yards away. It gave me a *dreadful* shock when I saw there were two *men* there — one hears of such *shocking* things happening to women these days, doesn't one? — particularly in lonely parts of the

'How did you know it was Meriton he was talking to?' asked the colonel.

'He walked past the end of Hanger's Lane a few seconds later,' said Miss Flappit. 'He left Mr. Veezey still standing on the bridge.'

'What did he say when Veezey threatened to kill him?' asked Alan.

'Nothing,' declared Miss Flappit. 'He only *laughed*. It was not a very *nice* laugh,' she added. 'Not a nice laugh at *all* . . . '

'What happened to Mr. Veezey after Paul had left him?' inquired Flake.

'He stood on the bridge looking down into the Dark Water for perhaps two or three minutes, and then he walked away,' replied Miss Flappit. 'It was *most* embarrassing!'

'Why?' grunted Ayling.

'He was crying,' said Miss Flappit.

There was a silence. In it, startlingly clear, came the measured strokes of a bell. Instantly, Miss Flappit became galvanized into activity.

'Good gracious!' she exclaimed. 'Can it be twelve o'clock already? Dear me, I really *mustn't* loiter any longer. I *should* be at the vicarage — I promised the vicar, *faithfully*, I wouldn't be late. Goodbye, Colonel Ayling; goodbye Miss Onslow-White. I trust, Mr. Boyce, you will enjoy your stay in Ferncross. Such delightful country.'

She wheeled the decrepit bicycle to the middle of the road, mounted it, and, after a preliminary wobble, went pedalling away towards the village, accompanied by sufficient rattles and squeaks to have satisfied Alice's White Knight.

★ ★ ★

Alan Boyce lay on the bed in his pleasant little room at Bryony Cottage. He had come up immediately after lunch, hoping to snatch an hour's sleep. But with the afternoon the heat had come back again. The window was wide open but there was no air to cool the room. Waves of heat beat down from the low ceiling: a humid heat, damp, sticky, and enervating.

His eyes felt full of hot sand, and there was a dull ache somewhere behind them, but his mind refused to be quietened. It was as though a wheel were spinning inside his brain — a wheel which kept forming pictures, like an old-fashioned kinetoscope that moved and jerked and changed.

He knew that he was suffering from overtiredness. The previous deadness of his mind had been replaced by an intense, vibrating activity, but eventually the deadness would return and, with it, a soothing oblivion. But, in the meanwhile, sleep was impossible.

He sat up, punched the damp, hot pillows into a more comfortable shape, took a cigarette from a packet on the table by the bed, lit it, and leaned back resignedly. The minute-hand of the little travelling clock on the chest of drawers was approaching three. In an hour the Onslow-Whites would be calling him for tea. He could hear the thin tenor of Henry Onslow-White's voice drifting up from the garden below — the garden where on the previous night Avril Ferrall's voice had come suddenly out of the thick, hot darkness to herald this queer business of the old, ruined house and Paul Meriton's death under the window of the Long Room.

Alan had been brought up in a severely practical school. Whatever the people of Ferncross might believe about the place they called 'Sorcerer's House', he dismissed it as a lot of superstitious rubbish. All this nonsense about 'lights', people dying . . . There must — there was bound to be a natural explanation. The light that had been seen when that tramp had been killed was as easily explainable as the poor guy's death. He had suggested a perfectly logical explanation, himself, when Flake had told him about it.

Flake . . . His mind always came back to Flake. *She* believed that there was something uncanny and dangerous about the ruined house, and so did Henry Onslow-White, although they both pretended to be sceptical. Even Simon Gale . . . Well, there was nothing unnatural about the death of Paul Meriton, except in the way that *any* murder is unnatural. It was impossible to believe in a ghost that left a trail of footsteps in the dust and did its killing with a loose banister torn from the staircase.

Somebody had hated Meriton, or feared him, to such a degree that murder had been the result. But what had induced this hatred or fear? What had Meriton done, and who was the person he had done it to?

Veezey?

It seemed incredible that the little weak-chinned man could have been capable of murder. But little weak-chinned men had been capable of murder before.

And Veezey had been heard to threaten murder.

Alan had never seen the bridge over the Dark Water where Miss Flappit stated she had overheard the threat, but he could imagine it, and Veezey, standing there after his hysterical outburst, crying . . .

Somehow, *that* was horrible.

Whatever Meriton had done, or contemplated doing, it must have been pretty drastic to have reduced even a man like Veezey to such a state of despair.

Drastic enough to lead to murder?

Perhaps the meeting at Threshold House had been an extension of the interview on the bridge. But if Veezey had killed Meriton, what had been the meaning of that whispered remark that he, Alan, had overheard Avril Ferrall make to her brother in the dark garden? She had said, ' . . . it's dangerous . . . '

What was dangerous?

Maybe it had nothing to do with the murder at all, but if it hadn't, what *had* it to do with? It wasn't the only thing either. Simon Gale had spotted a discrepancy in time that was peculiar. Meriton had left Bryony Cottage with the Ferralls just before eleven. According to Avril Ferrall they had left Meriton at the gate of his house just before twelve, when the rain was just beginning. For nearly an hour they had been doing — something. What? Perhaps Meriton had stopped at the Ferralls' house for a drink?

No, that wouldn't do. Alan remembered what Avril had said; '*It was getting late and the rain was beginning . . . Peter and I were very tired . . .* ' If Meriton had gone into their house for a drink, surely she would have mentioned it? It was the natural thing to do. But she hadn't.

That lost hour was queer.

Damn it, thought Alan irritably. Why should *he* worry about it? It was a job for the police. If Gale liked to stick his ugly nose into it, that was *his* concern.

He stubbed out his cigarette in the ashtray, swung himself off the bed, and looked out the open window. Facing him, across the intervening country, the ruined house sweltered in the glare of the sun; the window of the Long Room a dark, oblong patch in the old gable. Behind that ivy-draped window, night, there had been a light, and Meriton's blood had spattered the dusty floor . . .

It was back with him again.

The detective fever, once it gets into the system, is not so easily eradicated.

★   ★   ★

He had a cold bath — the amenities of Bryony Cottage did not run to a shower — put on a clean silk shirt and a pair of thin, worsted trousers, and felt better.

As he came out of his room he saw Flake by the head of stair. In spite of the stifling heat she looked fresh and cool.

'Hello,' she said with a quick smile. 'Did you have a sleep?'

'No,' he answered. 'Did you?'

She shook her head ruefully. 'It was too hot. And I kept on thinking of things.'

'I guess that was my trouble, too,' said Alan. He followed her down the narrow stairway. She was wearing a sleeveless summer frock of white silk, and a faint and very pleasant perfume wafted to his nostrils as she moved. Again he was conscious of the disturbing effect which this girl had on him.

As they reached the small, square hall, he heard the rattle of china from the direction of the kitchen. Flake looked round at him and smiled. 'Mother's getting tea. That's a habit you don't have in America, isn't it? The cult of afternoon tea.'

'No, we don't bother much about that,' he agreed.

'I should hate to go without my tea,'

she said. 'I think most English people would.'

'I guess it's a question of what you get used to,' said Alan. They went through the shadowed drawing-room and out, by the open French windows, onto the veranda. On the lawn, in a small patch of shade from a pear tree, the mountainous figure of Henry Onslow-White in a thin, open-necked shirt and crumpled tussore trousers, lay sprawling in a deck-chair, half asleep. A small table near him had been covered with a white cloth and, as Alan was following Flake down the veranda steps to the lawn, the small figure of Mrs. Onslow-White appeared from the kitchen carrying a laden tray.

'Let me take that,' said Alan, stopping.

'Thank you,' she said a little breathlessly. 'Would you put it over on that table while I go and fetch the sandwiches?'

He took the heavy tray from her and carried it over to the table. Flake had woken her father and he was struggling up, grunting from the exertion and, as usual, mopping his face. 'Must have dozed off,' he panted. 'My Lord, this infernal heat.'

A loud hail startled them. Alan, just setting the tray down on the table, nearly dropped it as he looked over his shoulder.

Round the side of the house strode the figure of Simon Gale. He had exchanged his emerald-green shirt and corduroy trousers for a tartan shirt and khaki shorts, and his bare feet were thrust into leather sandals. He looked, thought Alan, like something you might meet in a jungle.

'Hello!' he cried, striding across the lawn towards them. 'Pastoral scene in an English garden. I see you are initiating our young American friend in our traditional ways of life.' He squatted down on the grass, produced from a bulging pocket in the wrinkled shorts his battered tin of tobacco and cigarette-papers and, incredibly swiftly, he rolled a cigarette.

Mrs. Onslow-White brought the sand-wiches and a plate of cakes. 'Hello, Simon.' She smiled. 'You're just in time for tea.'

'Tea!' repeated Gale, contorting his face. 'D'you know what the Spaniards called it? They called it hay-water!' He found a loose match in his pocket and snapped it into flame with his thumb-nail.

'There's some beer in the kitchen,' said Henry Onslow-White.

'Aha!' cried Simon Gale, lighting his cigarette and blowing out a cloud of acrid smoke. 'Now you're talking! Receive the accolade for true hospitality!'

Flake laughed. 'I'll go and get your beer, Simon.' She ran off towards the house.

'What's the latest news about Meriton?' asked Henry Onslow-White lazily. 'Have they discovered anything fresh?'

'If you mean Chippy and Hatchard, no,' replied Gale. 'But the Flappit woman has been spreading some nonsense about Veezey.'

'She told us about that,' said Alan.

'Such a harmless little man,' remarked Mrs. Onslow-White, placidly pouring out tea. 'I'm quite sure *he* could never have done such a terrible thing.'

'Of *course* he could,' interrupted Gale.

'No man is harmless, given the right incentive.'

'Do you think Veezey had the right incentive?' asked Alan.

'How do I know?' Gale sucked in the smoke from his cigarette, then expelled it slowly through his nostrils. '*I* don't know what incentive he had. Maybe it was a good one. Maybe it wasn't. But you can't convict a man because somebody hears him utter a threat.'

'Meriton *was* killed,' remarked Henry Onslow-White quietly.

'I know he was,' said Gale. He seized a cucumber sandwich from the plate which Mrs. Onslow-White offered him and stuffed it into his mouth. 'So was the tramp.'

'The tramp?' began Henry Onslow-White, frowning.

'Ah-ha!' cried Gale, swallowing the sandwich with a prodigious gulp. '*That's* got you thinking, has it? The tramp, my boy, who was killed in *exactly* the same way as Meriton. If Veezey killed Meriton, then, logically, he must have killed the tramp.'

126

'Nonsense!' broke in the stout man. 'That was an accident.'

'You think so?' retorted Simon Gale. 'Are you prepared to accept such a colossal coincidence as that? Rubbish!'

Flake's return with two quart bottles of beer and a large tankard momentarily interrupted the argument. With a bellow of appreciation, Simon Gale filled the tankard to the brim, flung back his head, and poured the contents down his throat.

'Aha!' he cried, smacking his lips and pouring out more beer with a grin of delight. 'That's the stuff! Not as good as Jellyberry's draught, but a passable drink for a thirsty man.'

Alan waited until Flake had settled herself in a deck-chair beside him, and was sipping the tea which her mother had handed her, and then he said: 'Do you believe, then, that the death of the tramp and the murder of Meriton are connected?'

'It's just sheer common sense, isn't it?' demanded Gale. 'The tramp was found under the window of that room, dead, with his head smashed in. Meriton was found in exactly the same place with *his* head smashed in.' He drank a huge draught of beer and banged the tankard down on the grass beside him.

'Who *was* the tramp?' asked the American.

'They never found out,' answered Flake, helping herself to a sandwich. 'Did they?' She looked round at her father.

'No,' he said. 'I think you're absolutely wrong, Simon. The poor devil was seeking shelter for the night and fell out of the window. That's the most likely explanation.'

'It *is* queer, though,' said Flake, wrinkling her forehead thoughtfully, 'that they should both have died in the *same* way . . .'

'Queer!' exclaimed Simon Gale, picking up the tankard and waving it about excitedly. 'It's more than queer! It's such a flaming, thundering, unbelievable coincidence that only a mutton-headed imbecile could find it credible for an instant!'

Henry Onslow-White chuckled good-naturedly. 'Now, now, Simon,' he said soothingly, 'drink some more beer and cool down. I may be a 'mutton-headed imbecile' but *I* find it less easy to believe that Paul Meriton was mixed up with a nameless tramp than the other way.'

'The tramp wasn't *nameless* — has that struck you, Henry?' demanded Gale, deftly rolling himself another cigarette. 'He was only nameless to *us*, d'you see? He didn't suddenly come into existence in order to be bashed on the head at Sorcerer's House, y'know. He must have had a life and a name and a background. He *came* from somewhere. And, wherever that somewhere was, he must have come in contact with people. Until we know who, and what, and where, and why, you *can't* say that Meriton wasn't mixed up with him.'

'I guess that makes sense,' said Alan. 'But why didn't somebody from his unknown background notify the police that he was missing?'

'How do you know they didn't?' retorted Gale quickly. 'But supposing there was nothing to *identify* this unknown tramp with the person *they* knew? What then?'

'Now you've gone right over into the realms of fiction, Simon,' grunted Henry Onslow-White. 'You're suggesting that the man was disguised.' He snorted disparagingly.

'Perhaps he was,' said Gale. He refilled the tankard, took a prodigious gulp from it, and continued: 'Or perhaps it was the *murderer* who didn't want him identified? What about that?'

'But according to you, Paul knew who he was,' said Flake. 'Why didn't *he* identify him?'

'Why indeed? I say,' Gale raised one shaggy eyebrow and cocked an inquiring eye at them, 'what did you think of Meriton, hey?'

Rather to Alan's surprise it was Mrs. Onslow-White who answered him. She said in her gentle, placid voice: 'Poor Paul! I always felt so sorry for him. It must have been dreadful . . . that *tortured mind* . . . '

'You've hit the nail whack on the head, Maggie!' cried Simon Gale, smashing his closed fist into the palm of his hand.

130

'That exactly describes him.'

'It was Fay,' said Flake. '*She* made him like that.'

Simon Gale finished his beer. Very gently, this time, he put the empty tankard down on the smooth grass of the lawn. He said in a voice that had no trace of its usual stridency: 'Yes . . . Fay.' He scowled. 'I wonder what happened to her?'

'Everybody knows *that*,' said Henry Onslow-White. 'She ran away.'

'Did she?' said Gale. 'Y'know, Henry, I don't think she did anything of the kind.'

7

The moon, nearly at the full, rose high in a cloudless sky. With the sunset had come a cool breeze, dispersing the humid heat of the afternoon. The countryside, stretching away to hill and woodland, was a vast pattern in black and silver, with washes of dove-grey where the meadows lay; a land of highlights and dense shadows and a stillness that was broken only by the gentle rustling of leaves as a light breeze stirred them. There was a scent of hay.

To Alan Boyce it was a land of enchantment where anything was possible. If a knight in full armour had come riding out of the shadows of the copse by the white roadside, he would not have been surprised. This moon-drenched world was haunted with the magic of fairy-tale and legend . . .

He had been dawdling, absorbing the peace and beauty of the night, but the watch on his wrist warned him that, if he was to be in time for his appointment with Simon Gale, he would have to hurry.

Why Gale had asked him to come to his house at half eleven that night, he had no idea. That eccentric individual, after exploding his bombshell concerning Fay Meriton, had suddenly leapt to his feet and declared he must go. And he had gone, ignoring the chorus of protests that followed him. It was just before he turned the corner of the house that he had called casually over his shoulder: 'Can you come along to my house half past eleven tonight, young feller? You might be interested.'

Gale was so sure he would be there, that he didn't bother to wait for a reply, thought Alan, as he increased his pace.

Alan discovered, a little to his surprise, that he was beginning to like Simon Gale. There was something refreshingly genuine about him. Even his rudeness was the rudeness of the schoolboy, without hurtful sting to it. His immense gusto and vitality; the enjoyment which you felt he extracted from every moment of living, was a tonic.

Alan, following the directions Flake had given him, climbed a stile and struck off across a footpath skirting the edge of a field. This should bring him out by the bridge over the Dark Water where Miss Flappit had overheard Veezey utter his threat.

He came to it in a few moments. It was a narrow, humpy bridge of old stone spanning a wide, stagnant pool of black, green-scummed water. About it clustered great trees whose spreading branches shut out the moonlight and steeped the place in shadow. A few feet away from the beginning of the bridge, Alan could see the dark entrance to Hanger's Lane in which Miss Flappit had lurked. It was a gloomy and not very pleasant place. The road that led up to the bridge ran down to an abrupt turn and was lost to view.

It was here that the unfortunate motorcyclist had crashed into the parapet.

When Alan came to the middle of the bridge, he saw the broken stonework where the accident had happened. There was a dark, irregular patch that still showed. He was glad when he emerged once more into the bright moonlight.

Somewhere along here, according to his instructions, was Veezey's hut, and further on, Simon Gale's house. After walking about a hundred yards, he came upon the hut, set a good way back from the road on the left. It was a large army hut of corrugated iron, painted white with a round roof, and half-hidden under a profusion of creepers and vines. The small front door was approached by a white gate set in a wooden fence and a stone-flagged path that wound its way through the loveliest little garden that the American had ever seen. It was small, but perfectly planned and laid out. In the full light of day it must have been a blaze of colour. Now, in the moonlight, it had a dream-like quality.

Was the hand which had created that garden a murderer's hand?

Alan did not believe that just because a man was fond of flowers, he was incapable of violence. But he couldn't *see* Veezey, somehow, as a murderer.

There were no lights in any of the

windows. Veezey was probably the type who went to bed early and got up with the dawn.

Gale's house was quite a good way further on. Alan was beginning to think he must have missed it when he came suddenly to the gate. It was in the middle of a very high and straggly hedge: a solid gate of seasoned oak. On it, in large white letters, was painted: '*If you have been invited, come in. If you haven't, don't waste my time or yours.*'

Alan pushed the gate open. Beyond was a short path that led through a thick shrubbery to a long, low house that was backed by a mass of trees. It was shaped like an 'L' and the front door, of oak like the gate, was in the short arm. In the longer arm, a row of windows was brilliantly lighted behind drawn curtains.

Approaching the door, Alan saw there was neither knocker nor bell. The massive door presented an unbroken surface of ancient oak except for a very small keyhole set in a round metal plate. He had raised his hand to hammer on the door with his fist, when it suddenly opened and Simon Gale appeared on the threshold.

'Hello, hello!' he cried in greeting. 'You're late! Come in and have some beer.'

'How did you know I was here?' asked Alan curiously. 'I was trying to find a bell.'

'No bell, no knocker.' Gale grinned. 'Just a little gadget of my own, d'you see? Any weight on this step rings a buzzer in the studio. During the day it's switched through to the kitchen. Good idea, eh?' He led the way through a square hall, so stuffed with odds and ends that it looked like a junk shop, into an enormous room that obviously occupied the whole of the longer arm of the house. And it was like no other room that the American had ever seen before.

At one end, near a large window, stood a big studio-easel. Beside it, laden with jars of brushes, tubes of paint, palettes, all the paraphernalia of the painter, was a dinner-wagon on rubber casters. Against the nearby wall was stacked a pile of canvases of all sizes and shapes, and on the opposite wall, running under three of the six windows, was a carpenter's bench littered with all kinds of debris, and with a glue-pot in a tin saucepan standing on a gas-ring. Above the bench was a long rack stuffed with tools of all descriptions. Next to the carpenter's bench was a small lathe driven by an electric motor and, under the remaining three windows, an enormous desk with a typewriter and a telephone. It was piled with books and papers, and in front of it stood an office swivel-chair. Facing the desk, in the middle of the other wall, was a great open fireplace of red brick with several huge, comfortable-looking easy chairs scattered in front of it. A large barrel of beer on trestles occupied a place to the left of the fireplace, with a shelf over it containing a collection of pewter tankards and old German drinking mugs. There were books everywhere, crammed into shelves which had obviously been built wherever there was a vacant wall space, and piled in heaps on the floor and on numerous tables. The whole place was incredibly untidy, but with an untidiness that gave an impression of comfort.

'I suppose,' said Simon Gale, striding across the parquet floor and snatching two large tankards from the row on the shelf, 'you're curious to know why I asked you to come? We'll have some beer an' I'll tell you.' He filled the tankards from the barrel and thrust one into Alan's hand. 'Sit down,' he said, waving a huge hand towards the group of chairs.

Alan sat down. He said, balancing the tankard on his knee: 'I guess the reason you asked me here has something to do with Meriton.'

'A direct hit!' cried Gale, standing straddle-legged in front of the fireplace. 'You an' I are going to do some exploring, young feller.'

'Where?' asked Alan, although he had a fairly good idea.

'Sorcerer's House,' answered Gale shortly. He took a deep draught of beer and set the tankard down on the narrow brick ledge of the mantel. 'I've got a hunch that I'd like to have a really good look over that place.'

'What do you expect to find?' said Alan.

Simon Gale tugged thoughtfully at his beard. 'Ghosts and goblins.'

There was a silence. Alan drank a little beer, then said suddenly: 'See here. What did you mean this afternoon, about Meriton's wife?'

'That's been *troubling* you, eh?' said Gale. 'Do you know the story about Fay Meriton?'

'Some of it,' answered Alan, nodding. 'Flake told me.'

'Nobody knows it *all*,' said Gale. Abruptly, he began to stride about the room. 'Fay was a hysteric,' he said suddenly. 'D'you know what *that* means?'

'Somebody who's morbidly emotional,' said the American.

'It means more than that,' said Simon Gale, thumping his fist on the back of a chair, 'but that'll do to be goin' on with. But that's not *all* she was, d'you see? She was a sugar-coated pill. When you got through the sweetness, you found there was a hell of a nasty taste . . . And that poor devil, Meriton, worshipped the ground she walked on.' He stopped by the fireplace, picked up his tankard, and drained the contents. 'I painted her once,' he went on, staring into the empty tankard with a diabolical frown. 'It was a damned good picture. It was *Fay* — not what you could see, but all the rotten bits that were hidden. She was furious, and so was Meriton. I don't know what happened to that picture. Maybe they destroyed it.'

'What,' broke in Alan, 'makes you think she didn't run away? Everybody else seems to be certain that she did, with some man.'

'*I* never believed it,' declared Gale. 'I'd never have said anything while Meriton was alive, but I always had a theory. Look here, young feller, use your common sense. Old Ayling nearly had a fit when he heard she'd gone. He insisted on calling in the police to try and find her, and kicked up a hell of a rumpus. By all the Golden Apples of the Hesperides, d'you mean to tell me that they wouldn't have found her? Of *course* they would — *if she'd gone anywhere*

141

where she could be found.'

A chill seemed to Alan Boyce to have come suddenly into the big, untidy room. He knew the suggestion conveyed in Simon Gale's words, but he had to be sure. He said slowly: 'What do *you* think happened to her?'

Gale shrugged his wide shoulders. 'Perhaps the ghosts and the goblins got her,' he said. 'Finish your beer, young feller — it's time we were going.'

★ ★ ★

An owl hooted mournfully in the trees behind the house; otherwise, there was complete silence. Under the bright moonlight, Alan thought the ruined house looked even more dilapidated than when he had seen it in the full glare of the sun. Perhaps it was due to the *coldness* of the light and the hard effect of shadow.

He stood with Simon Gale amid the wild tangle of the garden, looking up at the broken window of the Long Room with its trailing ivy. Supposing a light were to spring up suddenly in that dark window — a bluish light?

They were standing where the lawn had once been, but which was now a knee-deep wilderness of coarse grass and nettles. The remains of a pergola, the roses long since reverted to their original briar, ran down one side in a tumbled ruin, and there were traces of flowerbeds just discernible under a mass of weeds.

It was a fitting graveyard for the dead house . . .

'Come on,' Simon Gale broke in abruptly on Alan's thoughts. 'It's the *inside* of the place I want to explore.'

He forced his way through a thicket of shrubbery and round to the front door. It wasn't unlocked tonight, as it had been when Alan, wet and tired, had leaned against it and nearly fallen into the dusty hall.

'H'm,' grunted Gale, when he pushed against it and it refused to budge. 'I suppose Chippy an' Hatchard locked it. Oh, well — better not muck about with the lock. There's sure to be a window we can get through.'

They found one at the back; a small

window that looked as if it belonged to a pantry. There was very little glass left in it, and what there was, Gale calmly proceeded to remove.

'There you are, young feller,' he said, when he had smashed the last splinter out with a stone. 'In you go!'

Alan pulled himself up on to the sill and scrambled through. He found that he was in a small room that might have been a larder. Dimly, he could see shelves running round the walls and a broken sink in one corner, full of rubbish.

'All right?' inquired Gale's voice outside, and without waiting for a reply, 'Hold on, I'm coming in.'

He found it less easy than the American had because of his size, but he managed somehow to wriggle himself through, and dropped down beside Alan, brushing cobwebs out of his hair and beard.

There was a door facing the window, and it was partly open. As they passed through into the darkness of a passage beyond, they heard the squeaking and scurry of rats. Simon Gale produced a torch and sent its light playing ahead of them. The passage was short, and ended in a huge kitchen with a great, rusty range that was falling to pieces. There was dust and decay everywhere. Large, irregular patches of damp blotched the walls, and there was a queer, unpleasant kind of reddish fungus, like those splashes on the floor of the Long Room . . .

'If anybody in the village sees our light,' remarked Gale with a sudden chuckle, 'it'll probably cause a minor panic. This should bring us to the hall.'

He shone the light onto a door leading out of the kitchen, which stood wide open. Cobwebs, the remains of a whole dynasty of spiders, draped it like a curtain. Beyond was another passage and, at the end of it, a closed door. There was a horrible, musty smell of rottenness. Gale tried the door and it opened. They came out into the vast cavern of the hall.

It was dimly visible, lit by a kind of spectral radiance that came from the moonlight filtering in through the staircase windows, and there was a stillness of utter desolation. It was at this moment, while they stood motionless by the door, that *fear* gripped the American. He could not have said what caused it, but it enveloped him suddenly, as though it were something tangible, something that had gathered out of the shadows.

Gale took a step forward and gestured with the torch towards a door on the other side of the hall. He said: 'We'll start over there. I should think it was the drawing room.'

Alan followed him over. The door stuck when he pushed against it, but between them they managed, eventually, to force it open. The hinges had sagged from the rotting frame, and it scraped the floor with a screeching noise that sounded abnormally loud in the hush of that silent house.

They saw a large, high-ceilinged room with the paper hanging in tattered strips from the walls. The greater portion of the ceiling had fallen in, leaving a gaping hole through which the blackened laths protruded, and forming a pile of old plaster on the floor. Soot heaped the fireplace. A rat scurried across the floor in the light, its beady eyes glinting, and vanished in a hole in the wainscoting.

'Nothing here,' grunted Gale, flashing his torch quickly round this wreck of a room.

'What,' asked Alan anxiously, '*exactly* are you looking for?'

'I don't know,' answered Gale evasively. 'Anything that's — *queer*.'

But they found nothing in the lower rooms; only the ruins of a past splendour and damp and dust and spiders. Slowly they mounted the great staircase. Alan thought that Gale would go into the Long Room, but he ignored it with an impatient gesture.

'What I'm looking for isn't *there*,' he said.

On the floor above there were five rooms, the principal bedrooms when the house had been — 'alive' was the word that came into Alan's mind. They were in a worse condition of dilapidation, if possible, than the rooms downstairs. There was nothing here, either, that could be called queer.

They came, at last, to the top floor

— the attic rooms in the gables. And the fear which had gripped Alan in the hall below, came back. He felt the surface of his skin grow cold and clammy with it. It was affecting Simon Gale, too. His beard bristled stiffly as the muscles in his face tightened.

But there was nothing in the rooms they entered to induce fear. In two of them the sloping ceilings were open to the sky, so that the moonlight streamed through, and the floors were sodden with the rain that had fallen on the previous night.

Nothing to induce that fear which was growing into terror.

And then they came to the locked room. Judging from the others, it was one of the smaller rooms. The door, more solid than any of the other doors, refused to move when Gale turned the handle.

'We've got to get this open,' he grunted. 'Come on with me.' He flung himself against the door. According to all the books Alan had ever read, the door should have burst open. But it wasn't as easy as all that. It took both their combined weights, and all their strength, before the screws holding the lock tore out and the door banged back against the wall with a crash that echoed through the house like the report of a gun.

Panting, they peered into the room. It was dusty and grimy, like all the others, but it was *furnished!* In the light from torch they could see chairs, a table, a cushioned divan . . .

And then Alan found himself staring at a large oil painting in a tarnished gilt frame that hung over the mantelpiece.

'By all the devils in hell!' breathed Simon Gale at his elbow. 'That's my painting of Fay Meriton.'

★   ★   ★

'I don't understand it,' declared Major Chipingham, rubbing irritably at his bald head. 'It's ridiculous! Why the devil should anybody want to furnish a room in a house that's practically falling down, eh?' He glared at each of them in turn.

It was the following morning, and the chief constable, Inspector Hatchard, Simon

Gale, and Alan Boyce were gathered in Gale's untidy studio. He had told Alan, on their way back from Sorcerer's House in the small hours of the morning, that he was going to inform Hatchard of what they had found, and had invited the American to be present.

'Well?' grunted Major Chipingham impatiently. 'Why doesn't somebody *say* something?'

'What do you expect us to say, Chippy?' said Gale. 'Do you expect we're going to give you an explanation for that room neatly typed in triplicate, hey? Don't be such a complete, utter, and flaming fathead!'

'Now look here, Gale — ' began the chief constable angrily.

'I'm telling you what *we found*, that's all,' Gale continued, ignoring the interruption. 'Facts, me lad, d'you see? You can find your own explanation for 'em.'

Inspector Hatchard said in his quiet, business-like way: 'You were a little ahead of us, sir! We were making a thorough search of the house today. There was no time yesterday.' He frowned. 'What made you look for that room, sir?'

'I wasn't looking for it,' answered Gale. 'I didn't know it was there.'

'But you must have had *some* reason for going to Threshold House, sir? If you weren't looking for this room, what *were* you looking for?'

'Anything,' said Gale, 'that might help to indicate Meriton's murderer.'

Major Chipingham exploded. 'What the devil,' he roared, thumping his clenched fist on the arm of his chair, 'has a ruddy room with a few sticks of furniture in it got to do with *that!*'

'Now, now, Chippy,' cried Gale. 'You haven't changed, have you? You never *could* see anything further than your nose. You're just as big a bonehead as you were at school. Why don't you try and *think!*'

'That's all very well, Gale,' retorted the chief constable, controlling his temper by a visible effort. 'You can rave and rant, and be as damn rude as you like. But it doesn't *get* us anywhere. We're practically certain that we know who killed Meriton — '

'D'you mean Veezey?' demanded Gale. 'Have you seen him?'

'Of course,' said Major Chipingham. 'After Miss Flappit — '

'What did he say?' broke in Gale. 'Did he tell you *why* he threatened to kill Meriton?'

'He says he never *did* threaten him, sir,' put in Inspector Hatchard.

'Naturally he's not likely to admit it,' said Major Chipingham, shrugging. 'The man's not such a fool as that. He does admit, though, that he and Meriton were on the bridge when Miss Flappit says she overheard — '

'Oh, he *does* admit that?' Simon Gale scowled ferociously. '*I'd* like to have a talk to him.'

'I think it would be much better if you didn't interfere,' said the chief constable crossly. 'Just leave this business to me.'

'I don't want to see you make a mess of it, Chippy,' cried Gale, propelling himself out of his chair with a bound. 'You're an obstinate, muddle-headed, pompous old stuffed shirt, but for some queer reason I like you.'

'Thank you,' interpolated Major Chipingham stiffly.

'I wouldn't like you to come a hell of a cropper over this thing, d'you see,' Gale continued, 'an' if you go after Veezey, you'll land with such a crash that all your confounded red tape won't bind up the pieces.'

'We haven't sufficient evidence to make any move yet, sir,' interjected Inspector Hatchard, as he saw his superior's face growing dangerously purple.

'I know you haven't,' cried Gale. 'All you've got is a threat, overheard by a gossiping old spinster who is more likely than not to have got it all wrong. An' while you go haring away after this red herring, the real murderer is hugging himself with glee.'

'If you're so certain it isn't Veezey,' began Major Chipingham, 'who do you — ?'

'There you go again, Chippy,' interrupted Simon Gale with an impatient gesture. 'Always jumping to conclusions. I'm *not* certain it isn't Veezey. What I'm saying is that you're approaching the thing in the *wrong* way.'

'How would you suggest we approach it, sir?' interrupted the quiet voice of Hatchard. From his tone, it seemed to Alan that he had a great deal of respect for Simon Gale's opinion.

'I'll tell you.' Gale took up a position in front of the fireplace and faced them with the air of a lecturer addressing a not very intelligent class. 'Somebody bashed Meriton over the head, and the first thing we want to know — I want to know — is *why*? To find the answer,' he went on, 'we've got to look for something in Meriton's life, something that *might* provide a motive for murder. And the first thing that jumps out at us, like a jack-in-the-box, is that business of Fay Meriton.'

The chief constable jerked up. 'What the devil are you talking about? She ran away with some man or other.'

'Did she?' broke in Gale. 'You're *sure* it was as simple as that?'

'I remember it very well, sir,' said Hatchard, with a light of sudden interest in his eyes. 'Colonel Ayling came to us to try and trace her.'

'But you couldn't,' said Gale. 'Or the mysterious man she was supposed to have gone off with, either. You couldn't find her, and nobody ever has.'

'I don't suppose she *wanted* to be found,' said Major Chipingham. 'Damned well ashamed of herself, I should think.'

'Women aren't ashamed of themselves for anything these days, Chippy,' said Gale. 'Two years ago, Fay Meriton vanished — poof! — like that.' He snapped his fingers. 'Where did she go? Or *didn't* she go?'

If he *wanted* to create a sensation, thought Alan, he'd done it. Major Chipingham's mouth opened suddenly, and his startled eyes bulged. Inspector Hatchard drew a sharp, quick breath, coughed, and leaned forward, his hands flat on his knees.

'*That* startled you, eh?' cried Gale, hugely delighted. 'You never thought of anything like *that*!'

'Well, as a matter of fact, sir,' said Hatchard, 'we did wonder at the time. But we couldn't do very much, you see.

155

There was that letter she left. That was genuine, you know, Mr. Gale. No fake about it; we had expert opinion on that.'

'I know.' Simon Gale nodded. 'But if that letter is *explained*, what then? Fay Meriton disappears from the face of the earth. Her husband allows it to be supposed that she's run away, and her father asks the police to try and find her. But there's no trace of her — because they *looked in the wrong places*.'

'Bosh!' exclaimed the chief constable explosively. 'The police were on the look-out for her all over the country.'

'Where,' said Hatchard, interrupting in his quiet voice, 'do you think we *should* have looked for Mrs. Meriton, sir?'

Simon Gale plucked a tankard from the shelf over the barrel by the fireplace. He squatted down in front of the barrel. He said, turning the spigot and watching the tankard fill: 'You might have tried Sorcerer's House.'

There was, for the space of several seconds, a silence. In it, the sound of the beer trickling into the tankard seemed abnormal.

'Damn it!' exclaimed Major Chipingham suddenly. 'You must be mad! Why, Paul Meriton was infatuated with his wife.'

'Hold on, sir,' said Inspector Hatchard respectfully but firmly. 'There may be something in this idea of Mr. Gale's.'

'Something in it!' The chief constable glared at him.

'Yes, sir,' said Hatchard. 'Don't you see, if it's true, it could supply a motive for Meriton's murder?'

Simon Gale straightened up and swung round, the brimming tankard in his hand. 'Pull yourself together, Chippy,' he said, grinning. 'Hatchard's right, y'know. If Fay didn't run away — if her body *is* hidden somewhere in that old house — it supplies a thundering good motive, hey?'

Queer, incoherent sounds issued from Major Chipingham's throat. 'Why should Meriton kill his wife? Good God! The feller was absolutely wrapped up in her. He worshipped her.'

'I know,' broke in Gale. 'But supposing something happened to disillusion him? Supposing he suddenly found out just what this woman he worshipped was *really* like?' He paused and took a deep drink from the tankard. 'What *then*?'

There came into Alan's mind a picture of the locked room in the old, ruined house, and what they had seen there in the uncertain light of the torch: the dusty furniture, softly upholstered easy chairs, and a divan strewn with crumpled cushions ... Shaded wall-brackets with half-burned candles still in their sconces ... A carpet into which the feet sank deeply ... And the picture ... A beautiful woman, but the mouth had a cruel twist and the eyes were not quite sane ... There had been the ghost of a dead perfume lingering in the thick air ...

'If somebody thought the same as you, sir,' murmured Hatchard, gently rubbing the top of his head, 'somebody who'd *also* been fond of the lady ... Well, now — that 'ud constitute a pretty strong motive.'

'Look here,' burst out the chief constable, 'this is all pure supposition. There's not an atom of proof. Anyway, why did the murderer have to wait *two* years?'

'Because he'd only just found out the *truth* about Fay Meriton's disappearance,' said Gale. 'That's easy. As for proof, well — '

He stopped abruptly as the door suddenly opened and a head was thrust in. A pair of small, malignant black eyes snapped at them.

'In the middle of me mornin's work,' hissed a shrill voice venomously. 'Drat 'im, drat 'im, drat 'im!'

'What *is* it, woman?' shouted Simon Gale with a ferocious scowl. 'Can't you see I'm busy?'

The nut-cracker jaws in the witch-like face worked convulsively. 'Busy!' The hissing voice rose nearly an octave, and was accompanied by such a horrible expression of maliciousness that the old woman's face seemed scarcely human. The thin lips compressed tightly and then suddenly spat out two words: 'Dr. Ferrall.'

'What about him?' snapped Gale irritably.

''e's at the door,' hissed the shrill voice. 'Buzz, buzz! In the middle of me mornin's work . . . Buzz, buzz . . . '

'Excellent!' cried Gale, in suddenly restored good humour. 'Dr. Ferrall, eh?' He rubbed his hands together with the glee of a small boy who has just been presented with an unexpected present. 'Shoot him in, Mrs. Gull, shoot him in.'

*   *   *

Alan thought Ferrall looked tired and ill when the appalling Mrs. Gull ushered him unceremoniously into the untidy studio. There were shadows under his eyes and worried lines across his fore-head. The thin streak of his moustache looked even blacker in contrast to the paleness of his face.

'Come in, Ferrall,' greeted Simon Gale jovially. 'Have some beer? Anyone else?'

'Not for me, thanks,' said Ferrall, and Major Chipingham shook his head. Inspector Hatchard also declined after moment's hesitation, but Alan thought he detected a wistful look in his eyes as Gale refilled his own tankard. 'I didn't know you had anyone here, Gale,' said Ferrall. 'I was passing — on my way back from visiting a patient — and I thought I'd drop in and — see how things were progressing.' He looked uneasily round the little group, the fingers of one hand twisting nervously at a button on his jacket.

'You couldn't have come at a better time,' cried Gale. 'What about you, Boyce? Beer?'

'I guess it's a little too early,' said Alan, shaking his head.

'Rubbish!' retorted Gale. 'It's never too early.' He raised the tankard to his lips, flung back his head, and drained it with deep satisfaction. 'How's Avril?'

'She's all right,' answered Ferrall.

'Been seeing any more lights?' demanded Gale, raising shaggy eyebrow quizzically. 'There were lights enough in that old house, if people had known where to look, eh? Not in the Long Room, though.'

'What do you mean?' asked Ferrall, and for a second, Alan could have sworn, fear flickered in his tired eyes. 'What did you mean — about lights enough in the old house?'

'You and Meriton were pretty good friends, eh?' said Gale, completely ignoring the question. 'You knew him before you came to Ferncross, didn't you?'

'Yes.' There was a tinge of surprise in Ferrall's voice. 'Why?'

'Were you equally friendly with Fay?'

Ferrall's eyes altered suddenly. A film of blankness came over them, leaving them completely without expression. He said with an exaggerated casualness: 'I didn't know her as well as I knew Paul, but I was friendly with *both* of them, naturally.'

'Were you friendly enough to know about the locked room?' Simon Gale shot the question with a forward thrust of his head, as though he were about to pounce. And the shot went home. Alan saw Ferrall stiffen slightly. It was only a momentary contraction of the muscles, but Hatchard had seen it too.

'I don't understand.' Ferrall drew his brows together in well-simulated perplexity. 'Locked room? *What* locked room?'

'It's not locked now,' said Gale. 'Boyce and I broke it open last night. D'you know what we found?'

'How should *I* know what you found?' retorted Ferrall. 'I don't even know what you're talking about.'

'I'm talking about the furnished room in Sorcerer's House,' answered Gale. 'A cosy little nest that somebody had been in the habit of using quite a lot. And there was a hurricane lamp with a blue-tinted glass which was put in the Long Room to foster the superstition and keep people away. Didn't Meriton ever tell you about it?'

Ferrall shook his head. 'No, I knew nothing about it,' he answered, but his hand went up to his mouth, and a nervous forefinger ran along the thin line of his moustache. 'A *furnished* room, you say? That's — that's an extraordinary thing . . . Why on earth should Meriton have wanted — ?'

'I don't think it was *Meriton* who used that room,' broke in Gale. 'He knew about it — Oh, yes, he knew about it — but it was *Fay* who went there. The place reeked of stale perfume.

'Fay?' repeated Ferrall, frowning. He shook his head. 'That strikes me as even more extraordinary.'

'Does it?' said Gale quickly. 'Didn't you *know* what was the matter with Fay?'

'Matter with her?' interjected Major Chipingham. 'What d'you mean — what *was* the matter with her?'

'She was mad!' snapped Gale curtly.

There was a sudden and rather ugly hush. The chief constable, one hand half-raised to his mouth, goggled at Gale. Hatchard leaned forward in his chair, seeming to take on an added alertness, as though a spring inside him had tightened. Ferrall stood quite still, his face as expressionless as a mask. But a tiny muscle twitched near his mouth.

Hatchard broke the strained silence. 'Do you mean . . . she was insane, sir?' he asked quietly.

'Yes.' Gale nodded. 'Oh, you wouldn't have known it, d'you see?' he continued, speaking rapidly and striding about the room. 'Fay Meriton was a hysteric — Dr. Ferrall 'ull tell you what *that* means — I

164

guessed it when I painted her. She was emotionally unbalanced even as a child. It was a throw-back. Her grandmother, on her mother's side, died in an asylum.'

'Is this true, Doctor?' Hatchard looked at the still motionless Ferrall.

Ferrall's answer was scarcely audible: 'There's a certain amount of truth in it — yes.'

'Good God!' exclaimeded Major Chipingham. 'You tell us that Fay Meriton was — '

'Never mind that for the moment, Chippy,' interrupted Gale. 'There's something I want to know, d'you see?' He stopped suddenly in front of Ferrall. 'When you drove Meriton home from the Onslow-White's place, on the night he was murdered, why did it take you nearly an hour? What were you *doing*?'

8

Ferrall's face darkened. Under the high cheek-bones the blood came up in dull red patches. His previous nervousness fled before the anger that suddenly swept over him. 'Look here,' he said a little thickly. 'I don't recognize your right to question me. What the hell business is it of yours?'

'Suppose we make it *my* business, sir,' interposed Inspector Hatchard suavely. '*I* should like to know what you and Mr. Meriton did during that hour.'

Ferrall's mouth set stubbornly, and Alan thought he was going to refuse to answer. But, as quickly as it had arisen, his anger left him. He shrugged and looked at Simon Gale with a wry smile. 'Sorry I lost my temper, Gale,' he said. 'I've had a pretty heavy week, and I'm feeling a bit tired. There's nothing very mysterious about what we were doing. It was a devilish hot night, as you know. We thought a run round in the car would cool us down. And that's what we did. We got to Meriton's gate just as the rain started. It's as simple as that.'

As simple as that, or very clever, thought Alan. A natural explanation that nobody could contradict. It didn't *quite* fit in, however, with the words he had heard Avril whisper in the dark garden, earlier: ' . . . *it's dangerous* . . . '

'I see, sir,' said Hatchard, but it was impossible to judge from his expression whether he was satisfied or not. He turned to Simon Gale. 'Now, I'd like, if you don't mind, sir, to get this straight.' Hatchard cleared his throat. 'Now, Mr. Gale,' he began, 'it's your opinion that to find the motive for Meriton's murder we've got to go back to Mrs. Meriton's disappearance nearly two years ago.' A faint, and quickly stifled, sound came from Ferrall. 'It's your idea, continued Hatchard, 'that Mrs. Meriton didn't run away, as she was generally supposed to have done, but that, for some reason or other, her husband killed her and concealed the body in Threshold House.'

'Good God almighty!' breathed Ferrall. 'You don't believe *that*, do you?'

'Please, sir.' Hatchard held up his hand. 'Let me finish! Your theory is,' he went on, turning again to Gale, 'that somebody who was very fond of Mrs. Meriton discovered what had *really* happened to her, and killed Meriton, the motive being revenge. Is that right, sir?'

'That's very well put, Hatchard,' said Gale. 'It's not *quite* as clear-cut as that, but you've got the gist of it.'

'It's ridiculous!' exclaimed Ferrall angrily.

'If I may be *allowed* to put in a word,' said Major Chipingham with heavy sarcasm, 'I think there's little point in going on arguing about it. Either Gale is right, or he's wrong.'

'Did you work that out all by yourself, Chippy?' demanded Gale with a shout of laughter. 'If you want to *prove* whether I'm right or not, the evidence is *there* — almost under your nose, d'you see? *Find Fay Meriton's body.*'

'If you had let me finish,' said the chief constable, very red in the face, but valiantly controlling his temper, 'instead of going off into one of your absurd ranting fits, that is exactly what I was going to say.'

'You'll only go wasting your time,' said Ferrall. 'Fay ran away — she left that letter behind to say so. How are you going to get over that?'

'Letters left behind by suicides and what-not have been explained away before,' remarked Gale. 'If there's no body, we won't have to bother about the letter. If there *is* a body . . . ' He shrugged his shoulders.

'If there *is* a body, sir,' said Inspector Hatchard thoughtfully, 'then I don't think we'll have to look very far for Meriton's murderer.'

'Eh, what's that?' said Major Chipingham. He frowned, and then his face cleared. 'Oh, yes . . . I see what you mean . . . '

So did Alan. That formidable old man with the aggressive, beak-like nose and determined mouth . . . Given sufficient incentive, he thought, Colonel Ayling would be quite capable of murder.

★ ★ ★

Like the quick-match which is used to ignite individual fireworks in a set-piece, the reason for the sudden activity of the police at Sorcerer's House flashed through the village of Ferncross.

In the Three Witches, Mr. Jellyberry, beaming in the midst of a clamour of speculation, dispensed beer with a prodigal hand and added his quota to the argument, nodding with ponderous agreement, or shaking his head in equally weighty negative.

Miss Flappit, in a seventh heaven of excitement, shot all over the village like a noisy and virulent wasp, buzzing and stinging wherever she alighted, until at the heralding clatter of her ancient bicycle, the inhabitants fled to the sanctuary of their houses; and even that long-suffering man, the vicar, locked himself in his study and refused to emerge.

People met in the small shops that dotted the narrow High Street, and, forgetting what they had come to purchase, entered into long discussions concerning this unheard-of sensation, and drifted out again without buying anything, to the annoyance of the shopkeepers and the detriment of trade.

Colonel Ayling, when the news reached him, scowled, set his face rigidly, and refused to discuss the matter at all; and little Mr. Veezey broke the habit of many years and bought himself three double whiskies instead of his usual two.

Many and varied were the stories that circulated in, and around, Ferncross during that period before there was any authentic news at all. A body had been discovered in the old water-butt; five bodies had been found buried in the garden; no bodies had been discovered, but a vast hoard of money had been unearthed from under the rotting floor-boards of an attic; the skeleton of a man, identified as that of Cagliostro, had been found, bricked up in the wall of the Long Room, and, on being moved, had vanished in a flash of blue flame.

These and many other stories, all equally exaggerated and without foundation, swept through the village with the speed of light. Sensation, *in excelsis*, had come to Ferncross.

The news spread, and an army of newspaper reporters invaded the village, filling the bars of the three public houses and clamouring round the rusty iron gate of Threshold House, insistent for information. Miss Flappit, baulked of her legitimate prey, found balm and solace among these new arrivals. The story of Veezey's threat on the bridge over the Dark Water was related with gusto, and that unfortunate individual found himself besieged. They tried the same thing with Simon Gale, but the appalling Mrs. Gull, in a fury of righteous indignation, turned a hose on them and they retired with their ardour considerably dampened.

In the midst of all this, a stolid Hatchard proceeded quietly and systematically with his search, assisted by four expert detectives requisitioned from the C.I.D. of the neighbouring town of Barnsford. Secure behind a police guard, which had strict instructions that nobody was to be allowed past the gate except with the express permission of Hatchard himself, they went methodically to work.

There was much speculation at Bryony Cottage concerning the outcome. 'I don't believe they'll find anything,' declared Henry Onslow-White. 'The idea of Paul Meriton killing his wife is simply absurd. Whatever she did, he wouldn't have hurt a hair of her head. It's just a wild theory of Simon's. I'm surprised the police took any notice of it.'

'I'm not so sure,' said Flake. 'I always thought there was something queer about Fay.'

'Maybe there was,' mumbled her father, his mouth full of toast and marmalade — they were having breakfast in the pleasant little dining-room — 'She may have been as mad as a hatter, but what *I'm* saying is that Paul *couldn't* have killed her. He just wasn't capable of such a thing.' He stopped breathlessly and wiped his mouth with his napkin.

'It might have been an accident,' suggested Alan. 'If she'd had a hysterical attack or something, and become violent. I guess it could have happened like that.'

'Why should he conceal the fact?' Onslow-White demanded. 'The natural thing to do, if that had happened, would be to call up a doctor and notify the police. Why didn't he do that?'

'He may have been scared that they'd think he killed her,' said the American. 'A man in a panic will — '

'Paul wasn't the type to get in a panic over *anything*,' broke in Onslow-White, shaking his large head. 'Fay Meriton ran away. There's that letter, in her own handwriting, to prove it. What more do they want?' He passed over his empty cup for more coffee.

'I don't think you're *quite* right, you know, dear,' remarked Mrs. Onslow-White placidly, as she took the cup. 'And I don't think Simon is *quite* right, either.'

'What do you mean, Mother?' asked Flake.

'Well, dear,' said Mrs. Onslow-White, smiling at her affectionately, 'I don't think Fay *did* run away, and I don't think Paul *killed* her.'

'Then what *did* happen to her?' asked her husband.

'I really don't know,' said Mrs. Onslow-White, pouring hot milk lavishly into the coffee. 'But whatever it was, it was neither of *those* things.' She handed the fresh cup of coffee across to her husband. 'You see,' she went on, 'Fay would *never* have left Paul. That would have meant giving up her house and the money, and she would never have done *that*.'

'The thing that really seems horrible,' said Flake, with a little shiver, 'is that room, tucked away in those mouldering ruins.'

Alan remembered that crawling of the flesh he had experienced when they reached the attic floor of the old house. And the focal point of that fear had been behind the locked door . . .

'What did she *do* up there, among the dust and cobwebs?' Flake went on, resting her elbow on the table and cupping her chin in her hand. 'Any normal woman would have been scared to death.'

But Fay Meriton was not normal . . .

'Well,' grunted Henry Onslow-White, dropping his crumpled napkin on the table and hauling himself out of his chair with difficulty. 'I'm going down to the village. Does anybody want anything?'

Mrs. Onslow-White was, apparently, in urgent need of a number of things. Alan and Flake left her giving a detailed list to her husband, and strolled out into the garden. It was a lovely morning. The heat — that airless, pressing heat — had gone, but it was still very warm.

'What shall we do?' asked Alan.

'Let's walk across the meadows to Threshold House,' she suggested, with one of those quick, sidelong glances which made his pulses tingle.

'You're a ghoul!' Alan laughed. 'But I feel rather the same way, myself.'

That walk across the sunlit meadows, although they were unaware of it at the time, was to lead them into the second, and infinitely more horrible, phase of this queer business. Even as they left the garden of Bryony Cottage, the beginning of what Simon Gale afterwards called 'the topsy-turviness' was taking place behind the high, enclosing wall of Sorcerer's House. But they knew nothing of this until later. In the bright, warm sunlight of that morning, Alan felt a surging of the blood; a joyous delight in the sheer fact of just living. Ghosts and goblins had no place here.

'Race you to that tree,' he cried suddenly.

He reached it yards ahead of Flake, and waited for her to come up with elaborate unconcern. When she did, with flushed face and dancing eyes, they both leaned against the thick trunk of the old oak and relaxed.

'Oh,' she said when she had recovered her breath. 'That was *nice* . . . ' She shook back her heavy, glossy black hair. 'I'm glad you came here.'

'So am I,' said Alan.

'Oh, look,' said Flake suddenly, 'there's Avril.'

Alan turned his head, following the direction of her gaze. Avril Ferrall was walking slowly towards them, her head bent and eyes fixed on the ground. She was moving like a sleep-walker, completely oblivious of her surroundings. Until she was within a few yards of them, she did not see them. When she did, it was with a start of surprise.

'Hello,' she said, her rich, deep voice dry and husky. Her eyes were cloudy and smeared, the lids puffy. Alan thought she looked very ill, and wondered what had caused her to look like that

'Isn't it . . . awful . . . all this?' She nodded in the direction of the old house. From where they stood they could see the ruined gable standing out clear in the sun against its background of trees, and the window of the Long Room, like an open, black mouth.

'Well, it's not very pleasant,' answered Flake. 'What's the matter, Avril? You look *really* ill.'

Avril brushed a hand across her face. 'I . . . I'm all right. I didn't . . . sleep very well . . . last night. I thought I'd come up here this morning . . . and try and find out what was happening . . . but there's a lot of reporters round the gate. I didn't want them to . . . see me, so I . . . turned back.'

'They wouldn't tell you anything, anyway,' said Alan. 'We shall all hear fast enough if they find . . . what they're looking for.'

'Yes, I suppose so,' said Avril. She looked at each of them uncertainly, and suddenly the tears welled up into the smeary eyes. 'Oh, God!' she burst out violently. 'Why did Paul have to die like that?' She turned away abruptly and ran, stumbling over the grass.

'What the heck's the matter with her?' said Alan. 'Has she gone crackers?'

'Don't you know what's the matter with her?' asked Flake in a low voice, staring after the jerky figure zig-zagging across the sunlit meadow. 'It's easy enough to see, *now*. She was crazily in love with Paul.'

They moved on in silence, but the greater part of the joyousness had gone out of the morning. Presently they came in sight of the entrance to Threshold House and stopped. Some sort of excitement appeared to be going on there. A clamouring group of newspaper reporters clustered round the rusty iron gate, out of which a uniformed police constable suddenly forced his way. Ignoring the barrage of questions which were shot at him, he stood looking down the narrow road. He was joined after a moment by a worried-looking Hatchard.

'I guess something's happened,' said Alan. 'Let's see if we can find out what it's all about.'

From somewhere in the distance there came a staccato pop-pop-pop-pop followed by a loud explosion, a succession of further pops and two more explosions even louder than the first.

'That's Simon's motorcycle,' said Flake, clutching Alan's arm. 'It always makes that noise.'

The popping and the explosions became louder. Presently, to the accompaniment of the most appalling din Alan had ever heard, and surrounded by a cloud of blue smoke, a motorcycle painted a vivid orange colour shot up the road, scattered the reporters, and skidded to an abrupt stop within an inch of Inspector Hatchard. The huge figure of Simon Gale, in shorts and an even more violent-coloured shirt than Alan had seen him in before, vaulted out of the saddle.

'Hello, hello!' he cried, thrusting the

motorcycle into the hands of an astonished reporter. 'Here I am, Hatchard. Where's Chippy?'

'Come on,' said Alan, grabbing Flake by the hand. 'We may be able to get in on this.' He rushed her up to Gale and the harassed inspector.

'Aha, it's you two, hey?' said Gale with a wide grin. 'Come on — let's get inside away from this rabble!' He flung a great arm round each of them and propelled them through the gate. Hatchard slipped in behind them and the police constable dragged it shut, and stood with his back against it, stolidly deaf to the howls of protest from the frustrated newspaper men.

'Now, then,' said Gale, turning to Hatchard, 'why did you send for me? Let's have it!'

'The chief constable's up at the house, sir,' said the inspector. 'I think we'd better wait until — '

'Rubbish!' cried Gale impatiently. 'Chippy won't mind. What's the news?'

'Well, sir,' said Hatchard. 'We've found the body.'

'You have?' exclaimed Gale, rubbing his hands in great delight. 'I'll bet Chippy's face was a sight for the gods when he heard that! Now d'you see what comes of *thinking*?'

'Yes, sir,' said Inspector Hatchard, with a rather peculiar look. 'We found the body of a woman. Only, you see, it's the *wrong* woman. It's not Fay Meriton!'

9

If the news that the police were looking for a body at Sorcerer's House had caused a sensation in Ferncross, the fact that they had actually found one caused an even greater sensation. That it should have turned out to be the *wrong* body only added to the general excitement.

The entire village buzzed like a gigantic wasps' nest, and no one buzzed more loudly than Miss Flappit. Wherever gossip and speculation was particularly rife, Miss Flappit materialized in the centre of it, joining in the wildest suggestions with zest, and offering even wilder and more unlikely ones of her own. Paul Meriton became, in turn, a monster — so diabolically evil that Landru and Christie had been almost archangels by comparison — who had spent his time murdering women and filling Threshold House with the bodies of his victims, or the victim himself of a homicidal maniac who prowled about the district with blood lust in his heart. Miss Flappit's convictions inclined to this latter theory and, with many a meaning look and innuendo, she made it clearly understood that in her opinion there was no need to look very far for the perpetrator of these horrible crimes. Again and again she retold the story of Mr. Veezey's threat on the bridge, and with each repetition it became more bloodcurdling.

'I know what *I* would do, if *I* were the police,' she declared, with a significant twitch of her shoulders and a sharp glint in her small eyes. And her listeners were left in no doubt.

The reporters, augmenting the guarded statement issued by Inspector Hatchard with such of these rumours as were printable, besieged the tiny post office to telephone lurid stories to their various newspapers.

The body, which remained unidentified, was that of a young woman whose age, according to the doctors, had been between eighteen and twenty. She had died from a heavy blow which had fractured the skull and, judging from the state of the corpse, had been dead for a considerable time. The body had been found buried under the tiles of a small out-building which had once been a wash-house, and it was the fact that these tiles had shown traces of having been re-laid that had caused the police to search there in the early stages of their investigation.

'You've been a *great* help,' said Major Chipingham sarcastically at a conference with Simon Gale and Inspector Hatchard, into which Alan Boyce had succeeded in wangling himself. 'All you've done, Gale, is to present us with another problem — as if we hadn't enough to contend with as it was! You've just made the whole thing more difficult, that's all you've done.'

'Now, just stop blowing off steam, an' listen to me!' cried Gale. 'If it hadn't been for me you'd never have known about this other murder.'

'And a fat lot of good it's done us,' broke in Major Chipingham, now purple in the face. 'All your damned clever theories about Fay Meriton — bah!'

'Don't you start shouting too soon, you old pessimist!' retorted Gale. 'You just wait an' see about Fay Meriton. What are you trying to tell me? That you'd rather not have found out about this other murder, because it makes it more difficult?'

'Now, now, sir,' interrupted Inspector Hatchard soothingly. 'That's not it at all. But it *has* rather put a spanner in the works, so to speak. You see what we're landed with now, sir? You thought we'd find the body of Mrs. Meriton, instead of which we find the body of an unknown young woman.'

'That only makes it more interesting,' said Gale.

'That's as may be, sir,' said Hatchard dubiously. 'But what we're faced with now is *two* murders instead of one, and — '

'Three,' said Gale, breaking in. 'You've forgotten the tramp. Three people, all killed in the same way. Two within a few weeks of each other, and the third one, Meriton, after a lapse of nearly two years.

It's a nice little problem.'

'And Meriton's the only one we can identify,' grunted the chief constable disgustedly. 'It may seem a 'nice little problem' to you, Gale, but so far as we're concerned it's a damned blasted headache!'

'What are you doing about trying to find out who the girl was?' demanded Gale, ignoring this outburst.

'We've asked for a list of all women between the ages of sixteen and twenty who were reported missing at the time she must have been murdered, sir,' answered Hatchard. 'The majority of 'em will have been traced by now, of course, which'll make it easier.'

'Pity you couldn't do the same about that tramp,' grunted Gale, pulling thoughtfully at his beard.

Hatchard shook his head. 'There's quite a few tramps 'on the road' that nobody 'ud ever miss,' he said. 'With a young woman, it's different. I expect we shall know who *she* was pretty soon, sir.'

'I hope it's going to help when we do,' grunted the chief constable pessimistically. 'I'm not at all sure that we're not up against a homicidal lunatic.'

'That's the popular belief in the village, sir,' said Hatchard. 'I must say that if we can't find a reasonable motive that covers all the — '

'No, no, no!' cried Simon Gale, sweeping his arm round in violent disagreement and knocking a pile of books off a small table. 'I won't have *that*! I told you at the beginning that there's a *pattern* to this business, d'you see? The murderer's working to a plan.' He flung himself into a chair. 'I've slipped up somewhere,' he muttered, scowling ferociously. 'I got hold of the wrong end of the stick.'

The telephone bell rang with eager insistence. Since Simon Gale appeared completely oblivious to the fact, Alan, who was nearest to the instrument, lifted the receiver.

'Yes?' he said into the mouthpiece.

The telephone demanded to know, metallically, if Inspector Hatchard was there.

'Hold on,' answered Alan. He turned to Hatchard. 'It's for you.'

The inspector got up and took the

receiver. 'Yes? Oh. What is it?'

The telephone chattered excitedly, and Alan saw Hatchard's face change.

'I see . . . Yes . . . yes . . . It may be very helpful.'

The chatter from the telephone ceased, and Hatchard put the receiver down slowly.

'What was it?' demanded Major Chipingham. Simon Gale had taken no notice whatever. He remained hunched up in his chair.

'They've just had an answer from Meriton's solicitors to our inquiry, sir,' said Hatchard. 'As near as they can tell, he died worth about seventy thousand pounds. There's a will, which he made about a year ago.'

'Who benefits?' asked the chief constable as Hatchard paused.

A queer look came into Hatchard's eyes. He said, speaking very slowly and distinctly: 'His wife gets the bulk of it, sir. But he left fifteen thousand pounds to — Dr. Ferrall.'

★　★　★

The inquest on Paul Meriton was held in an upstairs room at the Three Witches at ten-thirty on the following morning. It was not a large room, its normal purpose being a meeting place for various local clubs and societies, but it was the largest place available, since the school was unobtainable, and Ferncross did not possess a village hall. In consequence, only those people who were actually necessary to the proceedings were admitted; the remainder, which seemed to include the entire population, were forced to stay outside, gathered in little groups of avid discussion.

Miss Flappit was well to the fore. She flitted like a mosquito from one group to another, her dry, high-pitched voice clearly distinguishable above the general hum of conversation.

Colonel Ayling, his face rigid and devoid of expression, was listening, with an occasional grunted comment, to a small, fat man in a ginger-coloured suit of plus-fours, whose face looked like a well-polished apple. On the fringe of the small crowd, quite alone and looking, as usual, rather dazed, stood Mr. Veezey.

Alan Boyce and Flake arrived almost at the same time as Dr. Ferrall and Avril. They met, in fact, at the door, and only had time to exchange a hurried greeting before they were ushered to their seats in the improvised court-room. The coroner, a stout, capable-looking man, was already seated at his table, turning over his papers, and the proceedings began without delay.

They were brief and, to the reporters filling the back of the room, disappointing. Evidence of identification was supplied by Mrs. Horly, the deceased's housekeeper, a white-haired, comfortable woman with an ample bust, dressed discreetly in black, who gave her evidence quietly and without emotion. She was followed by Dr. Ferrall and the police surgeon, who testified to the cause of death, and then Alan was called. When he had related how he had come to discover the body, Inspector Hatchard got up and asked for an adjournment, pending further inquiries. The coroner, obviously primed beforehand, immediately granted his request and, except for a question by one of the jury — a local tradesman

— the proceedings came to an end.

'What about this other body?' demanded the juryman.

'That, sir,' replied the coroner, gathering his papers up, 'will be dealt with at a fresh inquiry.' And that was all.

Alan had expected to see Simon Gale, but there was no sign of him. They had left him on the previous day, after the telephone message to Hatchard about Meriton's will, still hunched up in his chair, scowling at nothing. The information that Ferrall was a beneficiary to the extent of fifteen thousand pounds, he had received with a non-committal grunt and, apparently, complete indifference.

Colonel Ayling joined them when they came out. 'Well?' he said, looking at them sharply from under his ragged brows. 'They adjourned it, did they?'

Ferrall nodded.

'I expected that,' grunted Ayling. 'The police are waiting for fresh evidence, I suppose. They won't find it, if they listen to that feller Gale too much. Why don't they tell him to mind his own business, eh?'

'I guess, if he had, they'd never have found this other body,' said Alan.

'An interfering mountebank, that's what *I* call him,' Colonel Ayling said angrily. 'Like all these fellers who think eccentricity is the hallmark of genius. Without all that posing an' bluster, nobody 'ud notice him, eh? Tried to make the police believe in a wild-cat theory that Paul had killed my daughter . . . Bah! *I* could have told 'em *that* was sheer rubbish.'

'Yes, indeed,' chimed in Miss Flappit from behind them. As usual she had materialized from apparently nowhere and overheard what Ayling was saying. 'I do so *agree* with that. If Inspector Hatchard would only listen to *me*, I'm quite sure that he would be able to make an arrest at *once*. There is no *doubt* in *my* mind concerning the guilty person.' She shot a quick and meaning glance in the direction of Mr. Veezey, who still stood, dazed and aloof, several yards away.

'Nonsense!' said Colonel Ayling curtly. 'Veezey wouldn't harm a fly. The whole trouble round here is there are far too many people with stupid ideas. Leave the matter to the police. That's what I say. It's their job, not the job of a lot of interfering incompetent amateurs!' He walked quickly away, pushing unceremoniously through the people who got in his path.

'Well, really!' said Miss Flappit, her small eyes glinting with annoyance behind her glasses. 'I do think Colonel Ayling is one of the *rudest* men. Anyone would think he didn't *want* this matter cleared up.'

'Let's go and have a drink,' suggested Ferrall, glancing at his watch, and rather pointedly ignoring Miss Flappit. 'Come on, the pub'll be open now.'

Leaving Miss Flappit to find 'fresh woods and pastures new' on which to drip the venom of her tongue, they went into the Three Witches. And the first person they saw, leaning up against the bar with a huge tankard in his hand, talking to Mr. Jellyberry, was Simon Gale.

'Hello, hello,' he greeted with a vast grin. 'What are you going to have, eh?'

'You weren't at the inquest,' said Alan

when the orders had been given.

'No,' said Gale. 'Jellyberry and I were having a quiet drink on our own.' He winked at the beaming landlord. 'I sneaked in the back way. There was nothing new to be learned from the inquest.'

'I thought you'd given up being the Great Detective, Simon,' said Avril, sipping her gin and French. She was still pale, and there were shadows under her eyes, but she looked better than when Alan had last seen her. Compared with Flake's more vivid beauty, her blue eyes and honey-coloured hair seemed rather washed-out, but there was no denying that she was very attractive.

'I never give anything up,' declared Simon Gale, 'until I've brought it to a successful conclusion, or discovered that it can't be done!' He drained his tankard and pushed it over to Mr. Jellyberry to be refilled.

'This is my shout,' said Ferrall, signing to the landlord to repeat the round. 'What makes you so interested, Gale?' he asked curiously.

'In this business?' Gale waved his arm in a vast gesture that embraced the whole affair. 'It's a problem, d'you see? And I like problems. Especially *human* problems. What made so-and-so do so-and-so? It's all the more exciting in this case because there's a hangman's noose for somebody at the end of it. Did you know Meriton was leaving you fifteen thousand?'

He flung the question quite casually, with scarcely a change of tone to his voice, but if, as Alan thought, he expected Ferrall would be disconcerted he was disappointed.

'Yes, I did,' answered Ferrall, collecting his change from Mr. Jellyberry. 'He told me he was going to when he made the will. I suppose the police told you — '

''ere he comes,' broke in the hoarse voice of the landlord, 'for 'the usual'. I was thinkin' it wouldn't be long.' He chuckled.

Alan looked round. Mr. Veezey had drifted into the bar. Uncertainly, he walked up to the counter, and the ritual of the two double-whiskies, and the hesitating search for the money, was conducted as before. Mr. Veezey drifted out again.

'Miss Flappit's chief suspect,' said Ferrall with a grimace. 'I'd sooner believe it was Miss Flappit than Veezey.'

'What makes him like that?' asked Alan curiously. 'As if he was in a kind of dream all the time.'

'Ah,' remarked Mr. Jellyberry, who had returned in time to overhear the question, 'It's my belief that 'e's not quite right in the 'ead, poor chap. Not that 'e's ever given any trouble. Got one interest in life, an' that's 'is garden.'

'I don't think he's cracked,' said Gale, shaking his head. 'Have you ever noticed his eyes? They're weak, but they're damned intelligent. There's a *brain* behind 'em.'

'I should never have thought poor Mr. Veezey particularly brainy,' said Flake doubtfully. 'He always seems to me rather . . . pathetic.'

'Like a lost child,' said Avril almost inaudibly.

'Well,' exclaimed Ferrall, finishing his

drink at a gulp, 'I must go. I've got patients to look after. You coming, Avril?'

She nodded. 'Yes, I must do some shopping if you want any lunch,' she said.

Simon Gale looked after them as they went out, with the cocked eyebrow look that Alan was beginning to know so well.

'Nice round sum, fifteen thousand, hey?' he grunted. 'I wonder if it was just a friendly gesture that made Meriton leave it to Ferrall — or whether there was any *other* reason?'

* * *

The Onslow-Whites went to Barnsford that afternoon, taking Flake with them, and Alan Boyce was left to his own devices. They had suggested that he might like to go with them, but they were calling on some friends, and he felt that he would rather stay in the peace of Bryony Cottage than make himself agreeable to strangers. Although he did not realize it, he was feeling the strain of exhausted nerves. The excitement of the last few days had been very wearing.

When they had gone he sat down in the pleasant old drawing room and wrote a long letter to his father.

The country's fine, and I guess you were right when you said this place had got everything. And how! There's already been a murder and the police have dug up the body of an unknown girl in the ruins of an old house that's supposed to be haunted! This morning I had to go to an inquest . . .

He finished his letter and went out into the garden. Making himself comfortable in one of the deck-chairs under the pear tree, he lighted a cigarette and let the peace of the summer afternoon soak into him like a hot bath. Outside this oasis there might be battle, murder and sudden death, but here, with the birds singing and butterflies chasing each other over the flowers, there was peace.

Bang! Pop-pop-pop . . . bang!

The American was startled to sudden wakefulness. *Bang!* The last explosion sounded as though the entire cottage had blown up.

'Hello, hello!' cried the voice of Simon

Gale. 'Anyone at home?' He came striding round the side of the house, a figure of immense energy, and grinned at Alan. The peace of the garden fled.

'They've all gone to Barnsford,' said Alan a little resentfully.

'So much the better,' said Gale, dropping into a chair beside him. 'It's *you* I came to see, young feller. I feel like talking. I want to clarify some ideas I've got about this Meriton business.' He whipped out his battered tin of black tobacco and a packet of papers and, almost with the effect of a conjuring trick, rolled a cigarette. 'I've been thinking,' he went on, 'and I've got a vague idea of the pattern. Part of it, anyway.' He scraped a match to flame on his thumb-nail and lit his cigarette. 'Mind you,' he said with a fiendish scowl at Alan, 'I'm only conjecturing, but it all fits. By all the cards in the Tarot, how it *fits* . . . '

'Well, let's hear it,' said Alan impatiently, annoyed at the interruption to his peaceful afternoon.

'You've got to keep this to yourself, young feller,' said Gale. 'I don't want

Chippy, or Hatchard, or *anybody* to know about it — yet. Because, d'you see, I may be wrong.' He blew a curl of burnt paper off the end of his cigarette and stared up into the branches of the pear tree. 'Now, look here,' he said, 'leaving the murder of Meriton out of it, what have we got? We've got two other murders — an unknown tramp and an unknown woman, both killed in the same place and in exactly the same way and, apparently, within a few weeks of each other. Right? There's only *one* difference in these two murders. While the body of the tramp is left lying under the window of the Long Room for anyone to find, the body of the woman is buried under the tiled floor of a wash-house. Suggestive, eh?'

'Do you mean,' said Alan, frowning, 'that it didn't matter about the tramp being found, but it mattered a heck of a lot that the woman shouldn't be?'

Gale slapped his knee. 'Double-twenty-first shot, young feller!' he cried. 'The woman's body was never *meant* to be found. It was only because I made a damn stupid mistake that it *was*. Anyone could have buried a dozen bodies in that old house, and nobody would have been the wiser. It was the one place, d'you see, that was absolutely *safe*. There's not a soul in the village who'd go near it. They're all scared to death of the ghosts and the goblins.'

'Fay Meriton wasn't scared,' said Alan. 'Not if she really used that room.'

Had she been up there, with the candle-flames flickering in the draught, while somebody worked feverishly in an outhouse below, re-laying a tiled floor . . . ?

'Of course Fay Meriton wasn't scared,' said Simon Gale with an odd inflection in his voice. 'There was no need for *her* to be scared. Because, d'you see, she was *responsible* for the ghosts and the goblins. I'll bet a used stamp to all the fleas on a stray cat that it was Fay Meriton who killed the tramp and the woman.'

10

Alan Boyce had seen what was coming, but when it came, it was nonetheless a shock. Fay Meriton, whose shadowy figure and queer personality had hovered in the background like an uneasy ghost, suddenly took on shape and substance, as though she had stepped out of the picture over the mantelpiece in that dusty attic room.

'D'you see what happened?' said Simon Gale, flinging away the end of his cigarette and deftly rolling a fresh one. 'D'you see how perfectly it fits? That insane streak in her that was responsible for the furnished room in Sorcerer's House, and the fits of hysteria, suddenly kicked bang over the traces. It turned homicidal, and the tramp an' the girl were the result.'

'But, surely,' objected Alan, 'if she became violent, everybody would have known?'

'No, no, no,' Gale cried. 'It doesn't work like that. Once it was over, once Fay had got the killing bug out of her system, she'd be more or less normal — until the next time the urge welled up. There have been dozens of similar cases, young feller. The homicidal maniac is usually as normal, outwardly, as you or I. An' then the blood-lust comes and, poof!' He snapped his fingers.

'Paul Meriton must have known.'

'Of course he knew!' broke in Gale impatiently. 'That's the reason why the poor devil always looked as though hell was burning inside him. He covered up for her. The tramp didn't matter — it was generally supposed that he'd fallen out of the window. His body was put there so that it *would* look like that. But the girl . . . *that* was different. If *her* body had been found a few weeks later, there'd have been a devil of a rumpus. The police *might* be persuaded that *one* accident had taken place, but they'd never accept *two*. So Meriton buried the body under those tiles in the outhouse. Wouldn't *you* have done the same, young feller, if you were desperately in love with your wife and you'd suddenly found out that she — ' He stopped abruptly and cocked an inquiring eye at Alan. 'Think what it would have meant,' he went on, after a pause. 'A trial . . . Broadmoor . . . a whole cartload of mud-slinging. He wasn't going to let her face *that*, so he got her away, after persuading her to write that note.'

'Where?' asked Alan curtly.

Gale flapped a huge hand at a wasp that was buzzing round his head. 'What would *you* have done with her? Remember, she was potentially dangerous. She might do it *again*. She couldn't be left at large.'

'A mental home,' exclaimed Alan.

'That's right,' said Gale, rubbing his hands. 'That's right, young feller. Now, d'you see why Meriton left that money to Ferrall?'

'Ferrall!' echoed Alan. 'Do you mean that *he* — '

'You've got to have the signature of *two* doctors to get a person admitted into a mental home,' said Gale. 'Understand?

I'll bet that Peter Ferrall could tell us the whole story. *He* knows where Fay is . . . an' that's why he's looking so flaming worried. If it all comes out, he's in for serious trouble, d'you see? Accessory after the fact.'

'Would any place — even a *private* mental asylum — have taken her in the circumstances?' said Alan doubtfully. 'The risk . . . '

'You don't suppose they told 'em the *true* circumstances, do you?' cried Gale, scowling ferociously at the wasp, which had returned for a further inspection. 'Of course they didn't!'

There was a silence. Alan realized that it fitted, this theory of Gale's. It fitted except for . . .

'Look here,' he said suddenly. 'Your theory explains the murder of the tramp and girl, but it doesn't explain *Meriton's* murder.

'Aha!' exclaimed Simon Gale. 'I only said I'd got *part* of the pattern.'

'And even that's only conjecture,' interrupted Alan.

'Quite right, young feller,' agreed Gale.

'But it covers the facts.'

It did — up to a certain point. But who had killed Meriton, and why?

'I suppose,' Alan said, as an idea struck him, 'that Fay Meriton couldn't have escaped?'

'And killed her husband?' Gale shook his head. 'No, that's too far-fetched. Where would she have hidden herself?'

'What about her father?' suggested Alan, with a sudden inspiration.

Simon Gale stared at him. 'Now that's something I didn't think of,' he exclaimed. 'By all the gold in Guatavita, I wonder . . .'

'Colonel Ayling probably knew all about it,' said Alan. 'I mean from the start.'

'No.' Gale was emphatic. 'He genuinely thought she'd run away. That I'm sure of. Besides, fond as he was of her, he would never have helped to hush up murder — whatever the cost might have been. But, if she had suddenly come back with some cock-and-bull story, *that's* a different matter.' He grabbed at his beard and pulled it through his fingers. 'We've got to go carefully over this ... I'm worried — damned worried, young feller. If Fay Meriton *is* somewhere round here ... ' He shrugged his shoulders, leaving the sentence unfinished.

But Alan knew what he meant, and his throat felt suddenly dry.

★ ★ ★

Nothing very much happened during the next few days. Alan spent his time reading, going for long walks with Flake, or chatting with the genial Mr. Jellyberry in the bar of the Three Witches. He saw nothing during this period of Simon Gale, but the talk they had had in the garden at Bryony Cottage was never very far from his mind. He was pretty sure that it had got somewhere near the truth.

He could not discuss the matter with Flake, because of his promise to Gale, but he brought up the subject of Fay Meriton, during one of their walks, and tried to learn all he could about her. They had been children together and Flake's dislike seemed to have dated from a very early age. Fay, she said, had always been selfish. If she couldn't have her own way, she would fly into a rage which quickly became hysterical and, even when this had worn off, would sulk for hours. In one of her fits of temper she had hit another little girl on the head with a jagged stone, and the child had had to have the wound stitched. She could, when it suited her, be very sweet, and as she got older, she discovered that this was a greater asset in getting what she wanted than her fits of hysterical rage, and she exploited it for all she was worth.

'Poor Paul thought she was wonderful,' said Flake, staring before her with hard eyes. 'She was determined to marry him, and she did. He couldn't resist the soulful expression she could turn on like a water-tap, and, of course, she really was lovely. She had that wonderful white skin which sometimes goes with red hair.'

The dislike which had started in childhood had grown to something very near hatred, thought Alan. There was a hardness about Flake's face when she talked of Fay Meriton that was not there at any other time. And that story of the child who had to have stitches in her head. That should interest Simon Gale.

But when Alan called at Gale's house later that day, the door was opened by the malignant-faced Mrs. Gull, who curtly informed him that Gale was out, and refused to give any other information whatever.

On his way back, he passed Mr. Veezey's hut, and saw its owner working in the garden. On an impulse, Alan stopped by the gate and called a cheerful 'good afternoon'.

Mr. Veezey jumped, like a startled rabbit, and looked round.

'I always admire your garden when I pass this way,' said Alan. 'I guess it must have taken you a long time to get it like this.'

Mr. Veezey blinked at him nervously. 'Oh — er — yes . . . thank you,' he said. He brushed a gloved hand across his forehead, leaving a streak of dirt. 'Er — you — er — you are from America, aren't you?'

'Yes,' said Alan, 'I'm staying with the

Onslow-Whites. I'm over here on business, but I'm having a short holiday first. My father has a publishing business in New York.'

Mr. Veezey's pimple of a chin dropped as his mouth fell open. He stared at Alan with an expression of sheer terror, mumbled something that was quite unintelligible and, turning, rushed into the house and slammed the door.

It took Alan a few seconds to recover from his astonishment. Was the man crazy? Why had he suddenly rushed away like that, as if all the fiends of hell were after him? He hadn't said anything that could possibly have offended the man. What on earth was the matter with him?

He tried to find an explanation for the extraordinary behaviour of Mr. Veezey during his walk back to Bryony Cottage, but the only one he could think of was that the little man was mad.

It was on the morning of the third day that Alan saw Simon Gale again. He had run out of the supply of cigarettes he had brought with him, and walked down to the village after breakfast to buy some more. As he came out of the small shop in the High Street, a stentorian hail greeted him, and there was Gale on the opposite side of the road, waving at him frantically.

'Where have you been?' asked Alan. 'I went along to see you the other afternoon, but — '

'I've covered a lot of ground since I saw you last, young feller,' said Gale. 'I'm just going to sample some of Jellyberry's beer. Come along with me.'

Alan glanced at his watch and found it was not yet ten. 'The pub won't be open yet,' he said, but Gale waved away the objection with a sweep of an arm.

'It's always open to me,' he declared. 'Come along, I've got a lot to tell you.'

Alan did not feel in the least like beer so early in the morning, but his curiosity was aroused.

They went round to the back door of the Three Witches and were admitted by Mr. Jellyberry, beaming as usual. Gale ordered beer, emptied the tankard at one draught, and said, with obvious relish: 'Ah, that's better! Now, Jellyberry, bring me another and then make yourself scarce. I want to have a private confab with our friend here, d'you see.'

Mr. Jellyberry refilled the tankard to the accompaniment of a rumbling chuckle. 'If there be anythin' more you want, just give me a call, sir,' he said, and he left them alone.

'Now, young feller,' said Simon Gale, 'I've been doing a bit of snooping. I've been delving into the history of Dr. Peter Ferrall,' he rubbed his hands gleefully, 'and I discovered something that bears out that theory of mine. Before he took over old Wycherly's practice here, Ferrall was connected with a private mental home at a place called Shilford in Hampshire. What d'you think of that, eh?'

'I guess it practically clinches it,' answered Alan. 'What are you going to do now? Tell Hatchard?'

'No, not yet.' Gale shook his head violently. 'I've got to see Ferrall first. If he was only trying to help Meriton, I don't want to get him into trouble, if it can be avoided.'

'It's going to be pretty difficult to keep

him out of it, isn't it?' said Alan doubtfully.

'Well . . . ' Gale took a mighty swig from the tankard. 'I'm concerned with finding out the truth of this business for my own satisfaction, d'you see? If it's only going to get people into trouble by making it public, without doing any good, I shall keep it to myself.'

'I don't see how you can do that.' Alan said dubiously. 'After all, it *is* murder.'

'I know it's murder!' retorted Gale, thumping the tankard on the counter so violently that some of the beer splashed over. 'But if Fay Meriton did the killing, what good's it going to do to get Ferrall dragged into court?'

'But you can't leave Fay Meriton at large,' protested Alan. 'She may do it again.'

'Aha, I agree with *that*,' said Gale. 'But there's no proof, yet, that Fay *is* at large. I've been to Shilford and had a look at this mental home. It's quite a small place — an old house that's been converted — kept by a Dr. Preston. There's only about a dozen patients, and a small staff.

There's a pub in the village where they sell passable beer, and I got into conversation with one of the male nurses. I brought up the subject of people escaping — not too obviously, of course — and he told me that nobody had ever escaped from his place.'

'I guess he wouldn't admit it, anyway,' interrupted Alan.

'Why shouldn't he?' demanded Gale belligerently. 'If Fay was a patient there, you don't suppose they knew *why* she was there, do you? They wouldn't have taken a risk like *that*. You can bet that Ferrall an' Meriton cooked up a story of some sort that never mentioned murder.'

'Well, if she didn't escape, who murdered Meriton?' demanded Alan reasonably.

'Yes . . . that's the tear in the balloon,' grunted Gale. He scowled into his tankard. 'Perhaps Ferrall can help us there. I'm going along to see him this afternoon. Like to come?'

Alan nodded. He said, after a slight pause: 'Did you know that when Fay Meriton was a child, she attacked another child, and they had to have stitches put in their head?' He related the story which Flake had told him.

Gale listened with great interest. 'Ah-ha!' he exclaimed when Alan had finished. 'The same method! The germ was stirring even then. You know, young feller, here's something worth thinking about. Did the evil in Fay Meriton communicate itself to that old house, or did a more ancient evil, that was already lurking there, take possession of her half-crazy mind? Perhaps *something* got out of Cagliostro's magic circle, and is still loose . . . '

* * *

Dr. Ferrall was out when they called at the house on the green that afternoon. Avril opened the door and seemed rather surprised to see them.

'Peter's gone to see a patient,' she said. 'I don't think he will be long. Do come in.'

They followed her into the drawing room, bright with flowers and chintz.

Large open French windows led into a neat, trim garden that lacked the artistic beauty of Mr. Veezey's. Avril must have been reading when they disturbed her, for a book was turned down on the arm of an easy chair drawn up to the open windows, and there was a half-empty box of chocolates on a low table nearby.

'What did you want to see Peter for?' she asked. There was a hint of nervousness in her manner and her eyes looked a little strained. Every time you saw this girl, thought Alan, you noticed something fresh about her. She wasn't instantly disturbing, like Flake — she didn't make you catch your breath because you didn't realize, until you'd met her for the third or fourth time, just how really attractive she was.

'We just dropped in for a little chat,' answered Simon Gale, perching himself on the arm of a settee which creaked ominously under his weight. Her nervousness increased, although she tried to hide it.

'Is there — is there any further news?' she asked. 'The police haven't made any fresh discoveries, have they?'

'Not a thing,' declared Gale, shaking his head. 'I'll bet Chippy's running around like a puppy chasing its tail! If he had any hair, he'd be tearing it out in handfuls.' He chuckled delightedly. 'What's the book you're reading?'

'*Whispered in Heaven*,' said Avril. She looked slightly surprised at this abrupt change of subject.

'Ah!' cried Gale, 'Maurice Charlton's latest, eh? Ever read any of his books, young feller?'

'No,' said Alan. 'Is he good?'

'Good!' repeated Gale with a surge of enthusiasm. 'He doesn't *write*. He tears off strips of life and confines them, by some flaming miracle, in the covers of a book! The whole thing glows with a passionate sincerity. Bah! I can't describe it! You must read him for yourself. Read *all* his books.'

'Read all *whose* books?' broke in Peter Ferrall's voice. He had come in quietly during Gale's outburst. 'I knew you were here, Simon. I could hear you on the other side of the green.'

'The praises of Maurice Charlton ought to be shouted from the house-tops!' said Gale.

'I thought you were doing that,' remarked Ferrall dryly. 'But I agree with you, he's excellent. Is this a social call, or . . . ?' He looked from one to the other of them with raised eyebrows.

Simon Gale hoisted himself off the settee arm. He said, without any dissembling: 'I want a word with you, Ferrall — in private.'

Alan heard the hiss of Avril's breath as she drew it in quickly, and saw the suddenly frightened look which came into her eyes. He felt thoroughly uncomfortable. This business of playing the detective was all very well in theory, but when it came to practice . . .

'It sounds rather ominous.' Ferrall tried to speak lightly, but he could not quite control his voice. 'You'd better come into the surgery.'

'Peter!' began Avril sharply. And then, 'Never mind . . . I'll get the tea ready.'

She walked quickly to the door and went out. There was a moment of awkward silence, and Alan began to wish he had let Gale handle the thing on his own.

'This way,' said Ferrall shortly. He led the way across the hall and opened a door on the other side. They entered a small room, plainly furnished with a desk, several chairs, and a square of carpet. In one corner near the window stood a padded table on rubber casters.

Ferrall shut the door carefully. 'Now then,' he said, leaning against the desk. 'What is it?'

'Look here,' said Gale. 'I want you to get it into your head that I'm not out to make trouble, d'you see? But I've got to know the truth.'

'I don't know what you're talking about,' said Ferrall. 'The truth about what?'

'The truth about Fay Meriton an' that private mental home at Shilford. That startled you, eh?'

Ferrall had nearly dropped the cigarette case which he had taken from his pocket. He said, recovering himself: 'What exactly are you getting at?'

'The tramp — and the girl whose body was found. They were both killed by Fay. That's why she had to be got away.'

'You're mad, Gale!' exclaimed Ferrall angrily. 'That's drivel!'

'It's easily proved,' interrupted Gale calmly. 'If Hatchard goes to that place at Shilford with a photograph of Fay, and they've never heard of her, then I'm talking drivel.'

Ferrall fumbled with a cigarette. His face had suddenly become drawn and old. His voice, when he finally spoke, rasped. 'Have you . . . said anything of this to Hatchard?'

'I've told you, I don't want to make trouble,' retorted Gale. 'Why d'you think Boyce an' I are here? We could have gone *direct* to Hatchard. Don't be a *complete* fathead, whatever else you've been.'

'Wait a minute,' muttered Ferrall. 'Let me think . . . ' He slid off the desk into the chair by it and stroked his brows as though he were trying to soothe an ache. 'I've always been afraid of this,' he said, after a long pause. 'I've cursed myself over and over again for ever having had anything to do with it. But once it was done, what could I do? If it had been anyone else but Paul . . . ' He looked up suddenly. 'You know what this'll mean . . . if it comes out?'

Simon Gale dropped a hand on his shoulder. 'Perhaps it won't have to come out,' he said, without any of his habitual bluster. 'Look here, suppose you tell us the whole story? You've lived with it a long time. It'll do you good to get it off your chest.'

'My God, you're right!' said Ferrall. 'Even when Paul was alive, it was a nightmare. Since his death . . . ' He made a weary gesture and sat up. He put the cigarette he had been fumbling with in his mouth, lit it, and inhaled deeply. 'You'd better make yourselves as comfortable as you can,' he said. 'This is going take rather a long time.'

11

'I knew Paul Meriton,' said Ferrall after a few moments' silence, 'before I took over Wycherly's practice — several years before. Things weren't too good with me then. I was working with Preston at Shilford, and the pay . . . ' He shrugged his shoulders. 'I got into a nasty jam. There might have been bad trouble if Meriton hadn't got me out of it. I'm telling you this so that you'll understand *why* I did what I did.' He drew on his cigarette and let the smoke feather slowly from his nostrils. 'One day I had a letter from Meriton telling me that Dr. Wycherley was retiring, and suggesting that I should buy the practice. He offered to lend me the necessary money. He knew I hadn't any of my own. I agreed, naturally. It was a good chance to get out of the rut, and I wasn't very happy at my job with Preston. I bought the practice, and settled down here. And I met Fay

. . . It wasn't long,' he continued after a pause, 'before I discovered that there was something wrong. There was nothing very much *outwardly*, but I'd had experience and I knew the signs.'

'I know!' broke in Gale, 'I recognized 'em, too — when she sat for that picture.'

Ferrall nodded. The strained look about his eyes was not so noticeable. He said, with a sudden expulsion of his breath: 'I'm glad to be able to talk about it — it's a relief. I've been worried sick ever since you started talking about Fay to Hatchard and Chipingham that day. I knew then that you must have guessed. I told Avril.'

'Does Avril know?' asked Gale quickly.

'She's known all along. She begged me not to have anything to do with it, but what *could* I do?'

So Flake had been wrong, thought Alan. It was not that Avril Ferrall had been in love with Meriton that had made her look so ill. It was worry — the fear of being found out.

'I soon discovered,' Ferrall went on, 'that the reason Meriton had suggested my taking over Wycherly's practice was because he wanted to have a doctor on the spot who was used to mental cases — somebody he could trust completely.'

'But surely at *that* time Fay hadn't shown any signs of homicidal tenden — '

'No, no.' Ferrall shook his head quickly. '*That* came suddenly — and completely unexpectedly. Of course, you can never tell in these cases, but I was quite unprepared for anything like *that*.' He stubbed out his cigarette in the ashtray on the desk. 'Fay, until then, was suffering from a paranoid psychosis. She had delusions in which she became the principal character in a series of *imagined* situations.'

'I guess that's over my head,' said Alan.

Ferrall smiled. It was a smile that twisted his mouth but left his eyes unchanged. He said: 'I'll try and explain. In its milder form it's very common and quite harmless. You've probably experienced something of the kind when you've imagined yourself in some unlikely situation, such as — er — being chosen to play for England in the Test — in your case, I suppose, it would be baseball — and saving the Ashes by a brilliant catch, or a stroke that gains the winning run — something of that sort. The point is that *you* are the outstanding personality — the hero. Most people have these pleasant daydreams at some time or other. It's an extension of childhood, during which these kinds of imaginings play a predominant part. But with Fay it was carried to an extreme.

'The majority of people,' Ferrall continued, after a pause, 'when they talk about hysteria, mean a crying or laughing fit brought about by overcharged emotions. *Real* hysteria is something very different. It is a nervous disease that *can* produce actual insanity.'

'So I hit the nail bang on the head, eh?' cried Gale.

'You did,' agreed Ferrall. 'And that's what worried me.' He lit another cigarette. 'The hysteric, you know,' he said, 'lives in a world of self-created illusion. For example, he or she may believe that it is impossible to walk, and *becomes*, to all intents and purposes, paralysed. Reality is subordinated to a fixed idea.'

'But Fay Meriton didn't suffer from *that* kind of illusion, surely?' said Alan.

'No, no, no!' said Ferrall impatiently. 'I merely used that as an illustration to show you just how the hysteric's mind works. Fay, at first, only tried to escape to a world of her own imagination because she was disappointed with reality. The result was that room in Sorcerer's House. It was there that she lived her *real* life.'

'The robbers' cave,' exclaimed Gale. 'The pirate ship, eh?'

'Exactly!' said Ferrall. 'I see you understand. That room was, to Fay, what the hide-out at the bottom of the garden, or the collection of chairs and boxes, is to the small boy. A world of make-believe. If it had stopped there . . . ' He shrugged his shoulders. 'But it didn't. I was much to blame for what *did* happen. I should have insisted that Fay was put under restraint earlier. But, although there were occasional scenes and hysterical outbursts, I didn't think there was anything *really* serious . . . nothing that would lead to . . . murder.'

'You should have known that when you're dealing with a hysteric, *anything* is possible,' grunted Simon Gale, scowling.

Ferrall's face clouded. For a moment, Alan thought he was going to lose his temper. Then he said, a little ruefully: 'I suppose I deserve *that*. But outwardly, you see, Fay was normal. Nobody would have suspected — nobody did — and Meriton begged me to keep the secret. He quite literally worshipped her. He was sure that she'd recover with care and watchfulness. He didn't realize that the basis of this disease is sexual, and that Fay had married the *wrong* man. It was no use telling him. He wouldn't have understood. And then . . . the tramp was killed.'

Ferrall got up. He walked over to a side table and poured himself out a glass of water. 'That night will stick in my memory until I die,' he said, facing them with the glass in his hand. 'And in Avril's. We'd gone to bed when Paul arrived, looking like death. Fay was with him, and her clothes were all smeared with blood.

She was in a terribly excited state, on the verge of a hysterical outburst, and I had to give her an injection to keep her quiet. Avril took her to the bedroom to lie down. And then Meriton told me . . . ' He sipped a little of the water, and put the glass down. 'He'd found her up at the old house, bending over the body of that tramp, with a piece of rusty old iron piping in her hand. Of course, she'd sworn that she hadn't killed him, but there wasn't any doubt about it in my mind. I knew then that the streak of insanity had suddenly taken a new and terrible turn. We sat up all night while Fay slept under the drug I had given her, discussing what was to be done. I urged Paul to take drastic action, but he wouldn't hear of it. There might be a mistake, he said. Perhaps somebody else had killed the tramp. He didn't really believe it; he was just trying to convince himself. It would easily pass for an accident, he argued. Why not give Fay the benefit of the doubt? He'd buried the iron bar and carried the body of the tramp and put it under the window of the Long

Room. It would *look* like an accident.'

'Where was the tramp *actually* killed?' demanded Gale.

'Near the front door,' answered Ferrall. 'Paul removed all traces of the blood-stains by the steps.' He went over to the window and stared out into the sunlit garden. 'I allowed myself to be talked over,' he said bitterly. 'I agreed to say nothing. If I'd only spoken out then, that girl would never have been killed.'

'Who was she?' asked Alan.

'I don't know.' Ferrall leaned against the frame of the window and thrust his hands into his pockets. 'She was on holiday, I think. She had a bicycle.'

'Did Meriton bury that, too?' said Gale.

Ferrall nodded. 'Yes, under the old rockery,' he answered. 'The girl was killed in the afternoon; I suppose she must have wandered into the grounds. You know how a place like that sometimes attracts people? Perhaps she was looking for somewhere to picnic. She had a packet of sandwiches with her, and a bottle of milk. It was a hot

afternoon. And she ran into Fay . . . '
The strained look had come back to his
eyes. 'Paul was frantic with worry. I
insisted that the police should be
informed, but he pleaded with me. He
suggested that we should get Fay into
the mental home at Shilford. It would
save all the scandal, the dragging of the
whole thing through the courts. We
argued and argued. In the end, like a
fool, I rang up Preston.' He passed a
hand wearily across his forehead. 'We
got Fay to Shilford that night. She was
quite willing. Meriton explained to her
what the alternative would be, and she
was frightened. He persuaded her to
write that note, because we had to
account somehow for her sudden
disappearance. Preston was a little
difficult at first, but I managed to talk
him round. Meriton was willing to pay
pretty stiffly. We never mentioned the
real reason, of course; we just laid that
Fay was subject to fits of violence.
Preston could tell when he examined her
that she was a psychopathic case, so
there was no trouble there. He and I

signed the certificate, and Fay was admitted. She's been there ever since.'

'Has she?' cried Simon Gale, leaping to his feet. 'That's the whole point, Ferrall. *Has she?*'

'What do you mean?' asked Ferrall sharply.

'Meriton was killed in exactly the same way as those other two,' said Gale. 'If — '

'And you're wondering if Fay was responsible?' interrupted Ferrall. 'Well, you can put *that* out of your mind. I don't know who murdered Paul, but it wasn't Fay. She's never been out of that mental home, Gale, since she went in nearly two years ago — not for a *single instant*. She's *still* there.'

⋆　⋆　⋆

'Now that you know the truth, Simon, what are you going to do?' asked Avril anxiously.

They were back in the drawing room. A tray of tea, the cakes and sandwiches untouched, stood on a low table beside her. Alan Boyce, with a cup of tea balanced on his knee, sat facing her. Dr. Ferrall stood by the fireplace, one elbow resting on the mantelpiece. Simon Gale, a ferocious scowl drawing down his bushy brows, strode restlessly about the room, winding the end of his beard round his fingers. Outside, in the sun-flooded garden, the birds made a chorus of sound in the trees.

'I don't know,' muttered Gale. 'I've got to think.'

Avril's worried eyes sought her brother's. He shrugged his shoulders. Alan got the impression that whatever the outcome, he did not care anymore. His expression was that of a man who had faced the worst that could happen to him and found a certain peace of mind in acceptance.

'You're quite sure,' said Gale, 'that Fay couldn't have got out of that home — not even for a short time?'

'Quite,' answered Ferrall. 'It was the first thing I thought of when I found out about Meriton. I telephoned Preston immediately.'

'By the Great Oracle of Delphi!' cried

Gale, suddenly smashing his fist into the palm of his hand. 'The pattern's clear up to a point, and then it goes all haywire. It's like a half-finished picture with the rest of the canvas blank.' He began to pace up and down the room again. 'Look here . . . during that hour, when Meriton drove around the country with you, what did he talk about?'

'Fay,' answered Ferrall. 'That's all he ever talked about to us — wondering if she'd *really* killed those people.'

'Did he say anything — anything at all, mark you — that might have suggested he was going up to that house later, or that he was meeting someone?'

Ferrall shook his head. He said: 'No. He used to go there and sit in that room, looking at the picture. But that was a long time ago. I don't think he went near the place for nearly a year.'

'So it was *Meriton* who hung the picture over that mantelpiece, eh?'

'Fay would never have had it there,' said Avril. She was frowning in a puzzled way and nibbling at her finger. 'She hated it. There *was* something, you know . . .

that night when Paul was killed.'

Simon Gale whirled round. 'Yes?' he cried excitedly. 'Yes? What was it — quickly!'

'It wasn't anything he *said*,' answered Avril slowly. 'But I got an idea that something had upset him. Something that *Fay* had told him.'

'You never mentioned it to me,' broke in Ferrall sharply.

'I've only just remembered,' she said. 'I . . .'

'Something that *Fay* had told him?' repeated Gale. 'When?'

'I suppose, when he last saw her.'

'He used to visit her once a week,' put in Ferrall. 'The last time would have been the day before he was killed.'

'And you think she told him something then that upset him?' demanded Gale, glaring at Avril with such a malignant expression that she shied away.

'It — it was only an impression I got,' she said. 'I — I couldn't be sure . . . I may be entirely wrong.'

'I've got to see Fay,' interrupted Gale, gnawing at his knuckles. 'I've *got* to see her, d'you see? Can you fix it?' He turned to Ferrall.

'I suppose it could be arranged,' answered Ferrall dubiously.

'Then do it,' said Gale. 'As soon as possible. Tomorrow. Does she know about Meriton?'

'No. Look here, you'll have to be careful about that. There might be very grave danger . . . '

'Do you think I'm a complete fathead?' growled Gale in high dudgeon. 'D'you suppose I'm going to blurt it out like a schoolboy over his first love affair? Rubbish! It may not be necessary to tell her at all.'

'She'll have to know,' said Avril, 'won't she? She'll wonder why he doesn't go to see her anymore.'

'Why,' said Alan, on a sudden impulse, 'did you say to Dr. Ferrall, that night in the garden at the Onslow-Whites', that something was dangerous?'

There was a sudden complete silence. Simon Gale stopped dead in the middle of his patrol of the room. He said, looking sharply at the American: 'What's that?

236

What's that, young feller?'

'That's what you said, wasn't it?' asked Alan.

'Did I?' Avril pursed her lips doubtfully, but her rich voice was not quite steady. 'I . . . must have been referring to this business of Fay.'

'That's right, you were,' said Ferrall. 'You were always warning me how dangerous it was.'

'That was it, eh?' said Gale. 'Look here, while we're on the subject of what happened in that garden, there's something *I'd* like to know. Why did you talk all that bilge about seeing a light in the window of the Long Room at Sorcerer's House? *You* knew very well what had started the local superstition — so did Meriton. It was Fay, when she used that room. And, later, it was Meriton himself. They fostered it between them. Why, by all the Powers of Darkness, did you have to make such a hullabaloo pretending that you'd seen a light there?'

'That's just it,' said Avril slowly. 'I wasn't pretending. I *did* see a light. And Paul was at Shilford that night — he always stayed the night at the hotel when he went to see Fay — so it couldn't have been he. *Somebody* was in Sorcerer's House. But it wasn't Paul.'

★   ★   ★

Peter Ferrall arranged for them to go to Shilford on the following afternoon. He telephoned Simon Gale in the morning, and Gale telephoned Alan Boyce.

Alan had some little difficulty in getting away. Flake, not unnaturally, wanted to know where he was going and, since he was unable to tell her the truth, and had to think of a not very plausible excuse, there was a certain amount of coolness between them.

The spell of hot weather broke during the night, and the morning was grey and cloudy. It was still warm, but the rain started to fall just after lunch. By the time Alan met Gale and Ferrall at the latter's house, it had developed into a steady downpour.

Avril did not go with them. Alan was rather sorry that she had not before the journey was over, for Simon Gale, apparently completely absorbed in his own thoughts, scarcely spoke a word throughout, and Ferrall was equally taciturn.

With the screen-wiper working madly they reached Shilford at a few minutes before six.

'Pull up at the pub,' grunted Gale, rousing himself at last. 'I feel in need of beer before we face this business.'

'I could do with a drink myself,' said Ferrall.

It was pouring in torrents when they got out of the car and entered the bar of the Shilford Arms. At that early hour it was nearly empty. Except for themselves and a middle-aged barmaid, there were only two men with briefcases talking in low tones to one corner.

Gale ordered drinks, beer for himself and whisky for Alan and Ferrall.

'I'm not looking forward to this at all, you know,' said Ferrall abruptly.

'It's got to be done,' answered Gale. To the fascinated astonishment of the barmaid, he poured the entire contents of the

tankard down his throat without appear-
ing to swallow.

'We'll have another, and then we'll go,'
said Ferrall, signalling to the dazed
barmaid, who was still staring at Gale
with slightly protruding eyes. 'I ought to
warn you,' he went on in a lower tone,
'that Fay isn't expecting us. Preston
thought it would be better if it looked as
though we had dropped in casually.'

Alan felt an absurd desire to laugh. Did
one 'drop in casually' to see the inmates
of a mental home? Like calling in at a
friend's house for a cocktail? What sort of
effect would it have on Fay Meriton who,
presumably, was under the impression
that nobody except her husband and
Ferrall knew where she was?

They finished the drinks and went back
to the car. The sky was lowering and
leaden-coloured. The rain, now that it
had come, looked as if it might go on for
ever.

The mental home was approached by a
narrow lane. A high wall of old red brick
with a coping of broken glass surrounded
it, and the entrance was guarded by a pair

of heavy iron gates. Just inside was a small lodge, and a porter came out of this when Ferrall rang the bell. He unlocked the gates, waited until they had driven through, and relocked them, returning as quickly as he could to the lodge.

They drove up a wide gravelled drive to the house, which was an ugly building, like an oblong box of brick with many windows, most of them protected by iron bars. In the driving rain it looked bleak and depressing. There were no trees or shrubs to soften the hard lines. Smooth lawns stretched away to the bareness of the surrounding walls. Nothing, thought the American, that would offer a vestige of cover for anyone trying to escape.

The massive front door, set flat between two shallow pillars, was opened by an elderly woman in a nurse's uniform who, after a word of greeting to Ferrall, led them across a bare hall shining with paint and polish to a door at the far end which bore the inscription in black lettering: '*Dr. Preston. Private.*'

The matron ushered them into a small room that was comfortably furnished as an office, and Dr. Preston rose from behind a large desk to greet them. He was a little man with a round red face and an enormous pair of shell-rimmed glasses, the lenses of which were so powerful that they gave him an odd, blind appearance. Rolls of fat bulged over his tight-fitting collar, and his paunch thrust itself aggressively between the fronts of his jacket. He had the appearance of having been as well scrubbed and polished as the hall, and his teeth, which he displayed generously at the slightest provocation, were so suspiciously white that even they could not possibly have been real.

'My dear Ferrall,' he exclaimed with the hint of a lisp, 'I'm delighted to see you. Shocking news about poor Meriton — shocking.' The genial expression changed to one of conventional distress and, as quickly, changed back again. It was, thought Alan, like the rapid application and removal of a mask. 'Mrs. Meriton knows nothing,' went on Dr. Preston. 'I considered it better not to tell her.'

'She'll have to know,' interrupted

Ferrall. 'She'll wonder why he doesn't come to see her.'

'Yes, yes, of course,' agreed Preston, 'but it must be done gently, gently . . .' He beamed at them with a great display of teeth.

Alan discovered that he had taken an instantaneous and violent dislike to Dr. Preston. There was something completely insincere about him. The real man behind the succession of masks which he assumed at will was, he thought, hard and calculating and a little unscrupulous. He had an idea that Simon Gale was rather of the same opinion.

'You will, naturally, wish to see Mrs. Meriton as soon as possible,' said Preston, when Ferrall had introduced them. 'The lounge, I think, would be the best place. You can be quite undisturbed there.' He pressed a bell on his desk, and after a short delay, the woman who had admitted them came in. 'Bring Mrs. Meriton down to the lounge, please,' he said, and when she had gone: 'Will you come this way, gentlemen?'

Rather like a procession in a department store, they followed him across the hall to a large room that reminded Alan of the lounge of a hotel. Everything was spotless and completely impersonal. You got the impression that nobody lived here, or ever *had* lived here.

'Mrs. Meriton won't be long,' said Dr. Preston, taking up a position before the empty fireplace. 'You will, no doubt, like to be left alone with her. It will be easier that way, perhaps, to — er — break the sad news.'

Alan felt a tingle of excitement run through him. Fay Meriton, whose elusive personality had been gradually building up in his mind, was about to emerge out of the mists and take concrete shape. What was she really like, this woman with the queer streak in her which had led to murder?

A footstep sounded from the hall outside. There was a pause, and then the woman of the picture came quietly into the room.

12

She was dressed in a simple black frock of angora wool with touches of white at the neck and wrists. It enhanced the creamy complexion and the heavy, dark red hair. She was pale, but it was a paleness that glowed with an inner warmth, as though there was sunlight somewhere under the smooth skin. There flowed from her, as she stood just within the doorway, an aura of femininity that was like a physical touch.

No wonder, thought Alan, Paul Meriton had been crazy about her. Only there was a queer look in the greyish-green eyes.

'Simon!' she exclaimed, as she saw Gale. 'Why have you come here?' Her voice was low and a little husky, but there was a slight vibration in it that suggested it might suddenly run high. 'Peter, why did you bring Simon?'

Her eyes flickered from one to the

other, completely ignoring Preston who, with all his teeth bared, was gently rubbing his hands.

'Simon wanted to see you, Fay,' said Ferrall. 'So I — '

'You told him I was here?' she interrupted sharply. 'Paul doesn't want anyone to know. Where is Paul? Why didn't he come with you? Who's this?'

The tone of her voice had risen. It was not shrill, but there was a hint of shrillness underlying it. She looked at Alan with eyes that had suddenly become suspicious and wary.

'He's a friend of mine,' said Simon Gale. He introduced Alan without any of his usual boisterousness. 'He's staying with the Onslow-Whites.'

Fay Meriton's eyes shifted uneasily and she gave a queer little twitch to one shoulder. She said: 'Why didn't Paul come? Why didn't he . . . ?'

'If you'll excuse me,' said Dr. Preston, moving between them and going over to the door, 'I'll leave you to have a little chat together. I shall be in my office if you should want me.' His teeth flashed with dazzling whiteness as he gave them a farewell beam, and then the door closed gently behind him.

With a swift movement that was almost a glide, Fay went to Ferrall and caught his sleeve. 'Why are you here?' she demanded, almost in a whisper. 'What has happened to Paul? Something's happened to Paul — what is it?'

Ferrall gently pulled his arm away. He took her hand and led her over to a chair. 'Sit down, Fay,' he said. 'You mustn't excite yourself.' She sat down, but without taking her eyes from his face.

'Paul's dead, isn't he?' she said suddenly. 'That's why you've come!'

'What makes you think that?' Simon Gale said.

'How did he die?' she asked, as though he hadn't spoken, still staring at Ferrall. 'Did *it* kill him too?'

It was the tone of her voice more than the actual words that made Alan's flesh creep. There was a breathless and rather horrible eagerness in it.

'Did *what* kill him?' demanded Gale quickly.

She turned half round in the chair to face him. 'The thing at the house,' she said. 'The thing that killed the tramp and that girl.'

'Now, Fay,' began Ferrall, much as he might have spoken to a child, 'you know that — '

'I didn't kill them.' She swung back to him with a quick, sharp jerk of her supple body. 'You all believed I did — Paul was certain I did — but I didn't.'

'I know,' said Ferrall gently.

'But you don't *believe* that I didn't,' she interrupted. 'You think I *did* kill them — like Paul did. I told him I didn't but he wouldn't believe me. He was sure, sure, sure . . .'

Her voice rose at each repetition of the word until that underlying shrillness came very near the surface. She'll go over the edge in a minute, thought Alan. Every nerve was vibrating at a dangerous pitch.

But she didn't. Somehow she managed to keep a thin margin of control. 'I told Paul, over and over again, that I didn't kill those people,' she went on, her voice dropping to its normal low huskiness. 'I found them . . . like that . . . '

Simon Gale came round to the chair opposite to her and perched himself on one arm. He said, almost tonelessly: 'Why did you let them bring you here, then?'

'I was afraid,' she answered. 'I was horribly afraid . . . If Paul and Peter wouldn't believe me, was it likely that anyone else would?'

'You were ill, Fay,' said Ferrall. 'You'd been ill for a long time. You didn't know, sometimes, what you were doing.'

'You see?' She looked at Gale and smiled, a mirthless smile that twisted the corners of her mouth without touching the greyish-green eyes. 'What chance would I have had with — with the police? It was the lesser of two evils. Sometimes I've wondered if it *was* the lesser.'

'It was the only thing to do,' said Ferrall.

'Tell me about Paul,' she said. 'When did it happen?'

There was no emotion in her voice, no expression on her face. Only the tightly clasped hands with the skin white over the knuckles showed any evidence of strain. And a little jerky movement of one foot.

Gale raised his eyes to Ferrall's and the latter shrugged his shoulders in reply to the inquiry he saw there. It was not so much an acquiescence as an acceptance of the inevitable. Briefly, and with as little detail as possible, Simon Gale told her.

Fay listened quietly. There was no movement now. She sat so utterly still that she might have been a figure in wax. Once, towards the end of Gale's recital, her lips moved but no sound came from them, and when he stopped speaking she still remained silent. The uncomfortable silence lasted for barely a minute, but Alan thought it was the longest minute he had ever experienced. Then she said, in a whisper that was almost inaudible:

'Poor Paul . . . Poor, poor, Paul . . . '

With a sudden, swift movement she got up and faced them. There was a glitter in her eyes and a tinge of colour in her cheeks. Her mouth, which had been beautiful, was suddenly ugly and distorted.

'For two years I've been shut up here

for nothing,' she cried, and at last the shrillness which had been so near the surface burst through. 'Do you understand, Peter? You and Paul shut me up here for nothing. For nothing, for nothing, for *nothing*!' She was screaming at them now and her eyes looked as though they had been varnished. 'Paul's dead . . . he's *dead*! And he was killed the same way as those others. You can't say I did *that*, can you? *Can* you? I didn't kill them, either. Do you hear — *I didn't! I didn't! I didn't . . .* '

Her voice cracked and she began to laugh, harshly, with a rising cadence that was punctuated by spasmodic sobs. The glazed eyes grew smeary and her face seemed to dissolve into a puckered ruin as she flung herself down into a chair and huddled there, alternately laughing and crying convulsively.

★　★　★

Simon Gale thrust a tankard of beer into Alan's hand and began to fill another for himself.

'Y'know, young feller,' he said, straightening up from the barrel beside the fireplace and glaring ferociously at his drink, 'I don't like it — I don't like *any* of it. There's something *wrong*.'

They had just come back from Shilford, a dreary and depressing journey with the rain still drenching down and visions of Fay Meriton crouched in the big armchair, shaking and shivering as though stricken with an ague.

Dr. Preston, hurriedly sent for, had had to give her an injection to quieten her.

Ferrall had dropped them at Gale's house and gone home, refusing to come in for a drink on the plea that Avril would be expecting him. It was a palpable excuse to avoid discussing the matter any further that night, and he knew that they were aware of it. Alan would have liked to go, too, but Gale was insistent.

'I want to talk,' he said. 'I'm worried. Let's have some beer.'

Sitting now, with the tankard balanced on his knee, Alan looked up at the huge figure, straddle-legged in front of the fireplace. 'You mean,' he said, 'that now you've seen Fay Meriton you're not so sure?'

'Got it in one,' said Gale. He swallowed a prodigious draught of beer. 'I'm not sure — not sure at all. There's something *wrong*, d'you see? Oh, she's as cracked as a coot,' he went on, as Alan opened his mouth to speak. 'It's not *that*. But *did* she kill those two — the tramp and the girl?'

'If *she* didn't, who did?' asked Alan. 'It's unlikely there would be *two* crack-brained people floating about the district.'

'Ah!' cried Gale, waving the half-empty tankard about, 'if Fay killed 'em, you don't need a motive. But if it was somebody else, unless, as you say, we're dealing with two crack-brains, we've got to find a motive.'

'That'll cover the murder of Meriton, too,' broke in Alan.

'Exactly!' Gale finished his beer and refilled the tankard. 'Look here, let's go over it all and see if we can't find the bit that's *wrong*. There's a queer streak in the Ayling family — Fay Meriton's family — and it pops up again in Fay. Nothing much at first — one or two

253

little oddities, perhaps, that nobody takes any notice of — nothing to warn them of the bug that's gnawing away at the brain. She marries Meriton and still nobody guesses that there's anything wrong. But she's a hysteric with the potentialities of a *dangerous* hysteric. The oddities increase — nothing that the outside world knows anything about. She's highly strung, that's all, and a bit over-imaginative. The room in the old, ruined house is just a rather childish game, like playing pirates, but Meriton begins to get uneasy. There are scenes and tempers over silly trifles or over nothing at all. He begins to suspect that his wife may be suffering from something more serious than over-strained nerves and arranges for Ferrall to take over old Dr. Wycherly's practice — just in case; it's a good idea to have a doctor whom he can rely on close at hand . . . And then the tramp is killed.'

Gale paused and took a long drink of beer. Alan sat silent, the tankard untouched on his knee. Before his eyes rose a picture of Fay Meriton as he had last seen her, shivering and shaking in the big chair, racked by gulping sobs and a horrible witless laughter . . .

'Meriton thinks that Fay's 'oddities' have taken a homicidal turn,' Gale went on, 'and Ferrall agrees with him. But he's not *sure*. She swears, black, blue, and all the colours of the spectrum, that she didn't kill the man, and Meriton isn't *sure*. But, a little while after, a poor, bloody girl on a cycling holiday is killed in exactly the same way, and Meriton *is* sure. The wife he adores is a homicidal maniac and nobody's safe while she remains at large. But he's not going to let her go through all the muck and scandal of a trial for murder. He buries the girl's body under the tiles, and the bicycle under the rockery, and, with Ferrall's help, he whisks Fay off to a mental home, explaining her sudden disappearance by letting it be thought that she's run away with some man or other. He produces a letter, which he's got her to sign, to bolster up the lie. Fay goes, because she's scared to death of what may happen to her if she doesn't, and for a time everything's peaceful. An' that's the end of part one. Part two, as they used to say in the old days, will follow immediately.'

He drained the tankard and banged it down on the mantelpiece. With his usual dexterity he rolled himself a cigarette, lit it, and expelled a mouthful of acrid smoke.

'Two years elapse,' he continued, striding about the untidy studio. 'Our heroine is still shut up in the mental home, and our hero, a little worse for wear under the strain, is visiting her once a week, but otherwise living a quiet and uneventful life. And then, *bang*! Out of the blue *he* gets a bat over the bean. Exactly the same as the tramp and the girl. But *this* time it *can't* be Fay. It *ought* to be, but it *can't* be. She's never been out of that damned mental home since they put her in. It's a nice little topsy-turvy problem, eh? All the right pieces in the wrong places. Bah!'

He flung himself down in a chair. Alan took a sip of his beer and set the tankard carefully on the floor beside him. 'I guess it's the motive you want,' he said.

'Something that will link the tramp and the girl *and* Meriton.'

'D'you think I don't know that?' grunted Gale impatiently.

'It might be easier if we knew the identity of the tramp and the girl,' said Alan.

'If, if, if!' exclaimed Gale, bounding to his feet and striding up and down the big room. 'If we knew *this*, if we knew *that*, if we knew something else ... I keep on thinking I've got it and then the blasted thing goes all haywire.' He flung out an arm and sent a small book-laden table crashing to the floor. 'I said it was topsy-turvy,' he went on, kicking a book out of the way but otherwise ignoring the accident, 'and, by the Seven Seals of St. John, that's an understatement! I expect to find the body of Fay Meriton hidden in Sorcerer's House and it turns out to be somebody else. I work out a fine, reasonable, logical theory to account for the murder of the tramp and the girl and *that* does a back-somersault on me.'

'Steady, now,' broke in Alan. 'You can't be sure of that. Fay may have been responsible for the tramp and the girl.'

'And then somebody else comes along and does the same thing to Meriton, eh?' Gale shook his head violently. 'It's too ragged. It doesn't *fit* nearly enough. It's inartistic.'

'Real life often is,' retorted Alan. 'Have you thought of it this way: Ferrall knew that Meriton had left him that money didn't he? Supposing he decided that he'd like a nice little windfall, and plagiarized Fay's method.'

'Of course, I've thought of that. It's so obvious that it hits you smack between the eyes. But it's not as simple as that.' He came back to the fireplace, refilled his tankard from the barrel, and straddled the hearth. 'There's a pattern, d'you see? If I can only find the *beginning* of the design . . . '

Alan took abother sip of his own beer. He said, with a shade of doubt: 'Maybe you're looking for something that isn't there.'

'It's *got* to be there!' said Gale. 'We've missed it because we're looking at the thing the *wrong* way.'

The buzzer which warned him that there was someone at the front door suddenly began to hum like an angry bee. Gale glared at it, muttered an imprecation and, without apology, strode out of the room. Alan heard the front door open and the sound of a mumbled voice that was instantly drowned by Simon Gale's deep bass: 'Come in, Hatchard!'

The door slammed, footsteps thudded along the hall, and Gale returned, followed by a tired-looking Inspector Hatchard wearing a soiled raincoat.

'Take your coat off, sit down, and have some beer,' said Gale. He went over to the shelf above the barrel and snatched down a large German beer mug.

'Thank you, sir,' replied Hatchard. 'I could do with a drop o' beer.' He removed the raincoat and deposited it with his hat on a vacant chair. 'Good evening, Mr. Boyce. My word, what a day it's been. Coming down in sheets, and plenty more to follow by the look of it.'

'You didn't come here to discuss the weather, did you?' demanded Simon

259

Gale, thrusting the now foaming mug into his hand.

'Well, no, sir,' answered Hatchard. He took a long draught of beer and smacked his lips appreciatively. 'I thought you might like to know that we've discovered the identity of that poor girl.'

'You have, eh?' cried Gale. 'Who was she?'

'She was a young woman named Christine Hunks. She lived with her family — mum and dad and a younger brother — at Hounslow, and was a waitress in a local restaurant.' Hatchard paused to take another pull at his beer.

'Go on,' said Gale impatiently.

'That's about all, sir. About two years ago, at the beginning of August, she left her home to go on a cycling holiday and that was the last they ever saw of her. They had one postcard.'

Alan suddenly saw a vivid picture of the girl wandering into the ruined garden of Sorcerer's House on that hot afternoon, with her milk and her packet of sandwiches. She had gone in search of peace and rest, and she had found — what? A crazy woman with a murder-bug gnawing at her brain?

'It doesn't help much, does it, sir?' remarked Hatchard. He rubbed at the bald spot on the crown of his head. 'There doesn't seem to be any possible connection between this young woman Hunks and anyone in Ferncross.'

'Was she in the habit of taking cycling holidays?' asked Gale, tugging at his beard.

'No, this was the first,' replied Hatchard. 'She'd only just bought a bicycle. It's a funny thing,' he added thoughtfully. 'Just shows what little things make big differences. She had a friend, a girl who worked in the same place, who was going with her. At the last moment this friend had an accident — fell down an' broke her ankle. If she hadn't done that, Christine wouldn't have been alone.' He emptied the mug and set it down. 'You know sir,' he said, 'I'm beginning to think we've got a lunatic to deal with in this business.'

'Who kills two people in rapid succession and then waits nearly two years for his next victim,' snapped Gale. 'Non-sense!'

'Nothing else seems to make sense,' said the inspector. 'What sensible motive could there be for anyone wanting to kill a girl like Christine Hunks?'

'She might have seen something she wasn't supposed to have seen,' said Gale. 'Have you thought of that?'

'And the tramp?' said Hatchard. 'Did *he* see something he wasn't supposed to have seen, too?'

'I don't know,' answered Gale. 'You asked for a sensible motive an' I'm giving you one, d'you see? Nobody 'ud want to kill a girl like that for gain. She could scarcely have stirred up sufficient hatred in anyone during the short time she must have been here. They're the chief motives for murder, eh? Gain, hatred . . . ' He stopped abruptly. 'By all the heads of the Lernian Hydra!'

'What is it, Mr. Gale?' asked Hatchard.

'I don't know . . . I've got to think . . . ' Simon Gale flung himself down in a chair and clutched his head between his hands. 'Look here, leave me alone, will you? I've just caught a glimpse of the whole pattern . . . the appalling, hideously cold-blooded design that was the motive for those three murders.'

* * *

The rain persisted throughout the following morning and the atmosphere in Bryony Cottage was a little depressing. Henry Onslow-White disappeared immediately after breakfast into his study with a muttered excuse that he had some work to attend to, and Flake joined her mother in the kitchen to help with the household chores, leaving Alan to his own devices.

She was quite obviously annoyed with him for absenting himself during the whole of the previous afternoon and evening without any very satisfactory explanation, and her attitude, in consequence, was verging on the frigid. He felt a little uncomfortable about it, but it was impossible to tell her where he had been. He spent most of the morning sitting on the bed in his room, smoking cigarettes and trying to puzzle out what Gale had suddenly hit on last night before he had unceremoniously thrown them both out. An 'appalling, hideously cold-blooded design,' he had described it. It might, of course, be merely his flamboyant and exaggerated way of talking, but Alan had an idea that he had meant it literally. There had been an expression on his face as though he had suddenly been confronted with a nightmare.

Through the rain-blurred the window of his room, Alan could see the jutting gable of Sorcerer's House with the ivy-draped window of the Long Room. Three people had died there — violently. And all three had died in exactly the same way. What, in Heaven's name, was the connection? What was the appalling design that Simon Gale had glimpsed? He was no nearer finding a solution by the time lunch was ready than he had been when he started.

The rain stopped in the early part of the afternoon and the sun came out. He asked Flake to come for a walk but she received the suggestion with a polite but firm refusal, and he gathered that he was not yet forgiven.

Alan went out on his own. It was very warm, indicating that the hot spell was returning. Almost unconsciously he turned in the direction of Simon Gale's house. He had no intention of calling. Gale had very clearly indicated that he wanted to be left severely alone until he had fully worked out the idea which had come to him. But it was a pleasant walk with the added attraction of passing Mr. Veezey's beautiful garden.

There was another mystery, thought Alan, as he strolled slowly along the hedge-lined road leading up to the Dark Water. Or was it part of the same one? There was certainly something queer about the little man. By no means normal, and abnormality took strange twists sometimes. There had never been any satisfactory explanation for the threat which Miss Flappit had heard him utter. It was true he had denied it, but, although Miss Flappit had probably embroidered on what she had heard, it was distinctly unlikely that she had made the whole thing up.

Alan came to the bridge over the Dark Water. He stopped, lit a cigarette, and leaning on the old stone parapet of the little humpbacked bridge, stared down at the wide pool of green-scummed, brackish water.

'*If you do that, I'll kill you!*'

That was what he had said — standing on this very spot. And Paul Meriton had laughed. What had he threatened to do to Veezey that had upset him so much? Upset him to such an extent that he had cried? Was this part of the 'appalling, hideous and cold-blooded design'?

Alan finished his cigarette and resumed his walk. The sun shone down hotly, drawing from the wet earth that wonderful scent which has no counterpart unless it was the tang of burning leaves on a frosty autumn afternoon. This green and pleasant land which lay in peaceful beauty on either side, stretching away to the distant hills, seemed the very antithesis of violence. But violence had happened here before and probably would again. He remembered the scorched earth and the blasted, tortured trees of the villages of France which he had seen just after the war.

'*Where every prospect pleases and only man is vile.*' Man had decidedly made a mess of his green and pleasant inheritance, and was spending vast sums of money and brainpower in an endeavour to wipe it out altogether.

Mr. Veezey was working in his garden when Alan came in sight of the gate. He looked up as he heard somebody approaching with his habitual nervous, half-scared expression. To Alan's surprise, he smiled rather hesitantly when he saw who it was.

'Nice now, isn't it?' said Alan cheerfully, pausing by the gate.

Mr. Veezey swallowed with difficulty. A little uncertainly, he moved nearer to the gate. He said, in his tremulous voice: 'I — er — I owe you an apology. I'm — er — afraid I was — er — rude the other day.' He gulped again and his fingers strayed to his small chin. 'I'm rather — er — shy, you know. People frighten me.'

This candid admission so embarrassed

Alan that he could think of nothing to say. Fortunately Mr. Veezey continued without waiting for a reply: 'You — er — seemed interested in — er — my garden,' he said diffidently. 'Would you . . . care to come in and — er — look at it?'

'I should, very much,' said Alan, and Mr. Veezey opened the white gate for his guest to enter.

'I — er — think gardening is the most pleasant and most rewarding of — er — all hobbies,' said Mr. Veezey, as he conducted his visitor round his small domain. 'There is always something — er — fresh and fascinating about it.'

Alan quickly realized that he was an expert on his subject and, as he waxed enthusiastic over his flowers, it was noticeable that his nervousness became less in evidence. At the back of the house was a small but perfect lawn, a velvety oblong of emerald green set in a profusion of carefully blended colour; and beyond this, screened by a mass of climbing roses, was a little kitchen garden and a tiny greenhouse, in which Mr. Veezey reared the seedlings and cuttings that formed the basis of his garden.

'Did you do all this yourself?' asked Alan.

'Oh yes, everything,' answered Mr. Veezey, with a note of pride in his voice. 'There was nothing here when I came. Nothing. Only rank grass, and a great many weeds and nettles. That is the pleasure, you know.'

'It must have taken you a long time,' said Alan.

'Eight years. I have enjoyed every minute of it. There was a time when I thought all my labour had been for nothing . . . ' His face clouded at the unpleasant memory, but he did not pursue the subject. Alan would have liked to ask what had happened, but he was afraid that it might jeopardize Mr. Veezey's friendly attitude and refrained.

It was over an hour before he left, and he found that he had thoroughly enjoyed the interlude. There was something very refreshing in the little man's simple and unaffected outlook. As he walked slowly back to Bryony Cottage, he wondered what had originally induced that almost

painful shyness. '*People frighten me* . . . '
There was something definitely psychological in that. Something, perhaps, that had occurred in childhood to an oversensitive nature. An outsized inferiority complex, thought Alan. That was what he was suffering from.

And an outsized inferiority complex, coupled to a sensitive and highly intelligent mind, could produce the most unexpected results — sometimes very dangerous ones.

13

The Onslow-Whites had almost finished tea by the time he got back to Bryony Cottage. Because the grass was still wet after the rain, the table had been set on the tiny veranda and, in spite of Alan's protests, Mrs. Onslow-White insisted that a fresh pot would be made for him. Flake, who although still far from her natural self, seemed a little less frigid than she had been earlier, went off to make it, and Alan settled himself in a vacant chair. He was telling them between mouthfuls of cucumber sandwich about his afternoon with Mr. Veezey when Flake returned with the fresh tea.

'So *that's* where you've been,' she remarked, setting the pot down in front of her mother. 'We rather wondered what had happened to you.'

'You mean *you* did,' grunted Henry Onslow-White, brushing cake crumbs from his trousers. 'You know, Boyce, you must be about the only person in Ferncross whom Veezey has been the least friendly with.'

'I thought, when you didn't come back in time for tea,' said Flake, 'that you'd gone off somewhere again with Simon.'

'Poor Mr. Veezey,' said Mrs. Onslow-White, shaking her head. 'It really must be dreadful to suffer such acute shyness. Such a drawback.' She handed Alan a cup of tea. 'I'm quite sure that he's a very nice man, but he must be terribly lonely.'

'I guess it doesn't worry him much,' said Alan. 'He seems to be happy enough with his garden.'

'Lovely place he's made of it,' said Henry Onslow-White. 'When he first came here it was nothing but a wilderness.'

'So he told me,' said Alan, stirring his tea. 'He said something else which I couldn't understand.' He repeated the little man's remark about all his labours being for nothing.

'Did he say that?' asked Flake quickly. 'I wonder if it could have had anything to do with Paul?'

'Why should it have?' inquired Alan.

'He owned the land,' answered Flake. 'Mr. Veezey wanted to buy it, but Paul wouldn't sell.'

'Paul didn't like Mr. Veezey,' remarked Mrs. Onslow-White. 'He couldn't understand him, of course. That meek manner irritated Paul. Meekness does some people, you know. I've always thought how wrong it is — that saying that the 'meek shall inherit the earth'.'

'Paul hated selling land,' put in her husband. His chair creaked as he reached over and helped himself to a cake. 'Perhaps Veezey 'ull be able to get it now from the solicitors.'

Here was something, thought Alan, that might explain the threat on the bridge over the Dark Water, which Miss Flappit had overheard. Supposing Meriton was trying to get his land back. Perhaps it was on a very short lease and he had refused to renew. To what lengths would Veezey have gone to keep his garden?

'I suppose all the property goes to Fay?' said Mrs. Onslow-White.

'They've got to find her first,' mumbled her husband through a mouthful of cake. 'That wild idea of Simon's — that Paul had killed her and hidden the body — proved to be a wash-out. I knew it would.'

'They *did* find a body, dear,' said his wife gently.

'Yes, I know,' grunted Henry Onslow-White. 'That was the most extraordinary thing.' He leaned back in his chair, pulled out a handkerchief and mopped his face. 'The whole thing's extraordinary. I wonder if they'll ever find out the truth about it?'

'I'm quite *sure* Alan and Simon will.' There was a slightly malicious note in Flake's voice. 'If they don't, it won't be for want of trying, will it, Alan?'

So she still resented the fact that he hadn't taken her into his confidence concerning his excursions with Simon Gale. Alan wondered what the result would be if he suddenly exploded his bombshell there and then — if he told them that Fay Meriton was in a mental home because her husband had believed

274

that she was responsible for the murder of the girl whose body had been found in the ruined house, and also for the murder of the tramp.

'Much better if Simon 'ud leave it to the police,' commented Henry Onslow-White. 'It's *their* job, and they should be left alone to get on with it.'

Alan decided that it was more diplomatic to say nothing.

After tea, Flake asked him if he would like a game of tennis. 'There are some pretty good hard courts just off the green,' she said. 'We ought to be able to find one vacant if we go soon.'

Now Alan rather fancied himself at tennis. He played regularly at home and, in the hope that he might get a game or two during his holiday, had brought his raquets with him. In the excitement of Paul Meriton's death, and all that had followed from it, any thought of tennis had been driven completely from his mind, but, at Flake's suggestion, he decided that a really strenuous set or two was just what he needed. It would be a relief from 'ghosts and goblins' and designs that were 'appalling, hideous and cold-blooded'.

He changed quickly and expected that he would have to wait for Flake, but when he came down she was waiting for him. And very attractive she looked in her crisp white shorts and sleeveless white blouse. He helped her drape a light dust coat round her bare shoulders, and they set off for the green.

Only two of the four courts were in use when they arrived, apparently by friends of Flake's, for they exchanged greetings and, dismissing all thoughts of murder and mayhem from his mind, Alan settled down to concentrate on the game.

Rather to his surprise, though why it should have been he couldn't have explained, Flake proved to be extremely good. She was fast and she could place a ball with unerring judgment. But it was her service that he found the most deadly. The ball came whistling over the net within a few inches of the top, and with the speed of a bullet.

They played three sets and although

Alan won two of them, it was only by exerting himself to his fullest capacity. 'I guess I didn't know you could play like that,' he said, pulling on his sweater. 'We must do this more often.'

She smiled, her face slightly flushed, and she was still a little breathless. The last remnant of her bad temper was gone. 'Paul taught me to play,' she said. 'When I was a schoolgirl. He was first-class.'

A stentorian hail shattered the peace of the evening and startled the birds in the trees. Alan looked round. At the entrance to the courts stood Simon Gale, waving furiously, and grinning like a malignant gargoyle.

'It's Simon,' said Flake unnecessarily. Even the people on the other side of the green must have been aware of the fact. She looked a little annoyed.

'Hello, young feller,' cried Gale. 'I've been looking for you. Henry told me I'd find you here.'

They collected their raquets and the box of tennis balls, and went over to him.

'It's really too bad of you, Simon,' greeted Flake.

'What is?' he demanded, raising his bushy eyebrows.

'Well, I suppose this means that you're going to commandeer Alan again for something or other.'

'Now, listen to me, my good wench,' said Gale, 'you can't expect to tie him to your apron-strings all the time.'

'All the time!' echoed Flake. 'I haven't seen very much of him at all lately.'

'And you don't like it, eh?' remarked Gale, hugely amused. 'Well, you won't have to put up with it much longer. But tonight's important, d'you see? I've got a little job that I want him to help me with.'

'Oh, well . . . ' She spoke lightly, but the flush had deepened under her eyes. 'I suppose I can walk home by myself.'

'You'll do nothing of the sort,' said Alan.

'Of course she won't,' agreed Gale. 'Come along, we'll go and call on Jellyberry.'

Without waiting for a reply, he seized each of them by an arm and propelled them at a furious pace across the green towards the Three Witches. The bar was not very full, and Mr. Jellyberry welcomed them with a beaming smile.

'Now,' said Simon Gale, cocking an inquiring eyebrow at Flake, 'what would you like?'

For a moment she looked mutinous, and then her face cleared and she laughed. 'Something long and cold,' she said.

'A gin and ginger beer with ice in it, Jellyberry,' ordered Gale, 'and lots of beer for Mr. Boyce and me.'

While Mr. Jellyberry proceeded ponderously to execute the order, Alan produced cigarettes, gave one to Flake, took one himself, and lighted them both. He was itching to know what Gale wanted him for, and so, quite obviously, was Flake. But Gale made no effort to enlighten them. Rolling one of his cigarettes with his usual dexterity, he blew out clouds of evil-smelling smoke while he expatiated in his booming bass on the way tennis ought to be played.

For a long time they listened to this, and then Flake's curiosity could stand the strain no longer. She said, as Alan ordered another round of drinks: 'Look here, Simon. You didn't come chasing after Alan to lecture him on how to play tennis, did you?'

Gale grinned at her over his tankard. 'Didn't I, my girl?' he demanded.

'Oh, stop being irritating! If it's anything to do with — with the murder, why can't I know about it? After all, I was in it at the beginning.'

'Do you know what the beginning was?' he asked. '*Do* you? If you imagine it was when you and young Boyce found the body of Paul Meriton under the window of the Long Room that night, you're miles out.'

'Do you know what the beginning was?' asked Flake quickly.

'I think I do, *now*. I think I know the beginning, the middle and almost the end.' He looked at his watch abruptly, and swallowed the remainder of his beer. 'Drink up!' he said. 'We'll see you home, and then we can get busy.'

'What,' asked Flake, 'are you going to do?'

'We're going to search Meriton's

house,' answered Gale, 'and if we don't hurry up, Mrs. Horly will have gone to bed.'

'But the police did that, didn't they?' said Flake.

'Yes, they did,' agreed Simon Gale. 'But they weren't looking, d'you see, for what I'm looking for.'

'What *are* you looking for?' asked Alan.

'I'm looking, young feller,' replied Gale, quite seriously, 'for something that isn't there!'

* * *

Mrs. Horly, clutching a faded dressing gown to her ample bosom, was a little disgruntled at their sudden and unexpected arrival at Ferncross Lodge. She had been on the point of going to bed, and she was not inclined at first to let them in. But Simon produced a letter of authority from Inspector Hatchard, in the face of which she capitulated; not, however, without a great deal of under-breath rumblings and mutterings.

On the way back from Bryony Cottage, where they had left Flake in a fever of unrequited curiosity, Alan had tried to get Gale to explain his cryptic remark concerning the object of this expedition, but he definitely refused.

'I'm not trying to emulate the detective in a crime story,' he declared. 'But I've been wrong about this business before, d'you see? Now, I'm not talking until I'm *sure.*'

'When will that be?' demanded Alan.

'Pretty soon, I hope,' answered Gale. 'By the six horns of Satan, it's *got* to be soon.'

And that was all Alan could get out of him.

They stood now in the dining room at Ferncross Lodge with Mrs. Horly hovering uncertainly in the doorway. It was a long, raftered room with lead-paned windows and panelling of aged oak. The furniture was old and solid, and silver gleamed in the light from the wall-brackets. Two massive candelabra stood at either end of the refectory table, and Alan thought that candlelight was the *right* illumination for this room. Electricity was an anachronism.

'Are you likely to be very long, sir?' inquired the housekeeper, looking at Gale rather curiously. Having recovered from her first, not unnatural, resentment at this disturbance, she was obviously anxious to find out the reason for it.

'That depends.' Gale ran his fingers through his hair and scowled at the sideboard. 'Where's the bedroom?'

'If you mean Mr. Meriton's — ' began Mrs. Horly.

'Of course I mean Mr. Meriton's,' interrupted Gale. 'I presume it was also Mrs. Meriton's before she went away, hey?'

'Yes, sir. It's upstairs, over the drawing room.'

'I want to see it,' said Gale shortly.

'I'll show you.' Mrs. Horly pulled the dressing gown tighter round her waistless figure and led the way out into the hall. Pausing at the foot of the broad staircase to switch on a light for the upper landing, she began to ascend, guiding herself by the banister rail. Crossing the landing, she opened a door, switched on another light, and stood aside.

'This is the room, sir,' she said a little breathlessly.

They looked into a large room, softly glowing in the light from pink-shaded wall-brackets. Here elegance was the predominant note — a light and airy elegance of pastel shades and Regency stripes. It was a woman's room and the draped dressing table in the window embrasure, with its triple mirror and crystal lamps, was still littered with creams and lotions, perfume, and a big cut-glass powder bowl. There was a faint and lingering scent that reminded Alan of the locked room in Sorcerer's House.

Fay Meriton . . .

'It's just as it was when Mrs. Meriton left,' said Mrs. Horly. 'Mr. Meriton wouldn't have nothing touched or altered.'

Simon Gale nodded. Going over to the dressing table, he inspected the contents of its glass top.

'You say nothing has been moved, eh?' he asked, without looking round.

'Only the things that Mrs. Meriton

took with her, sir,' replied the house-keeper.

Pulling aside the drapery, Gale disclosed a row of drawers down each side of the table. They were none of them locked and he opened them rapidly, one after another, and peered inside. Alan wondered what he expected to find — or *not* to find, if one took what he had said literally.

His curiosity remained unsatisfied. Without any comment, Gale left the dressing table and turned his attention to the wardrobes. There were two of them, a large and a small one. There was a key in the lock of each, and he opened the small one first. It was fitted with trays for shirts and underclothes, socks and handker-chiefs, collars, all the various things that a man needs. There was a compartment in which several suits hung on hangers and, at the bottom, a rack of shoes. Simon Gale, watched by two pairs of curious eyes, rummaged about among the contents for some time, gave a grunt at last, and closed the door. The other wardrobe was, except for a couple of dresses and some old shoes, empty.

Gale shut this door, too, and turned to Mrs. Horly. 'I've finished here,' he said. 'I want to have a look at the drawing room. Come on, young feller.'

'I'll just turn off the lights, sir,' began the housekeeper, but Simon Gale was already halfway down the stairs. Alan followed him, leaving Mrs. Horly, breathing heavily, to bring up the rear.

The door to the drawing room faced the dining room door across the hall, and Gale had already opened it and was switching on the lights when they joined him. It was a large room, running the full length of the house, with a window at either end; and here, again, in its furnishings and colour scheme, was the unmistakable evidence of a woman's hand.

Simon Gale appeared to be interested in only one object — a bureau that stood cater-cornered near the further window. He strode over to it, dragging a bunch of keys from his pocket.

'I got these from Hatchard, d'you see?' he explained, as he tried them in the lock.

'They were Meriton's.'

The third key turned easily, and he pulled down the flap. The inside of the bureau was fitted with pigeon-holes in which papers were arranged neatly. While Alan, with a feeling of acute embarrassment at this prying into a dead man's affairs, looked on from the doorway, Gale proceeded calmly to go through them, muttering unintelligible comments to himself as he did so.

Having exhausted the contents of the pigeon-holes, he opened two shallow drawers that ran beneath them. One of these contained a cheque book and some old cheque stubs, which he scarcely glanced at; the other held a bundle of letters tied round with a piece of pink string.

Mrs. Horly's heavy breathing behind Alan stopped. She said, with a little gasp: 'They're letters Mrs. Meriton wrote, before she and Mr. Meriton was married.'

Gale whirled round with the packet in his hand. 'How do you know that?' he demanded.

'Inspector Hatchard found 'em, sir,' explained the housekeeper. 'I heard him tell the man who was with him what they was.'

'You can't read them,' protested Alan, as Gale began to untie the string.

'Don't get excited,' retorted Gale. 'I'm not going to. I only want to be sure there's nothing else mixed up with 'em, d'you see?' He inspected them rapidly, retied the string, and put them back in the drawer. He shut up the flap of the bureau and locked it.

'Now,' he said, shoving the keys back in his pocket, 'where do you sleep?'

The question was so unexpected that it was a second or two before Mrs. Horly replied. 'At the top of the house, sir.'

'Listen,' continued Gale. 'On the night Mr. Meriton was killed, what time did you go to bed?'

'Just after ten o'clock, sir — like I usually do.'

'Did you hear Mr. Meriton come home?'

She shook her head. 'I was asleep.'

'Asleep!' interrupted Gale sharply. 'There was a thunderstorm. Didn't it wake you?'

'No, sir,' answered Mrs. Horly. 'You see, Dr. Ferrall had given me some sleeping tablets.'

'Oh, he had, eh?' cried Gale, thrusting his head forward with an expression that was so fiendishly malignant she jumped. 'When did he give them to you?'

'In the morning. I'd been sleeping badly, and Mr. Meriton asked him to give me something.'

'So you never heard *anything* that night? Nothing at all?'

Again she shook her head. 'No, sir. The police asked me that,' she added.

Gale frowned and tugged at his beard. 'One last question, and then we'll go. Apart from Dr. Ferrall, who else called to see Mr. Meriton that day?'

'Nobody, sir.'

'All right, Mrs. Horly. That's the lot,' said Gale, to her obvious relief. 'You can go off to bed and get your beauty sleep!' He chuckled in great good humour. 'Come along, young feller.'

'I guess that was a waste of time,' remarked Alan, as they walked down the short drive to the gate.

'You guess wrong!' retorted Gale. 'Come back to my place, and we'll have some beer!'

Alan agreed, not because he particularly wanted beer, but because he hoped that Gale might prove a little more communicative. What *had* he learned as the result of his search?

'*Doctor Ferrall had given me some sleeping tablets.*' Was it a coincidence, or had it been vitally necessary that Mrs. Horly should sleep soundly that particular night? They only had Avril and Peter Ferrall's word for it that Meriton had ever gone back home on the night of the murder. Supposing, after that drive in the country to seek relief from the heat, which *again* rested on the unsubstantiated word of the Ferralls, something had occurred, and they had gone straight to Sorcerer's House? It seemed improbable that a girl like Avril could be a party to sheer, cold-blooded murder, but it was not impossible. And there *was* a pretty strong motive. A plain and straightforward motive. Meriton had left Ferrall quite a lot of money, and Ferrall had known about it. Mrs. Horly, sleeping her drug-induced sleep, couldn't testify as to whether Meriton had come home that night or not.

'Look out, young feller!' Gale's shout scattered Alan's thoughts. A car, furiously driven, came hurtling round a bend in the road and missed him by a few inches. Dazed by the glare of the headlights, as they were suddenly switched on, Alan staggered and would have fallen if Gale's grip on his arm hadn't saved him. The car, with a screech of skidding tyres and a squeal of scorching brake-drums, pulled up. A head was thrust out of the window, and a voice — Ferrall's — called with urgency: 'Gale . . . Gale!'

'What the devil are you doing, driving about the country like the son of Nimshy?' roared Gale. 'Trying to get yourself a few patients?'

'I've just been up to your house.' Ferrall's voice was hoarse and agitated. Now they had come up with him, they could see, in the reflected glare from the car's headlights, that his forehead was glistening with little beads of perspiration.

'Preston telephoned me half an hour ago. It's Fay!'

'What about her?' snapped Simon Gale.

'She's dead!' answered Ferrall.

14

Alan never forgot that scene: the road, glaringly white in the brightness of the car's headlights, with every little stone and bump accentuated by black shadow; the startling green of the grass verge, and the dark tracery of trees against the rapidly deepening blue of the summer night. And the face of Ferrall, white and strained, thrust out through the car's window, as he made his curt announcement. It was as though Alan's brain had become a photographic plate, registering every tiny detail for eternity.

Simon Gale suddenly struck his hand sharply against the side of the car. He said, in a hard, dry, rasping voice: 'How did it happen?'

'She took some sort of poison.' Ferrall moistened his lips. 'Look here, Gale, we've got to talk this over. Come back with me.'

'It can't be hushed up *now*, you know,'

said Gale. He jerked open the door of the car and motioned for Alan to get in. 'It'll *all* have to come out.'

'I know.' As Gale followed Alan into the car, Ferrall pressed his foot on the clutch and moved the gear lever from neutral into first. 'God almighty, do you think *I* don't know?'

The car started with a jerk that threw Alan hard against the back of his seat, and sped down the silent road. Gale's face was set; his expression was that of a man consumed by a black, and rather terrible, anger.

Poison! An ugly word — with ugly associations.

Ferrall brought the car to an abrupt stop outside the house on the green, and slid from the driving seat. As he opened the wooden gate, Alan remembered the first time he had come to this house, with Flake. It had been Paul Meriton who had died that night. Now, it was Fay.

Avril opened the front door before they were halfway up the path. Even in the orange light that flooded down from the hall lamp, she looked white. And her hands were shaking. 'Come in,' she said, almost in a whisper. She looked at Ferrall. 'Have — have you told them?'

He nodded. 'Yes.'

'It's — terrible, isn't it?' Avril's eyes flickered from Gale to Alan and back. Her voice went into a strange and unnatural key at the end of the sentence. She had to clear her throat before she could speak again. 'What — what *can* we do?'

'I ought to go to Shilford,' said Ferrall, in a curious flat tone. 'I shall *have* to go.' He took out his handkerchief and wiped his face and the palms of his hands. 'There'll have to be an inquest.'

'Look here,' said Simon Gale. 'The first thing you'd *both* better do is swallow a good, stiff brandy, and then tell me all about it. Have you got any brandy?'

'There's some in the dining room,' answered Avril tremulously. 'Simon . . . there must be *something* we can do. This is going to — to ruin Peter.'

It could do more than that, thought Alan. Did she realize the *real* seriousness of the position? By doing what he did, he's made himself an accessory after the fact to two murders.

Unless it could be proved that Fay *hadn't* committed them.

Gale had marched off to the dining room, and when they followed him, he was already at the sideboard. He found the brandy, glasses, and a couple of bottles of beer in a cupboard below. Pouring out two generous portions of brandy, he thrust a glass each into Avril's and Ferrall's hands.

'Now,' he said, pouring out beer for himself and Alan, 'let's have it — *all* of it. All I know, at present, is that Fay's dead from some kind of poison. How did she get it, what was it, and when did she die?'

Ferrall drained his brandy at a gulp and set down the empty glass. He said, with a little more colour in his voice: 'Preston didn't tell me very much. I don't know what the poison was she took, or where she got it. She usually had a glass of hot milk and a sedative at nine o'clock every night — it was part of Preston's treatment. When they took it up to her tonight, she was dead.'

'What *was* the sedative?' demanded Gale.

'Phenobarbitone,' answered Ferrall. 'She took a half-grain tablet, night and morning. It's effective for cases of nervous excitement.' He took out his case and fumbled for a cigarette. He was still shaky but the brandy was working, soothing away the shock, dulling raw nerves.

'Give me a cigarette,' said Avril. He held one out to her and she took it, lighting it in the flame of his lighter.

'She could have died from an overdose of this stuff?' asked Gale.

'She *could*, but . . . ' Ferrall paused. 'But Preston would have seen that, at once, surely? But he didn't say what the posion was.'

'Does it *matter* what it was?' broke in Avril impatiently. 'We shall know soon enough. Dr. Preston's called in the police and *they'll* find out what the poison was. The main thing is that Fay's dead.'

'And that's going to raise such a rumpus that the echo 'ull be heard in hell!' cried Simon Gale, slapping his knee.

'We can't stop it, d'you see? It's bound to come out that, all this time, Fay Meriton has been in a mental home.'

'But nobody except us knows *why* she was put there,' said Alan quietly.

Avril, the cigarette raised halfway to her lips, stopped. Hope brightened the dull weariness of her eyes. She said: 'Do you mean . . . about the . . . ?'

'Dr. Preston doesn't know,' Alan went on, 'the *real* reason why Fay Meriton was put in that home. Only Meriton, Ferrall, and you knew about the tramp and that girl — and *Fay*.'

'Wait, now,' interrupted Gale. 'It's not going to be as simple as that, young feller. You think, if we all keep our mouths shut, the murders won't come out, eh? Rubbish!'

'Why should they?' began Ferrall.

'Because the police are not all bone-headed imbeciles!' cried Gale impatiently. 'They're halfway to believing that those killings were done by a homicidal maniac, d'you see? What do you suppose they're going to think when you hand them a maniac on a plate, eh? It won't take them very long to connect the whole thing up, and then you're sunk.' He tugged at his beard, screwing up his face in concentration. 'What we've got to do,' he said, after a short silence, 'is get hold of Hatchard at once.'

'Hatchard?' echoed Ferrall.

'Yes. We've got to tell him the whole story, d'you see?'

'But, Simon,' exclaimed Avril in dismay, 'we *can't* do that.'

'It would be suicidal.' Ferrall flung his cigarette into the fireplace. 'They'll arrest me straight away as an accessory after the fact.'

And probably for Meriton's murder, too, thought Alan.

'They're likely to do that anyway,' retorted Gale. 'Look here, all you've got to fear is that Fay was responsible for killing those two — the tramp and the girl. There's nothing else they can get you on. Both you and Meriton were quite within your rights to put Fay in that home. She was definitely a psychopath needing treatment.'

'That's all very well,' broke in Ferrall

irritably. 'But the fact remains that she *did* kill those two people.'

'That's just the point,' snapped Gale. '*She didn't!*'

For a moment there was dead silence. Suddenly motionless, as though some magical influence had come into the little dining room and turned them to stone, Avril and Ferrall stared at him with eyes that looked queerly blind.

'Fay Meriton never killed *anyone*,' he declared. 'That's the whole damnable, cruel, devilish thing about this business, d'you see? She was deliberately sacrificed to satisfy . . . ' He stopped and thumped the table in a sudden and uncontrollable anger.

'To satisfy — what?' asked Alan.

'An obsession!' answered Simon Gale.

Ferrall was the first to recover from the shock of Gale's announcement. 'You don't know what you're talking about!' he said. 'It's absolute nonsense!'

'Oh, is it?' cried Gale. 'Did you, or anyone else, *see* Fay Meriton commit those murders?'

'No, of course not. But — '

'She was found bending over the bodies,' went on Gale, striding about the room in a sudden excess of nervous energy. 'Because both you and Meriton knew that she was a paranoiac, you took it for granted that she'd killed them. She told you over and over again that she hadn't, didn't she?'

'Naturally,' said Ferrall. 'She probably didn't *know* she had. Very often in these cases there is a complete mental black-out.'

'There is, eh?' cried Gale. 'Well, this was a case where there *wasn't*, d'you see? Fay Meriton spoke the literal truth.'

'I wish I could believe you.' Ferrall shook his head. 'It would get me out of a very nasty position. But it *could* only have been Fay. Unless you're trying to tell me there was *another* homicidal maniac at large.'

'I'm not suggesting any such balder-dash!' broke in Gale. 'It was no lunatic. You don't understand, do you? The whole of this infernal, cold-blooded scheme was carefully *planned* so that Paul Meriton would believe just what he *did* believe

301

— that his wife was a homicidal maniac.'

Avril uttered a little, gasping cry. 'Nobody *could* be so utterly cruel and callous.'

'This person could,' retorted Gale grimly. 'There was sheer, black hatred behind it.'

'Is this just a theory, Gale,' broke in Ferrall, 'or can you *prove* it?'

'No,' Simon Gale almost snarled. 'By all the Bulls of the Borgias, I *can't*! That's what worries me. There's not a tittle of *real* evidence, d'you see.'

'Then how do you know it isn't just another wild theory?' Ferrall said.

'Because it fits,' answered Gale. 'It fits *all* the facts. It accounts for the murder of the tramp and the girl *and Meriton*.'

Alan, who had been listening in silence, decided to break in with a leading question. 'Who is it who had this black hatred for Meriton?'

'You've got it *wrong*, young feller,' said Gale. 'Nobody had any black hatred for Meriton.'

'But you said — '

'Meriton's murder was never intended,

302

but, d'you see, the whole devilish scheme went *wrong* when Fay was smuggled into that mental home, and Meriton and Ferrall covered up for her.'

'Do you mean, Simon,' said Avril, 'that this hatred was directed against *Fay?*'

'Yes, of course!' he cried, seizing his beard and twisting it between his fingers. 'And the murderer must have wondered what the hell had happened when Fay *wasn't* arrested and dragged through the muck and mud-slinging of a murder trial, found 'guilty but insane', and finally bunged into Broadmoor. *That* was the plan; that's what was *intended* to happen.'

'I think you've got hold of a mare's nest,' said Ferrall sceptically. 'What could Fay have *done* to make anyone hate her like that?'

'Listen!' Avril suddenly raised her hand and motioned them to keep quiet. A car had stopped outside the house. They heard a door slam and then the click of the gate-latch. Footsteps sounded on the paved path leading to the front door, and a second later the bell rang insistently.

'Who is it?' whispered Avril.

'May be a patient.' Ferrall got up with a frown. 'I'd better go.'

He went out quickly and, listening, they heard the front door open. The unmistakable voice of Inspector Hatchard reached them. It said, politely, but with an underlying note of authority: 'Good evening, sir. Can I have a word with you?'

Avril's hand went up to her throat and the tinge of colour that had crept into her face drained away.

'Come in,' said Ferrall, and they heard the door shut. There was a moment's pause and then Hatchard entered the room with Ferrall behind him.

The inspector's eyes moved quickly over the little group. If he was surprised to see Gale and Alan there, no sign of it appeared in his face. 'Good evening, miss . . . Good evening, Mr. Gale . . . Good evening, sir.' He turned to Ferrall. 'Perhaps you would prefer that I saw you in private, sir?'

'It's all right, Hatchard,' broke in Gale. 'We know what you're here for.'

'Do you, sir?' Hatchard's eyes, under the overhanging brows, were expressionless, but, the American thought, there was a subtle difference in his manner. 'I'm afraid it's rather serious.'

'The police telephoned you from Shilford, eh?' said Gale.

'Just so, sir.' Hatchard cleared his throat. 'Mrs. Meriton died in a private mental home at Shilford earlier this evening. She died from poison. I understand that it was Dr. Ferrall and Mr. Meriton who arranged for her to go into this mental home, which is run by a Dr. Preston, and that she has been there for the past two years.' He looked inquiringly at Ferrall, but it was Gale who answered.

'That's right, Hatchard. We told you that Mrs. Meriton was a hysteric.'

'Yes, sir.' There was a faintly reproachful note in Hatchard's voice. 'But you didn't tell me that she was in this home, nor did Dr. Ferrall. I was allowed to believe, like everyone else believed, that Mrs. Meriton had run away.'

'Now, now!' said Gale. 'At the time

you're talking about, I didn't know where she was.'

'But Dr. Ferrall did!' said Hatchard. 'While we were searching, at your suggestion, sir, for Mrs. Meriton's body, Dr. Ferrall knew where she was all the time.'

'You weren't wasting your time, Hatchard,' said Gale. 'You *found* a body,'

'Yes, sir, we found a body,' agreed the inspector. 'And it's still got to be explained how it got there. However, that's not what I'm here for at the moment. I'm here to inquire into the death of Mrs. Meriton, who died from cyanide poisoning this evening.'

'Cyanide!' exclaimed Ferrall, and Simon Gale's eyes suddenly narrowed.

'How on earth did she get hold of cyanide?' Gale demanded

Alan felt that something had come into the little dining room — something that was sinister and pregnant with fresh terrors. A sensation that was like the physical touch of a cold hand.

'I can tell you how she got hold of it, sir,' said Hatchard soberly. 'It was sent to her, contained in a box of chocolates, which arrived by the second post this morning.'

'I should have *known* it!' said Gale. 'It was murder!'

'Yes, sir,' agreed Hatchard quietly. 'It was murder. The chocolates were posted in Barnsford.' He paused and looked at Ferrall.

'What I should like you to explain, sir, is how your card came to be in it?'

15

Ferrall stared at Hatchard in a silence that seemed to stretch out unendurably. He said presently, swallowing hard: 'My — my card?'

'Yes, sir.' Hatchard's voice was stolid. 'It was inside the box.'

'I never sent Mrs. Meriton any chocolates.'

'Of course you didn't!' cried Gale. 'Don't be a blithering ass, Hatchard! People don't send poisoned chocolates and enclose their cards.'

'I never said that Dr. Ferrall sent the chocolates,' answered the inspector. 'I only asked him how his card came to be in them.'

Ferrall shook his head. 'I don't know.'

'*That's* obvious enough,' said Gale. 'Fay Meriton would have wondered, d'you see, if she'd received an *anonymous* box of chocolates. Nobody was supposed to *know* where she was, eh? But, coming from Ferrall was a different matter. I say, Hatchard, they were mighty quick in finding cyanide in those chocolates, weren't they?'

'It was Dr. Preston who cottoned on to it, Mr. Gale,' said Hatchard. 'He saw the chocolates had been tampered with — most of the top layer had been cut in half and stuck together again.'

'Why didn't he say anything to me about it?' said Ferrall.

The card, thought Alan. He wasn't sure he hadn't sent them.

'I don't know, sir. Maybe he hadn't found what it was when he telephoned you. He thought, at first, it was suicide.' Hatchard turned to Gale. 'What made you say you should have *known* about it, sir?'

'It was the logical sequence, d'you see?' answered Gale. 'The logical sequence to the other murders — the tramp, that girl Hunks, and Meriton.'

'Are you suggesting, sir, that they were all killed by the same person?'

'I know they were, and I should have foreseen that an attempt would be made on Fay Meriton.' Gale frowned and ran his fingers through his hair. 'But, d'you see, I didn't think our murderous friend knew where she was.'

'Are you,' said Inspector Hatchard, 'trying to tell me, sir, that you know *who* the murderer is?'

'Oh, yes, I know who it is,' answered Gale with an impatient gesture. 'The trouble is that I've no evidence to prove it.' He rubbed his forehead. 'I suppose you'll be going to Barnsford post office to see if they can remember who posted those chocolates, eh?'

'I shall be attending to that first thing in the morning,' answered Hatchard. 'Look here, sir, if you know who the murderer is, it's your duty to inform — '

'If I told you, you couldn't do a damn thing about it,' said Gale irritably. 'If I had any real evidence, it would be a different matter, d'you see? As it is — ' He stopped abruptly. 'I say, you'll have to see Ayling, won't you? He'll have to be told.'

'I'm going to call on Colonel Ayling when I leave here, sir,' said Hatchard. 'I should like Dr. Ferrall to come with me. There'll be a certain amount of explaining to do,' he added significantly.

'Let me come, too,' said Gale quickly. 'With Boyce.'

Hatchard hesitated.

'Look here . . . ' Gale leaned forward with his knuckles pressed against the edge of the table. 'If you let me handle this, I'll guarantee to hand you the killer on a plate, and with enough evidence to satisfy the Lord Chief Justice himself, within forty-eight hours. But you've got to do it *my* way, d'you see? If you don't, this cold-blooded devil will slip away for good and you'll be left high and dry with an unsolved murder case on your hands. What about it?'

If he was bluffing, thought Alan, he was putting up a good one. But if he didn't have any evidence *now*, how the heck was he going to get it in forty-eight hours? He looked across at Avril. She had been sitting with her hands tightly clasped in her lap, staring down at the floor. Now, she raised her head and a look of panic flashed in her eyes.

Hatchard still hesitated. At length he nodded. 'All right, Mr. Gale, I'll take a chance on it.'

'You won't regret it, Hatchard,' cried Gale, rubbing his hands. 'I shan't let you down.'

'Well, I don't mind telling you, sir,' said the inspector, 'that the chief constable's talking about calling in Scotland Yard. I'd sooner finish this job off my own bat, if it can be done. Of course, when he hears about this fresh business of Mrs. Meriton, he may insist on doing so at once.'

'Don't you worry about Chippy,' said Gale. 'I'll fix him.'

'Well, then, sir, it's getting late, and I think we ought to go.'

'Ayling will be in bed,' said Ferrall, glancing at his watch. 'It's nearly twenty minutes past eleven.'

'Afraid I can't help that, sir,' said Hatchard. 'There won't be any time tomorrow.' He picked up his hat. 'My sergeant'll drive us there. I left him outside in the car.'

'Come on, young feller.' Gale motioned to Alan, and strode over to the door.

Ferrall looked at Avril a little anxiously. 'You'd better go to bed, dear,' he said. 'We may be some time.'

She shook her head. 'I shouldn't sleep,' she answered. 'I'll wait up for you.' She followed them out to the front door. Looking back, as they drove away, Alan saw her standing, bathed in orange light, staring after them. He got the impression that she was crying.

★　★　★

There were no lights in Colonel Ayling's house when the police car pulled up outside the gate five minutes later. The moon was up, and under its brilliance the house stood out alone, white and gleaming, with a shingled roof that looked dully pink in the moonlight. It was a low-built house with a shaven lawn that ran down to a trimmed hedge of golden privet, and there were symmetrical flower beds. A neat garden, but with none of the loveliness of Mr. Veezey's.

Their footsteps crunched on the gravel of the path as they walked up to the front door. It was not, thought Alan, going to be a particularly pleasant interview. As Hatchard had said, there was a lot of explaining to do, and that formidable old man was not going to be easy. Ferrall evidently thought so, too. His face was deeply troubled.

Hatchard found the bell-push at the side of the door. Faintly they heard the bell ring somewhere inside. Nothing happened. Hatchard tried again, keeping his finger on the push. Still nothing happened.

'Try the knocker,' suggested Simon Gale. 'Here, let me do it.'

He stretched across Hatchard, grasped the knocker and beat a loud tattoo. It had the desired effect. Somewhere above them a window went up with a bang. The upper half of Colonel Ayling, in a magenta pyjama jacket, his bald head glistening in the moonlight, leaned perilously out and demanded to know, angrily, who they were, and what the so-and-so they wanted.

'Very sorry to disturb you, sir,' called up Inspector Hatchard, 'but — '

'It's Hatchard, isn't it?' demanded Ayling. 'Who's that you've got with you? Gale? What the devil do you want at this hour of the night?'

'It's about Fay,' said Simon Gale. 'You'd better come down, Ayling. We can't talk to you from here.'

'Fay?' There was a sudden sharp rise in Ayling's voice. He ducked in under the frame of the window and closed it. At length they heard his muffled footsteps crossing the hall and the door opened.

'Come in,' he said. 'Be as quiet as you can. I don't want my wife disturbed.' He stood aside to let them pass him, closed the door, and led the way to a room on the right of the hall. It was large, old-fashioned drawing room, over-crowded with Victorian furniture and bric-a-brac. Colonel Ayling switched on the light in the centre chandelier, shut the door carefully, and stood facing them.

'Well?' he said. 'What have you to tell me about my daughter? Have you found her?'

'Yes, sir — I'm afraid we have,' answered Hatchard.

315

Ayling's jaw muscles tightened and his thin lips compressed. He said, in a voice that was rendered toneless in an effort to mask all emotion: 'Does that mean she's dead?'

'Yes, sir,' Hatchard answered.

'How did it happen? Where?'

And Hatchard told him.

Ayling's face was quite expressionless as he listened. Once, when Hatchard was explaining how Fay Meriton came to be in the mental home at Shilford, he turned his head and looked at Ferrall; but it was only a brief glance, and almost instantly his eyes went back Hatchard.

When the inspector came to the end of his concise recital, there was a moment of complete silence. Ayling stared straight before him. When he spoke, his words were prefaced by a sighing hiss, as though had been holding his breath. He said:

'There is no doubt that my daughter died from eating the chocolates?'

'No, sir,' replied Hatchard.

'She was, therefore, deliberately murdered.' The steady toneless voice might have been discussing the weather. 'Have you any suspicion why and by whom?'

'Well, sir,' began the inspector, 'we hope to be able to trace the person who posted the parcel in Barnsford.'

'You won't find the killer *that* way, and you know it!' broke in Gale impatiently. 'Look here, Ayling — '

'I can understand, Inspector,' said Colonel Ayling, completely ignoring Gale, 'why you brought Dr. Ferrall with you, but I cannot see *any* reason why you should have brought Mr. Gale and Mr. Boyce.'

'I came because I want to ask you some questions,' said Gale. 'I believe that — '

'I do not acknowledge your right to ask me *any* questions,' interrupted Colonel Ayling, turning upon him frigidly. 'I consider this interference in matters which do not concern you intolerably impertinent.' His voice was cracked; the almost inhuman control he was exercising was dangerously near breaking point.

Gale raised his eyebrows and scowled. 'You don't *want* to find the person who murdered your daughter and Meriton?'

'I prefer to leave it in the hands of the

317

proper authorities,' retorted Ayling. 'I dislike the intrusion of amateur sensation-seekers!' He moved forward. It was, thought Alan, like an automaton moving. 'I should be obliged,' Ayling continued, and there was the faintest tremor in his voice, 'if you would leave me. This has, naturally, been a great shock. Not only that my daughter is dead, but *how* and *where* she died. I should have been told about that, Ferrall. Even with my daughter's consent, you and Meriton should not have acted on your own initiative.'

Ferrall remained silent. What *could* he say, thought Alan, without telling the old man the *real* reason why his daughter had been taken to the mental home at Shilford?

'I'm afraid, sir,' said Hatchard, 'that you'll be required at the inquest.'

Colonel Ayling inclined his head. 'I will do anything that is necessary. Now, please, will you go!' He escorted them to the front door, wished them 'good night' and closed it behind them. That rigid control had remained to the last, but Alan had a feeling that once the door was shut it had snapped.

In the moonlit, symmetrical front garden they looked at each other.

'Well, that's that,' said Ferrall. He sounded relieved.

Hatchard nodded. 'Not a very pleasant job.' He made a wry face. 'You didn't seem very popular, sir,' he added to Gale.

'Ayling's never approved of me,' answered Gale, shrugging. 'I'm everything he dislikes, d'you see. I've got to have a talk with him, though.'

'I guess,' put in Alan, 'you won't find it easy. Mrs. Ayling must be a sound sleeper.'

'She always takes a sleeping tablet,' said Ferrall. 'I doubt if anything would wake her until after the first effects have worn off.'

They walked down the gravel path to the waiting police car with the yawning sergeant at the wheel.

'What were the questions you wanted to ask Colonel Ayling, sir?' asked Hatchard curiously, as they got in. 'Are they important?'

Gale flung himself into a corner of the back seat. 'One of 'em was,' he answered. 'It's so important, d'you see, that I've *got* to have an answer. It's the one question on which this whole case hinges — Why did Fay marry Paul Meriton?'

16

Henry Onslow-White and his wife had gone to bed when Alan got back to Bryony Cottage, but Flake was waiting up for him. She insisted on making coffee and sandwiches, and while he ate and drank, she plied him with questions.

There was little he could tell her. He described the search of Meriton's house, but so far as he knew, this had ended in rather an anti-climax. He said nothing at all concerning Fay Meriton's death. It would have involved a long explanation which he couldn't go into without disclosing why she had originally gone to the mental home at Shilford, and he thought that Simon Gale would prefer that it wasn't mentioned. The news was sure to leak out soon about the murder, but in the meanwhile he concluded it was better to keep a still tongue.

'Well,' remarked Flake, when he had finished, 'you seem to have spent a long time doing nothing! What *is* Simon up to, Alan? Do you really think he knows all about it, as he says?'

Alan shrugged. 'I guess I can't make up my mind,' he answered. 'You know him better than I do.'

'You never can tell with Simon,' said Flake, frowning. 'The only thing you *can* be sure of is that he's thoroughly enjoying himself.' She got up from the arm of the chair on which she had been perched. 'I'm going to bed,' she said. 'I'm very disappointed, Alan. I expected some sensational news. I'm beginning to think this business will *never* be cleared up. Perhaps there *isn't* a natural explanation.'

'Say,' protested Alan, 'you're not suggesting that Meriton was killed by something supernatural?'

'That old house has always been — queer,' she said seriously. 'It's evil. Even in bright sunshine you can feel it — as though it was *saturated* with something horrible.' She shivered suddenly.

'There was nothing supernatural about those footprints in the dust on the stairs,' said Alan practically. 'Somebody went to the house with Meriton on that night.'

'I know,' said Flake. 'But things can get into people. When Cagliostro lived there, Threshold House must have been the focal point of all kinds of horrors.'

'That,' said Alan, smiling, 'is a nice thought to go to bed with!'

She laughed. 'Look here, shall we go and play tennis after breakfast, if it's fine?'

'And blow all the horrors away?' He got up. 'O.K. There's nothing I'd like better.'

But there was to be no tennis for either of them on the following morning. Just before seven o'clock, heavy black clouds blew up from the east, and when Alan came down to breakfast the rain was falling in a steady downpour. At twelve o'clock it cleared up a little and, restless from mooning about the cottage all the morning, Alan persuaded Flake to come for a walk.

'What we both need,' said Alan, as they came within sight of the Three Witches, 'is a drink. Let's go and see Jellyberry.' At the back of his mind was the hope that he might run into Simon Gale, but that unpredictable individual was not in the bar. Mr. Jellyberry, his fat face wreathed in smiles, greeted them with his usual geniality.

'You did ought to 'ave bin in a bit earlier,' he remarked, after he had attended to Alan's order and set before them a gin and tonic and a whiskey and ginger ale.

'Why?' asked Alan, wondering if Gale had been looking for him.

'There was a chap in a motor car looking for Mr. Veezey,' replied the landlord. 'Come in to inquire the way to his 'ouse. Come all the way from Lunnon, he said.'

'That's unusual,' said Flake. 'I don't think Mr. Veezey's had a visitor since he's been here. At least, if he has, nobody's ever seen them.'

'That's what I be thinkin',' said Mr. Jellyberry, leaning his massive arms on the counter. 'Nice-spoken chap, 'e were.'

Alan, who was unused to the intense curiosity that lurks in the heart of everyone living in an English village, was rather surprised that the visitor should have created so much interest.

'I guess even Veezey must have *some* friends,' he said.

'Ah,' said Mr. Jellyberry with unexpected shrewdness, 'but this chap, I wouldn't say he'd be a friend, like what you mean. 'e didn't seem to know much about Mr. Veezey. Full o' questions, 'e were.' He gave a rumbling chuckle. 'But 'e got mighty few answers out o' me for 'is trouble, I can tell you!'

Alan was raising his glass to his lips when he saw the sudden change in the landlord's face. Mr. Jellyberry leaned forward and a sepulchral whisper issued from his mouth: ''e's come back!'

A short, dark, rather stocky man, wearing a fawn raincoat, came across to the bar and ordered a pink gin. His face, normally probably quite pleasant, was marred by an expression of extreme bad temper.

'Did you find Mr. Veezey's 'ouse, sir?' inquired the landlord as he mixed the drink.

'I might have saved myself the trouble,' retorted the dark man, frowning. 'He shut the door in my face as though I was trying to sell vacuum cleaners! What's the matter with the man, eh? Doesn't he realize the value of publicity?'

Alan looked at Flake. No wonder Mr. Veezey had shut the door. The mention of the word 'publicity' must have struck terror to his timid soul.

'Of course we know he's a genius,' went on the dark man, gulping half his pink gin, 'but even a genius needs to keep his name before the public.'

A genius? thought Alan. Little Veezey? Surely there must be some mistake. He said, turning to the dark man: 'Excuse me, sir, but are you talking about Mr. Veezey?'

The dark man swallowed the remainder of his drink. 'Yes,' he replied. 'He writes under the name of Maurice Charlton. I wanted to get a full-page interview out of him for *The Planet*. You'd think he'd have jumped at it, wouldn't you?' He sighed and shook his head. 'Oh, well. Queer people, some of these writers. I must be off. No good wasting any more time.' He nodded briskly and hurried out.

Maurice Charlton! Alan remembered

the book that Avril had been reading on the day he and Gale had called to see Ferrall about Fay Meriton, and Gale's enthusiasm. '*He doesn't write. He tears off strips of life and confines them, by some flaming miracle, in the covers of a book.*'

And that was Veezey! That was why he had scuttled away like a frightened rabbit when Alan had mentioned that his father was a publisher. Scared to death of fame and any sort of publicity. '*People frighten me.*'

'I guess,' said Alan, 'we'd better forget what we've just learned, or, at any rate, keep it to ourselves.'

Mr. Jellyberry's large forehead was wrinkled in perplexity. 'Well, Mr. Boyce, sir,' he said doubtfully, 'I don't quite get the 'ang of it. But if it be that Mr. Veezey's done something 'e's ashamed of . . . '

'No, no,' put in Flake quickly. 'It's nothing like that. Mr. Veezey writes books and they're very famous books.'

'Writes books?' said Mr. Jellyberry in astonishment. 'Well now — I always thought there was sump'n a bit queer about him.'

'He doesn't want people to know,' said Alan. 'I guess it would embarrass him if they all started staring and whispering. You know how very shy he is.'

'Ah,' said Mr. Jellyberry, his face clearing. 'I see what you mean. My wife's sister's 'usband used be a powerful shy man, an' when 'e come back from the war, 'aving got a medal, it were planned to give 'im a welcome at the station with a band an' all. But 'e seen what were going on an' never got out of the train. Jest stayed put an' let himself be carried on to the next station.' He laughed. 'There's them that don't mind a bit o' fuss, an' there's them that do. I'll be keeping me mouth tight about Mr. Veezey, sir.'

Alan left the Three Witches, hoping that he had done his best to preserve Mr. Veezey's secret.

★ ★ ★

The postman delivered three letters at Bryony Cottage on the following morning. There was one for Henry Onslow-White, one for Flake, and one for Alan.

328

Alan's was a hastily scrawled note from Simon Gale: '*Be at my house, without fail, at nine o'clock tonight. You might as well be in at the death.*' That was all, and, to Alan's surprise, it had been posted in London. That last sentence quite obviously meant that Gale was going to keep his word. He had guaranteed Hatchard that he would hand him the murderer on a plate within forty-eight hours. Alan experienced a tingling of excitement. It was tempered by a certain amount of anxiety. Gale seemed to be very cocksure that he had found the right answer, but he had admitted that there was no evidence. Had he found the evidence he lacked, and would it be sufficiently convincing? Supposing Gale should turn out to be wrong? As the morning wore on, Alan found that he was getting more and more nervous.

Just before lunch, Henry Onslow-White, who had been down to the village, returned in great excitement and with news that did nothing to alleviate Alan's anxiety.

'What d'you think?' he announced

jerkily, mopping his face. 'Fay Meriton's been murdered. Ferncross is seething with it.'

So, thought Alan, the news had leaked out. Would this upset Gale's plans?

'Murdered!' exclaimed Flake in blank amazement. 'Where?'

'At Shilford — in some kind of mental home,' answered her father breathlessly. 'It appears she's been there all the time. She never ran away at all.'

'I never thought she had,' remarked Mrs. Onslow-White placidly. 'I've always said so.'

'I don't believe it. How was she murdered?' asked Flake.

Henry Onslow-White explained in great detail and with much mopping of his face. Whoever had been responsible for disseminating the news had done so very thoroughly. The only fact that had not come out, apparently, was that Ferrall's card had been in the box of chocolates.

'I suppose,' said Flake, looking at Alan reproachfully, '*you* knew all about this?'

'How should I?' he answered evasively.

She didn't press him, but he was sure that she was unconvinced.

'It's a most extraordinary thing,' declared Henry Onslow-White. 'I shouldn't wonder if the police never find out the truth. There's that girl and the tramp and then Meriton himself, all murdered, and now Fay.' He discussed it throughout lunch with immense enjoyment.

The morning had been heavy and sultry with the sun obscured behind a haze of cloud, but in the early afternoon this cleared away and from a steel-blue sky the sun blazed down with almost tropical heat.

Flake, who had complained of a slight headache during the morning, went up to lie down, and Alan, concluding that it was far too hot for a walk, sprawled on the lawn in a patch of shade and listened to Henry Onslow-White's noisy slumbers from the deck-chair under the pear tree.

The afternoon dragged slowly by. To Alan, in a fever of impatience for nine o'clock and his appointment with Simon Gale, the hands of his watch seemed scarcely to move at all.

Flake, looking rather pale, came down for tea. Her headache, she said, had got worse. She put it down to the thundery heat, and decided to have a cool bath and go to bed early.

Alan was relieved. He had been wondering what excuse he could make to get away and see Gale.

'What are you going to do?' she asked, and the question came so aptly on his thoughts that he started.

'I guess, when it gets cooler, I'll probably go for a walk,' he answered. He thought she looked at him a little suspiciously, but concluded that, after all, it was possibly only his guilty conscience.

He left Bryony Cottage at half past eight. The moonlight was as brilliant as it had been on the previous night, but the heat was stifling. And away on the horizon woolly clouds were gathering.

As he neared Simon Gale's house his pulses increased their beat and his breath came a little faster. '*I'll guarantee to hand you the killer on a plate* . . . ' In a short while, if Gale kept his promise, the mask would be torn from somebody's face.

Gale was alone when Alan arrived and, for some reason, Alan felt disappointed. What he had expected, he scarcely knew, but it acted on him in the sense of an anticlimax.

'You're a little early, young feller,' said Gale, who was in high spirits. 'Never mind! Have some beer!'

Alan hesitated.

'You'd better,' remarked Gale. 'You'll need it before the night's over!' Without waiting for a reply, he strode across to the barrel and filled two tankards. Thrusting one into Alan's hand, he raised the other to his lips. 'Here's to the end of all the ghosts and goblins!' he cried, and he poured the contents down his throat.

'Look here,' said Alan, 'what *is* going to happen tonight?'

Gale looked at him. There was a glitter in his eyes, and his beard seemed to quiver with suppressed excitement. He said, in an unusually quiet voice: 'Presently, young feller, you and I are going on a little excursion. And at the end of it we're going to meet the murderer.'

'Where?' demanded Alan.

'At Sorcerer's House.'

Alan drank a little of his beer. There was a dryness at the back of his throat. 'How do you know he'll be there?' he said.

'Don't you worry about that!' cried Gale, with a sudden return to his normal boisterousness. 'I've arranged it all, d'you see? By the four sons of Horus, Chippy'll be handing me out medals tomorrow for making him famous!'

He really was a nice guy, thought Alan. He said: 'Did you know that it's leaked out about Fay Meriton? The whole village is full of it.'

Gale waved his free hand impatiently. 'Of course I know,' he said. 'I took a great deal of trouble to see that it did!' He looked at his watch. 'Come on, young feller, drink up! It's time we were off.'

The clouds had piled up thicker when they left the house. Low down on the horizon, they were black and angry. The night was very still. The leaves of the trees were unstirred by even a breath of wind, and the air was heavy with heat. As they passed Mr. Veezey's hut, Alan remembered the surprising revelation at the Three Witches on the previous day, and told Gale, who was intensely interested.

'So he's Maurice Charlton, eh?' he said. 'It doesn't surprise me as much as you seem to expect. I told you once that there was intelligence behind those weak eyes of his. Have you ever thought what a queer thing the human mind is, young feller? At one end of the scale you get a flaming genius like Veezey, and at the other a cold-blooded devil like the person we're going to meet tonight.'

He did not speak again until they reached the gate to Sorcerer's House. Then he said, pausing with his hand on the rusty iron: 'We may have a long wait. But we couldn't risk not getting here in plenty of time, d'you see?' He opened the gate sufficiently wide to enable them to slip through into the neglected drive. 'Whatever you see or hear,' he whispered warningly, 'keep quiet!'

It was dark here. The thick, interlacing branches of the trees formed a canopy through which little light penetrated.

From the tangled mass of shrubbery on either side came a heavy odour of rotting vegetation, and there was the sound of things stirring in the bushes. The heat was stifling. It was a moist and clammy heat, like the heart of a tropical jungle, and there were night insects which flew blindly, flicking their faces. The sweat was pouring down Alan's face when they reached the end of the drive, and the palms of his hands were wet.

Before them, starkly black against a moon now hazy with cloud, reared the ruined hulk of Sorcerer's House. Gale led the way over to the massive door. It was unlocked and partly ajar. Pushing it open, they stepped into the cavernous hall. The smell of the old house rushed to meet them, and there was a sudden scurry and squeaking of rats. In the dim light from the staircase windows it looked very much the same as it had done on that other night, when they had found the locked room.

The locked room? Was it *there* that they were going to await the coming of the murderer?

It was deadly still in the old house. Even when they mounted the stairs there was scarcely a creak from the ancient woodwork. They had been built in the days when workmanship was solid and lasting.

The American's heart began to beat faster as they passed the landing from which the corridor led to the Long Room. The Long Room where the spatters of blood on the dusty floor still showed where Paul Meriton had died.

With a hand that shook in spite of his efforts to keep it steady, Alan took out his handkerchief and wiped his streaming face before he followed Simon Gale up the next flight. Without pause, Gale continued on until at last they came to the attic floor — the floor with the room in which Fay Meriton had escaped from a world of reality into a dream world of her own creation.

And there was a light under the door!

Alan felt Gale grip his arm and lead him away from that closed door, behind which lurked — what?

Silently, with that restraining hold on

his arm, Alan was guided towards the next room, the door of which stood partly open. Simon Gale pushed him gently inside and followed. The grimy window scarcely admitted any light, and the empty room, with its broken ceiling, was almost in darkness. Over the broken roof, which when they had come here before had been open to the sky, someone had draped a tarpaulin.

Gale's shadowy figure beside him made a warning gesture, the grip on his arm relaxed, and Gale went noiselessly, across the floor to one of the walls — the wall that divided this room from that other room where *someone* waited.

Alan watched him press his face close to the wall and stand there for a moment, motionless. Then he turned and beckoned.

With his heart thumping so that its beats sounded loudly in his ears, Alan went over to him. And then he saw that two small, round holes had been bored through the plaster and the lath beneath. He caught the faint glint of a light. At a motion from Gale, he applied his eyes to the holes and found that he was looking into the locked room. And it was all he could do to suppress the startled exclamation that almost forced its way from his lips.

The room was exactly as he had last seen it, except that there were fresh candles burning in the wall-sconces. The picture hung over the mantelpiece in its tarnished gilt frame; there were the chairs and the table and the cushioned divan.

And sitting on the divan, reading a magazine, was Fay Meriton!

17

Fay Meriton!

But Fay Meriton was dead!

Alan felt a creeping of the flesh and a stirring of the hair on his scalp.

She was dressed in the black frock of angora wool, with white at the neck and wrists, which she had worn when he had seen her at Shilford. The yellow light from the flickering candles, scarcely enough to drive away the thick shadows, glinted faintly on the heavy, dark red hair.

'*Whatever you see or hear, keep quiet.*' Alan remembered Simon Gale's whispered warning as they entered the drive. Gale, then, had expected this. He had known that Fay Meriton would be here — in the locked room. The holes had been made in the wall so that they could see. There must have been a mistake, somewhere. She had *not* died from eating those chocolates, after all.

'*You and I are going on a little*

excursion. *And, at the end of it, we're going to meet the murderer.'*

But Fay Meriton *couldn't* be the murderer. She had been in the mental home at Shilford when Meriton had been killed. The whole thing was mad and impossible. The American felt his brain reeling with the confusion of his thoughts.

The woman on the divan was nervous. He could see, now that he had partially recovered from the first shock of surprise, that her hands, holding the magazine, were trembling. Her eyes kept shifting from the printed page towards the door.

Gale's hand, light but reassuring, pressed his shoulder, and he turned away from the spy-holes in the wall. He wanted to demand an explanation for the apparently impossible presence of the woman in the other room, but he had been warned to keep quiet. What else was it that Gale had said? *'We may have a long wait.'* What were they waiting *for?*

Up here, under the roof, the room was heavy with heat. It pressed down until the stale air seemed to have acquired a weight and substance. The dim figure of Simon

Gale had moved soundlessly, over to the window. He was standing motionless, a dim silhouette, his fingers twisted in his beard, his head bent slightly forward as though he were listening. But there was dead silence both here and in the house below.

Vividly there rose in Alan's mind a picture of the empty, cavernous hall and the wide staircase. The staircase from which the murderer had snatched his weapon.

The murderer?

Was someone, in the vast desolation of the ruined house, creeping stealthily nearer? Nearer to the woman sitting, alone, in the adjoining room?

Was that the explanation for her presence here? Was she the tethered kid, waiting for the lion's spring?

But surely there could have been no doubt that Fay Meriton had died. Dr. Preston couldn't have made a mistake — the local police couldn't have made a mistake. It was impossible! But not more impossible than the fact that she was sitting on that divan, only a few yards away.

Never in his life had Alan experienced such a longing to talk. Questions that he dared not put into words clamoured for utterance. But the ban of silence which Gale had imposed could not be broken.

With the slowness of a snail dragging itself along a garden path, the time moved on. When Alan looked at the luminous dial of his watch, convinced that it must be nearly midnight, he was surprised to find that it was barely ten o'clock.

The atmosphere of the room was getting thicker and heavier. There was now scarcely any glimmer of light from the grim window. Those stormy clouds on the horizon must have spread and obscured the moon.

A quarter past ten . . . half past ten.

Alan felt the tension becoming unbearable. This long wait in enforced silence in that dark, hot room was playing havoc with nerves, already keyed to breaking point.

Eleven . . .

If something, *anything*, didn't happen soon . . .

And then it did!

In the silence of the room, with a loudness that seemed startling, but was in reality scarcely audible, the soft note of a buzzer sounded twice.

From where Simon Gale was standing, almost invisible in the darkness, came the sharp hiss of suddenly indrawn breath. He moved quickly to Alan's side, and his beard brushed the American's cheek as he whispered, close to his ear:

'The killer's in the house *now*.'

There was a tightening in Alan's chest. He sensed, rather than saw, Gale go swiftly and noiselessly to the partly open door, and followed him. Peering out at the dark landing, he could just make out the head of the staircase looming up from the blackness below. On the floor to his left was the faint gleam of yellow light, fanning from under the door of the room in which Fay Meriton sat — waiting.

Alan held his breath and listened.

Dead silence!

Beside him, so close that he could feel the tense rigidity of his body, Simon Gale was listening, too.

It was a very faint sound that first

reached their straining ears, but it was unmistakable. Someone had begun to mount the stairs!

Alan found himself staring at the outline of the stairhead with a horrible anticipation. Who would presently emerge from that well of darkness?

But Simon Gale was pulling him back into the room and closing the door. He drew Alan quickly over to the wall and rapped sharply on it with his knuckles.

'Watch from here,' he whispered.

Once more Alan looked through the spy-holes into the adjoining room. Fay Meriton was no longer reading, or pretending to read. The magazine lay on the floor at her feet. Half-turned, she was watching the closed door with an expression that was a mixture of fear and expectancy. One of her hands had closed tightly on one of the cushions.

Footsteps became audible, first on the staircase and then on the landing outside. They hesitated, stopped, and then went on again. With a sudden, swift movement, the woman on the divan rose to her feet, and the hand that had been gripping the cushion went up to her throat.

The door began to open, slowly . . .

That moment, while the door swung back on its hinges, seemed to extend into eternity. There was a nightmarish quality about it. The furnished room in the old, ruined house, lit so dimly by the flickering candlelight; the woman, standing, still as a waxwork figure in the shadows by the divan . . . And that slowly opening door, through which would come the murderer. It was grotesque, unreal; a picture that was to linger in Alan's memory long after it was all over.

And then Flake entered the room.

The blood drained from Alan's brain and a misty blackness swirled before his eyes. He couldn't have said whom he had expected to see come in through that door, but his wildest imaginings hadn't prepared him for Flake.

Something *must* have gone wrong somewhere. *She* couldn't be the murderer.

Gale's voice, so soft as to be nearly inaudible, whispered in his ear: 'Steady, young feller.'

The dizzy haze of that first shock cleared. Flake was standing just within the doorway, facing the woman by the divan. She was dressed in a simple summer frock. Over the glossy black of her hair she wore a scarf of some flimsy material, and her face was dead white. Her dark eyes, by contrast, looked darker — and larger. She said:

'Well, I'm here, Fay.'

'I thought you'd come.' Fay Meriton's voice was very low — so low and with a faint huskiness that it barely carried through the spy-holes in the wall.

'I had to, didn't I?' said Flake. 'After the letter you wrote? She took a step forward. 'It gave me rather a shock. How did you know it was *me*, Fay? I mean, about the tramp and the girl?'

The woman by the divan moved a little further away from her. But her eyes never left her face.

'You've always hated me, haven't you?' she said, still in the voice that was almost a whisper.

Flake laughed. Alan had never heard her laugh like that and, in spite of the heat, he felt a sudden chill.

'Yes,' she said, 'I've always hated you, Fay. Even when we were at school. You always got the things I wanted. At last you got Paul! I've always hated you, but I never thought you knew it.' She took another step forward. 'You know a lot of things, now, don't you, Fay? I don't know how you found them out, but you have. You told me what you knew in that letter.'

'You killed that girl and the tramp,' said Fay. 'You wanted people to think *I'd* done it. You hoped there'd be a scandal and I'd be arrested and tried and either hanged or sent to Broadmoor. And then, with me out of the way, you might stand a chance with Paul.' The hand at her throat plucked nervously at her dress. 'But it all went *wrong*. You never expected that Paul would *save* me from that, did you? In the way he did. You must have wondered when that poor girl's body wasn't found.'

Flake was breathing a little faster. Alan could see the quickened rise and fall of her breast under the thin dress. But she was quite cool. She said: 'I did. I couldn't understand what had happened.'

'And in your anxiety to find out you gave yourself away to Paul.' Never once did that low voice rise above a husky whisper. Alan had to strain his ears to hear all that she said. 'That's why you had to kill him.'

For the first time emotion showed in Flake's white face. Her eyes clouded and her mouth twisted as though in pain. Her voice, clear before, was husky when she spoke. 'I had to kill him,' she said. 'Oh, *God* . . . I had to kill him . . . *Paul!*' For a moment the tears gathered in her eyes, but she choked them back.

'And so all that you'd done was for nothing,' said Fay. 'You *still* didn't get what you wanted.'

A change came over Flake. Her face distorted into such a look of sheer, black hatred that Alan, watching, was appalled. She took a third step forward so that now she was quite close to the woman by the divan.

'Not entirely for nothing, Fay,' she said. 'There's still *one* thing I want that I *am* going to get. I thought I'd got it when I heard you were dead. I still don't know how it is you're not. You *should* be after those chocolates I sent you. Everybody thinks you are. And you're going to die, Fay — now — like Paul died . . . '

She had kept one hand behind her, hidden by her frock. Now she brought it out, gripping a short piece of iron bar — that strong right hand that could send tennis balls over a net with the force of a cannon shot.

'Sorcerer's House has got a bad reputation,' she said. 'Three people have died here. Now there's going to be *a fourth*!' She raised the bar of iron. Fay's scream echoed through the old house, and she cowered back as Flake sprang forward.

And then so many things happened that Alan, dazed and confused, could afterwards remember exactly *what* took place. Gale's deep, bellowing roar . . . A rush of feet on the landing, and the excited shouting of men's voices . . . The screaming curses of a woman . . .

How, amid that babel of sound, Alan managed to get into the other room — that room with the flickering candles

— he never knew, but he found himself there, with Gale and Hatchard and Major Chipingham. There were two other men holding Flake, who was struggling, between them.

And sitting on the divan, with her dark red wig awry, fumbling with trembling fingers to light a cigarette, was a woman — not Fay Meriton, but a complete stranger.

18

'Well, well,' said Simon Gale, filling four brimming tankards from the barrel beside the fireplace. 'I don't mind admitting that I'm glad it's over.'

'You did a very good job of work, sir,' said Inspector Hatchard, eyeing the tankards expectantly.

'H'm ... yes. Quite unorthodox, of course,' remarked Major Chipingham, frowning at the thought. 'We couldn't have done it.'

Alan said nothing. He was still feeling dazed and shocked from what he had heard and seen.

The sky was beginning to lighten in the east; pink shreds of cloud heralded the coming sun, and they were sitting in Gale's big, untidy studio. Flake, ice cool after her first paroxysm, had been taken in the police car to Barnsford with Inspector Hatchard, who had attended to such official formalities as were necessary and then returned, at Gale's request, to join them.

'You can't realize it yet, eh, young feller?' said Gale, as he distributed the beer. 'You thought she was a nice, simple kind of girl, didn't you? Well, you heard her when she was off-guard. I couldn't say anything to you, d'you see? I was afraid you'd give it away, even if you didn't mean to.' He took a mighty swig from his tankard. 'The beginning of all this goes back a long way. To the time when Flake Onslow-White and Fay Ayling were children. You've got to understand that, to get the hang of it. Flake was good at games, but Fay was just a little bit better. Flake was pretty bright at her lessons; but Fay was brighter. So it was in everything, d'you see? Fay first, Flake a very close second, but second . . . And the hatred began to build up.

'But hatred — the *real* kind, the *dangerous* kind — is a deep and quiet thing. You've got to remember that, young feller, to understand Flake. She didn't go around screaming with rage against Fay;

it would have been better if she had. She kept it all bottled up inside her. Her *vanity* wouldn't let her show it. And in that one word, 'vanity', you've got the whole thing. But she was practical and cool-headed, as well. Fay, on the other hand, was highly strung, sensitive, and hysterical. She was mentally unbalanced, a legacy from the grandmother who died in an asylum, and she was *cruel*. She took a delight in showing off — in proving how clever she was, snatching things from her friends.' He paused to swallow the remainder of his beer. '*She* was given to bursts of hysterical rage if anything displeased her — yes, but it was out and over. But *Flake* . . . D'you remember telling me, young feller, about Fay hitting one of her school friends over the head with a jagged stone?'

Alan nodded. He remembered very vividly the day that Flake had told him that — and other things. He had sensed her hatred for Fay Meriton then.

'I don't believe she ever did,' declared Gale, going over to the barrel and refilling his tankard. '*That* was a little bit of Flake, d'you see? Cool and calculating, even as a child. Can't you see it? Fay in a rage with her school friend, and Flake, choosing her opportunity when neither could tell what was happening, creeping up behind the other child and — whack!' He made a sudden downward gesture with his hand. 'And then accusing Fay. That was the start, d'you see? *That's* what was later *repeated* in the case of the tramp and the girl.'

'It's appalling,' muttered the chief constable, shaking his bald head. 'I would never have believed it possible.'

'Didn't I know that?' retorted Gale. 'Isn't that why I had to stage my bit of hocus-pocus at Sorcerer's House? *No* one would have believed it, d'you see? The crowning thing, the thing that finished it, and turned Flake into a murderess, was Paul Meriton. She fell violently, hell for leather, head over heels in love with him. If you can hate so deeply that it becomes an obsession, you can do the opposite — if you've got a nature like Flake's. And that's what her feeling for Meriton became. But, once again, Fay was *first*.

Flake knew that she wasn't in love with Meriton — that she only married him to score once more over *her*. And the acorn of hatred flourished into a full-grown oak! I told you that was what the whole case hinged on — why Fay ever married Meriton. From that moment Flake began searching for a means to split it up.'

'Surely,' said Alan, almost inaudibly, 'she could have done it some *other* way?'

'Maybe she could, young feller,' said Gale, 'but, d'you see, she wanted something that would finish Fay for *ever*, not only in Meriton's eyes, but in the eyes of the *whole world*. And she didn't have to wait long for an idea. It was practically thrown in her lap. By all the Holy Saints, can you imagine her hugging herself when she found out about Fay's constant visits to her hide-out in the locked room at Sorcerer's House? Fay, the paranoiac, who lived in a world of illusion . . . And *might* be capable of anything with that insane maggot eating into her brain. If it were possible to make people believe that Fay was a homicidal maniac? Even Meriton's devotion wouldn't be proof against *that* — or so she thought. Fay would be an object of horror and disgust. So the plan matured and, biding her time, she killed the tramp.'

He paused to drink some beer. Nobody spoke. Hatchard was staring into his tankard and gently rotating it. Major Chipingham frowned down at his fingernails. Alan shivered, not entirely from the chill of dawn which seemed to have suddenly crept into the big, untidy room.

'She killed the tramp,' Simon Gale went on, 'and *nothing happened*! No outcry, no arrest! Can you imagine how she felt? And she couldn't do anything about it. It must have given her an awful shock when she learned that the body had been found under the window of the Long Room when *she* had left it by the front door. But it was nothing to the shock she got later when she killed that poor girl, Hunks, and the body wasn't found at all! That must've been paralysing! And on the top of it Fay disappears, leaving a letter saying that she's run away. Flake must have been in the devil of a stew, hey? The amazing thing is that she managed to carry on behaving normally.'

'It's incredible!' grunted the chief constable. 'A young girl like that . . . '

'You don't understand, Chippy,' cried Gale. 'You've got an old-fashioned idea of youth. Youth is cruel and relentless *unless* it's balanced by a strong sense of the difference between right and wrong. The old religious teaching helped to do that. Left in its natural state . . . ' He snapped his fingers. 'You can blame Henry and Mrs. Onslow-White, if you like. Flake was spoilt as child.'

'She must have been mad, sir,' said Hatchard, with his eyes still fixed on the swirling liquid in the tankard.

'No, no,' said Gale, shaking his head, 'she was nothing of the sort! She was, and is, cool-headed and intelligent. But, d'ye see, she's cold-bloodedly self-centred. There's nothing *mad* about her, except that overwhelming hatred of Fay and her obsession for Paul Meriton.'

'And yet, sir, she killed him,' said Hatchard.

'She killed him because she *had to*,' retorted Gale. 'And it nearly broke her heart. You saw yourself what effect it had on her. Look here, try and put yourself in her place. For nearly two years she lived in a fever of uncertainty. The whole of her precious plan had gone *wrong*. Fay had gone, and she didn't know *where*. She guessed that Meriton had had something to do with the fact that Hunks's body hadn't been found, but she didn't know *what*. The strain must have been almost unbearable. And to make things worse, Meriton began to get suspicious.'

'How?' asked Major Chipingham tersely.

'I don't suppose we shall ever know, exactly,' answered Gale. 'But I believe Fay had told him about that childish effort of Flake's, when the school-friend had to have stitches in her head, and it started him wondering. Remember, he wanted desperately to *believe* in Fay's innocence. I think he began asking a lot awkward questions, and Flake saw not only her scheme tumbling about her ears, but *herself* in the position she had planned for *Fay*. It may have been *her* idea, or it may have been Meriton's, that meeting at Sorcerer's House. I'm inclined to believe

it was Meriton's. He had to have it out
with her and it was the one place, d'you
see, where he was certain no one would
see or overhear them. And what must
have happened was that Flake completely
lost her head. She gave herself away.'

'How?' asked Major Chipingham again.

Gale shrugged his shoulders. He drank
deeply from his tankard and then said,
frowning: 'How can anybody tell what
exactly took place at that interview? I'll
tell you what *I* think she did. The only
thing that would have made Meriton
sure. *She inadvertently mentioned the girl
Hunks.* Now, d'you see, only Meriton, the
Ferralls, and Fay knew anything about
that. The only other person who *could*
have known was the person who *really*
killed her. And for two years Fay, whom
Meriton practically worshipped, had been
shut up in a mental home for something
she *hadn't done*. Can you imagine how
he felt? Can you imagine his rage and
horror and what he threatened to *do*? She
had to kill him, d'you see? It was the only
thing she could do to save *herself*.'

'She didn't follow me that night,' said

Alan, speaking almost to himself. 'She was already there.'

'That's right, young feller,' said Gale. 'She'd just toppled Meriton's body out the window of the Long Room and left the house, when she heard you coming up the drive. She hid in the bushes, waited until you'd found the body, and then pretended that she'd followed you.'

There was a silence. In it, Major Chipingham cleared his throat. Alan saw a vivid picture of the rain-soaked drive and the light of the torch wavering on wet bushes. And Flake's voice coming out of the darkness: '*Is that you, Mr. Boyce?*'

'What about the footprints, sir?' Hatchard, gently rubbing the bald spot on the top of his head, broke the silence. 'In the dust on the staircase. They were too big for a woman's.'

'Remember what sort of a night it was?' answered Gale. He whirled round on Alan. 'What shoes was she wearing when you saw her?'

Alan remembered. He remembered everything about that night. 'Crepe-soled tennis shoes,' he said.

'I'll bet she *started* out with Wellingtons over 'em,' cried Gale. 'An old pair of Henry's, probably — and she ditched 'em before she met you. Somewhere under the dead leaves in that tangled shrubbery, eh? There are no flies on that girl, you know. She'd think of the dust, and what sort of footprints she'd left.'

'H'm,' grunted the chief constable. 'But she didn't go there with the intention of killing Meriton?'

'She didn't know *what* was going to happen, but she was pretty *sure* it wasn't going to be pleasant, d'you see?' replied Gale. 'She was in the Long Room at Sorcerer's House the night before. When Avril saw the light. That was probably when she put the banister handy — just in case. Oh, yes, she'd take precautions.'

'Like she did over the parcel of chocolates?' remarked Hatchard, nodding several times. 'That was clever, sir. Posting it through the wide slit of the post-box at Barnsford that was intended for newspapers and magazines. Made it impossible to trace the sender by inquiring at the post office.'

'And Ferrall's card,' said Gale. 'So that Fay wouldn't wonder who'd sent 'em.'

'How did she know *where* to send them?' asked Alan. 'If she didn't know what had happened to Fay?'

'But she *did*, d'you see?' broke in Gale. 'I'm quite sure that she learned, somehow, possibly from Mrs. Horly, about Meriton's periodical absences, and followed him. But it took her nearly two years to find out.'

'Well,' said Major Chipingham grudgingly, 'you seem to have worked it out pretty thoroughly. Can't understand what first put you on to her. Should never have thought of her, myself.'

'I don't suppose you would, Chippy,' said Gale, grinning. 'Thinking was never your strong point! I was looking for a motive, d'you see, that'd cover the killing of the tramp and the girl, as *well* as Meriton, and I was flummoxed. I couldn't find one, until we were talking about that poor devil of a waitress, Hunks, and I said the principal motives for murder were gain and hatred. And suddenly I got it! Somebody had hated

Fay Meriton so *much* that they'd planned those two murders for the sole purpose of making people believe *she'd* done 'em. If that really *was* the truth, and *Meriton* had found out, then the motive for *his* murder was clear, *and* it linked up with the other two, d'you see? The question was, who hated her and why? I spent the greater part of the night sitting and thinking. Boyce had told me about the incident of the little girl and the stitches, which Flake had told *him*. Well, that fitted, if Fay had killed the other two. The murder of the tramp and Hunks was an *extension* of the same method, d'you see? But, *supposing* Fay had *never* hit the child. Supposing it was a story that had been made up by *Flake*. By all the signs of the Zodiac, that put a different complexion on it! I began to remember a lot of odds and ends — little things that didn't mean much by themselves, but, when you put 'em all together, added up to a hell of a lot. They began to form *a pattern*, d'you see? I'll admit that I had an advantage, Chippy, over you and Hatchard. I *knew* these people inside out. Flake had been very clever at concealing her *real* feelings, but she hadn't been entirely successful. From things she'd said, now and again, I knew that she actively disliked Fay.'

Yes, thought Alan, she couldn't quite conceal that.

'I knew, also, d'you see, that she'd had a youthful passion for Meriton,' continued Gale. 'Marshalling together all these stray bits and pieces I began to build up a theory — the theory you saw justified at Sorcerer's House a few hours ago.'

'Damn it all!' exploded the chief constable. 'You had no evidence at all! Nothing concrete! And yet you had the infernal audacity to — to . . . ' He tried to find a suitable word to express his disgust, and spluttered into silence.

'Now, now,' cried Gale, 'you're not *quite* right you know, Chippy. I hadn't enough evidence to satisfy *you* and *Hatchard*, but I had enough to satisfy *me*, d'you see? I talked to the old school mistress here, and I had a long telephone conversation with the headmistress of Longdean, where Flake and Fay went, after. And I got the same story — Flake was always just lagging behind Fay in everything, with Fay poking sly fun at her because of it. There was one thing I wanted to make sure about. I wanted to satisfy myself, as near as I could, that Meriton hadn't given Flake any encouragement in thinking that, with Fay out of the way, there would be a chance to step in. I was pretty sure he hadn't, and, after Boyce and I paid our visit to Ferncross Lodge, I knew I was right. Meriton had never had eyes for any other woman, poor devil! You only had to look at that bedroom, just as she'd left it, and those carefully preserved letters in the bureau, to know that. I told you, young feller, that I was looking for something that wasn't there, eh? And then came Fay's death from the poisoned chocolates, and that clinched the matter, so far as I was concerned. It was a *woman's* method, d'you see.'

'I wonder how she got hold of the cyanide, sir?' muttered Inspector Hatchard thoughtfully.

'Wasps!' said Gale. 'There was a nest of 'em in the garden at Bryony Cottage.

Henry got hold of some cyanide from one of the farmers early in the summer to get rid of 'em. Probably there was a bit left over. I remembered that, and it was *another* pointer to Flake, d'you see.'

'It wouldn't have been enough on its own, sir,' said Hatchard, shaking his head.

'No, no, everything had to be water-tight and copper-bottomed,' cried Gale. 'There wasn't enough *real* evidence to convict a one-legged sailor. So I had to take a chance and play out my little show. By the orgies of Bacchus, I was worried. If Flake had ignored that letter, I was sunk.'

'What,' asked Alan, '*was* the letter?'

'Ah-ha,' said Gale, rubbing his hands together in great delight. 'It was a Machiavellian effort, young feller! I got a pal of mine in London to copy Fay's handwriting. It told Flake, d'you see, *exactly* what she'd done, as though Fay *knew all about it*. And it asked her to come and see Fay in the room at Sorcerer's House that night. I'd started the gossip in the village about Fay's death from the chocolates, and I counted on the fact that Flake would be so confused as to what had *really* happened, that she'd *have* to come and find out. I got hold of an actress I knew who was Fay's build, and sufficiently like her, with a dark red wig, to pass in the dim candlelight of that room; put her in Fay's dress, which Hatchard got for me; and coached her in what she was to say. I didn't tell her that Flake would probably make a murderous attack on her. I thought we could look after *that*. Poor Miriam, she was so scared I don't suppose she'll ever speak to me again.' He scowled suddenly. 'I was scared, too, until I heard that buzzer we rigged up, Hatchard. I was afraid Flake *might* be sensible enough not to turn up, hey?'

'The whole thing was damned risky,' growled Major Chipingham disapprovingly. 'If you'd told me what you were up to — '

'You'd have stopped it, eh, Chippy?' said Gale. 'And Flake would have got away with it. As it is,' he added, suddenly serious, 'unless the defence can convince a jury she's insane, which is absolute bosh and rubbish, she'll hang.'

★　★　★

Miss Flappit's decrepit bicycle rattled to a shrill and squeaky halt, and her angular and wasp-waisted figure dismounted from the saddle. She greeted her bosom friend, Miss Cringe, in an excited falsetto.

'My dear,' she said, 'how *nice* to see you. I am about to do my morning shopping. Where are you going?'

Miss Cringe admitted that *she* was about to do *her* morning shopping, too, which, considering she was carrying a basket, was very obvious.

'You know,' remarked Miss Flappit, eyeing her critically through her thick spectacles, 'I don't think you're looking *quite* so well this morning, dear.'

Miss Cringe, who knew that this was the opening gambit preparatory to telling her that she looked old, smiled with the honeyed sweetness of an alligator about to devour a tasty morsel. 'I'm feeling *quite* well, dear,' she replied. 'Are your eyes giving you any trouble? They really look so very *strained*. Perhaps you need stronger glasses at your age?'

369

Miss Flappit, on the point of delivering a devastating reply which might have endangered a beautiful friendship, suddenly found her attention distracted. On the other side of the road she saw Alan Boyce and Avril Ferrall. In the joyous anticipation of being able to re-tell a choice tit-bit of gossip, her annoyance was forgotten — at least temporarily.

'They are always *together* these days,' she said significantly, leaning nearer to her friend.

'He went to stay with Doctor Ferrall and his sister after that *dreadful* scandal over the Onslow-White gal, didn't he?' said Miss Cringe. 'That was a truly *shocking* thing.' She clucked her disapproval.

Alan and Avril, quite oblivious to the fact that they were being discussed, passed by. His hand touched hers and, almost unconsciously, their fingers interlocked.

'Did you see *that*, dear?' whispered Miss Cringe breathlessly.

Miss Flappit's eyes glinted. She drew in her breath almost ecstatically. 'You should have seen what *I* saw last night!' she declared. She whispered in her friend's ear.

Miss Cringe's small and reddish-rimmed eyes goggled. 'No!' she said.

'Yes!' said Miss Flappit.

THE END

GRIM DEATH
MURDER IN MANUSCRIPT
THE GLASS ARROW
THE THIRD KEY
THE ROYAL FLUSH MURDERS
THE SQUEALER
MR. WHIPPLE EXPLAINS
THE SEVEN CLUES
THE CHAINED MAN
THE HOUSE OF THE GOAT
THE FOOTBALL POOL MURDERS
THE HAND OF FEAR

We do hope that you have enjoyed reading this large print book.

Did you know that all of our titles are available for purchase?

We publish a wide range of high quality large print books including:
Romances, Mysteries, Classics
General Fiction
Non Fiction and Westerns

Special interest titles available in large print are:
The Little Oxford Dictionary
Music Book, Song Book
Hymn Book, Service Book

Also available from us courtesy of Oxford University Press:
Young Readers' Dictionary
(large print edition)
Young Readers' Thesaurus
(large print edition)

For further information or a free brochure, please contact us at:
Ulverscroft Large Print Books Ltd.,
The Green, Bradgate Road, Anstey,
Leicester, LE7 7FU, England.
Tel: (00 44) **0116 236 4325**
Fax: (00 44) **0116 234 0205**

Other titles in the
Linford Mystery Library:

ZONE ZERO

John Robb

Western powers plan to explode a hydrogen bomb in a remote area of Southern Algeria — code named Zone Zero. The zone has to be evacuated. Fort Ney is the smallest Foreign Legion outpost in the zone, commanded by a young lieutenant. Here, too, is the English legionnaire, tortured by previous cowardice, as well as a little Greek who has within him the spark of greatness. It has always been a peaceful place — until the twelve travellers arrive. Now the outwitted garrison faces the uttermost limit of horror . . .

THE WEIRD SHADOW OVER MORECAMBE

Edmund Glasby

Professor Mandrake Smith would be unrecognisable to his former colleagues now: the shambling, drink-addled erstwhile Professor of Anthropology at Oxford is now barely surviving in Morecambe. He has many things to forget, although some don't want to forget him. Plagued by nightmares from his past, both in Oxford and Papua New Guinea, he finds himself drafted by the enigmatic Mr. Thorn, whom he grudgingly assists in trying to stop the downward spiral into darkness and insanity that awaits Morecambe — and the entire world . . .